Among The Dead Part Two:

Fear No Evil

Ryan Colley

PAPERBACK EDITION

ISBN-10: 1999819128
ISBN-13: 978-1-9998191-2-5

***

Edited by Ashley Conner
www.ashtheeditor.biz

And Monique Happy
www.moniquehappy.com

Cover art by www.fiverr.com/oliviaprodesign

DEDICATION

As always, this is for my mum, sister, and partner.

My grandparents, who are always awesome.

As well as the various Stubbs in my life.

ACKNOWLEDGMENTS

Thank you to Ashley Conner and Monique Happy for their amazing job editing.

Thank you to everyone who proofread and beta read for me.

Finally, a thank you to you, the reader – you beautiful person.

PREVIOUSLY …

I made an idiotic and selfish decision. Possibly the worst of my life. I left my mother and sister to fend for themselves when the dead began to walk. For what? To save Alice, the love of my life. It all seemed so simple – I would turn up at her house in Essex, during the apocalypse, and I'd be the hero. It didn't work out how I had planned. But I made a friend on the way – Officer James Morrison. He was an upstanding man of the law, and he was truly incorruptible.

In the face of the undead, he remained true to who he was. We became close. We became brothers. He was killed by a drunken disgrace of a human – General Harrington. I had sworn to kill him, and I intended to keep my promise.

I made my way through the living hell that was London, where nearly all life ceased to exist, and all the way to Essex. It wasn't the oasis I'd built it up to be. It wasn't any better than London for that matter.

I made it to Alice's house. I was injured and had a huge shard of glass sticking out of my leg. I walked up her blood-strewn driveway and to her front door which had been left ajar. I could hear movement inside …

CHAPTER 1

I slowly pushed the door open, one hand clamped tightly around the pistol.

Oh God.

The horrific stench hit me first. It was something I could never get over, regardless of the numerous times I'd encountered it. It was the smell of death. A miasma that no words could describe. *Rotten meat.* They're just words. There's no way words could describe it in a way that another could even begin to comprehend it. Yet those were the only words to describe it. Rotten meat – it didn't even come close. There were so many other foul odours mixed with the death. Urine. Faeces. Blood. Clinical words to describe a non-clinical situation. I couldn't think about it.

The second thing that engulfed my senses was the blood! Blood was everywhere. I had never seen so much of it and prayed I never would again. Was there even enough blood in a human body to spill that much? No … there had to be multiple bodies. The blood was deep and had begun to soak into the skirting board, climbing up the walls into the wallpaper. Pushing the door caused waves in the blood which rippled and lapped over the lip of the frame and escaped into the outside world. The house looked as though blood had leaked out of the walls and flooded the hallway, as if the walls were crying at the horrors it saw.

On the floor was a body, front down and face obscured. Dread and terror submerged my mind, almost sending me over an edge I knew I could never return from. I had no idea who the body belonged to. It could've been anyone. Was it Alice, the woman I'd travelled so far for? Or another of the Kingsley family, whose death would leave her feeling broken? I didn't know.

Another figure was draped over the body. It looked like a caring mother figure from the way it leaned over the body. It was almost protective. However, the *caring* figure was clearly anything but. It was undead. Tatters of a blue nightgown hung heavily from the woman's body. The piece of ruined, bloodstained clothing was too big for her frail body. The weight of the blood made it appear as if the gown was trying to escape her. She was older, probably could've been someone's grandmother. Her skin was loose and her breasts were sagging. No, her *breast* was sagging. Where the other breast once had been was now a bloody gash of a wound, as if it had been ripped from her when she was still alive. More than likely it had been. Most of her hair had been torn out at the scalp. A flap of bloody skin fell away from the skull, moving each time she did with a wet slap.

And, oh God, the zombie did move and showed no signs of stopping. It moved to dig its fingers into the bloody crater of the dead person's back and pulled pieces of offal out. It jerked the ichor-covered strips up to its mouth, shovelled it in, and chewed mechanically. Several pieces fell into the bloody stew on the floor and made a loud slopping noise. As loud as it was, it did nothing to distract me from the terrible grinding noise that the zombie made when chewing. The sound of teeth on teeth. Bone on bone. The undead woman barely remembered how to chew. Yet it did its best to carry on.

The door continued to swing open as I let go and stared in horror. It finally stopped when it hit the wall with a thud. The zombie snapped its head towards me, and I was reminded of a cat and the way it would turn its whole head rather than move its eyes. Its jaw went slack and the innards it had been chewing fell from its mouth and to the floor. Wet thuds resounded from where the flesh impacted with the blood. I was unable to move, terror gripping me. The zombie stared just for a moment, before its face twisted into a snarl. Its blackened lips pulled back over its broken teeth. The gash across its face, which exposed the sinew and bone beneath, seemed to tear further and grew wider as the zombie began to howl. Primal rage controlling every action of the creature. It climbed to its feet, congealed blood pulling away in globules as it made its uneasy ascent, and staggered towards me. I was still frozen but couldn't understand why. I had faced the undead so many times before! If it had been any faster, I would've been a dead man. Fortunately for me, the zombie kept slipping on the bloody floor, followed by the occasional stumble because of its uneven and uncoordinated steps.

Fear finally released my hand and I was spurred into action by thoughts of my imminent demise. I yanked my machete up high, the weight a familiar comfort, and a sudden calmness came over me. Just as quickly as I'd brought it up, I slammed it down. The machete crashed into the skull of the undead, splitting it like an overripe melon. And just like an overripe melon, the putrid innards spilt out and onto the floor in front of me. Blackened brain mixed with reddish-brown gore. If I had any sustenance in me to vomit out, I would have. Starvation had its advantages, I suppose. My machete was wedged in the skull of the zombie, like a twisted version of The Sword in the Stone. I placed one foot on the zombie's neck and pulled my machete out with such force that, had there been any onlookers, they would've crowned me the next King of Britain. Flecks of rotten brain matter flicked up and daubed me. I panted, adrenaline leaving my body with each heartbeat and exhaustion beginning to take over. The wound in my leg felt heavy, and I was hungry. I needed to stop. I just needed a break, but I knew I wouldn't get it anytime soon.

I heard shuffling behind me and wheeled around on one foot, the slick blood on the floor nearly causing me to slip over. I saw a few undead heading towards the front door, so I grabbed the door and slammed it shut, then slid the bolt across. It wouldn't hold long, but it would provide me some time to do … whatever it was I was going to do.

As I looked down at the two corpses, the reality of the situation hit me hard and I dropped my machete, submerging it in blood. I gripped and rolled the zombie I'd just killed off of the other body. I felt my chest tighten and breathing quicken as the moment of revelation grew nearer. As I rolled the second body over, it squelched in the blood.

Please don't be Alice. Please don't be Alice. Please don't be Alice.

I was relieved by the disgusting mess that was once a human. Although half its face was gone, part of its skull was caved in, and most of its chest cavity had been pulled away, I could see it wasn't Alice. It was another young woman who I'd never seen before. I let go of her body the moment I realised she held no significance to me. Relief flooded through me, but it still left the question of where was my Alice?

I picked up my machete, blood slick on my hands, and stepped over the dead woman, ignoring her glassy gaze. I walked further into the hallway, to the left, and into the lounge. Empty. Barely any blood, just the leftover devastation which was expanding from the hallway. No one was in there, alive or dead. I had a quick glance around the room, and something was niggling away at me. I continued looking around the familiar room but couldn't put my finger on it. Something was definitely amiss. I hated the cryptic sensation. Whatever it was, it would have to wait. I crept onto the next room but didn't dare to call out for someone in case *others* were in the house. Then I moved towards the kitchen.

Alice's kitchen was huge. I mean massive. I could probably get to maximum running speed from the length of it! It was modern, with up-to-date worktops and an expensive cooker. The sort of kitchen I had wanted to own someday. A faint hope that the world would return to normal and I would own a kitchen like that still glimmered deep inside me. The tiled floor, which I'd slid across in my socks many times, was also slick with blood. I had my machete raised and could already see the source. A zombie stood at the far end of the kitchen, staring out the window. I doubted it was admiring the once perfectly pruned garden.

I sprinted towards it, making huge bounds as my feet pounded the tiles. I sunk my machete into the back of its skull before it'd even begun to turn around, splitting the skull and destroying the brain. It collapsed to the floor. At first glance, I thought the zombie was Alice's father, Mark. It was short, frail, and grey-haired like Alice's father. However, her father wasn't a butch undead woman. I felt bad mistaking a woman for Mark but doubted he would mind considering the circumstances.

I checked the two smaller side rooms for any sign of the Kingsleys. The dining room and pantry were devoid of life. Nothing indicated their presence, yet something still felt wrong. I ignored the mysterious feeling and moved back to the hallway and towards the stairs. I couldn't hear any movement above. No creaking of floorboards or shifting of the house, so I ran up the stairs, taking two at a time. I could hear the undead outside, thumping against the door. It wouldn't be long before the house was breached. Would I still be inside when it was?

CHAPTER 2

I stood on the landing. Four doors were in front of me in a horseshoe shape. The door to my immediate left was Mother and Father Kingsley's room, Mark and Lydia. The next one over, in front and to the left, was Alice's room. Next to that was the spare room, in front, to the right, and used for storage. The door to my immediate right was the bathroom.

I knew from past visits that all the rooms were about the same size. Both bedroom doors had artwork and a name stuck to the woodwork which indicated whose room it was. The landing I stood on was so narrow that two people would struggle to pass each other. The only thing on it was a bookshelf. It wasn't the biggest of gaps and I would have to walk sideways to fit through it, but that also meant the undead would have to come at me one at a time.

All the doors were closed. That worried me. Not because closed doors were out of the norm, but because I didn't know who or *what* was on the other side. I thought – hoped that if there'd been any undead in one of the rooms, then they would've stirred at the commotion downstairs and alerted me to their presence. I still clutched the machete, which was the best comfort blanket available. I placed my hand on the door handle of Lydia and Mark's room.

"Nothing ventured," I sighed, twisting the door handle, "nothing gained."

I pushed the door.

And nothing was gained. The room was empty, as in no one was there. It looked like it had been torn apart. Could there have been looters already? I doubted it. It seemed too early for that, and nothing of value seemed to have been taken. I moved onto the bathroom next. When I opened the door, my heart jumped into my throat and adrenaline flooded my body. Similar scenario to the first room.

I headed towards the spare room. I was leaving Alice's room until last, knowing I was delaying the inevitable. When opening the spare room door, my heart barely made any irregular movement. It didn't even skip a beat. I suppose there are only so many times your system can be shocked before it becomes desensitised. Maybe if I survived long enough my body would just get rid of that feeling altogether?

I stared into the spare room curiously. I still had the feeling that something wasn't right. The room was a mess. The cupboard was tilted over and the contents of the drawers were strewn everywhere. I couldn't shake the unmistakable feeling that something was wrong. But it wasn't the mess. It was something else. I could feel the solution creeping around the edge of my brain, teasing me with the almost-answer before darting back into the recesses of my mind. *Dammit.*

I left the room and moved on to Alice's. The thought of something amiss was bothering me. It was frustrating, even more so in a scenario as crucial as the one I was in. I stared at Alice's door. I didn't want to open it. There were so many reasons for that. What if Alice wasn't inside? What if it became painfully obvious what her fate was? What if it became clear that I would never know what happened to her? Different scenarios. Different outcomes. With all those potential futures, I didn't know which one I wanted. The preferable outcome would be that Alice and her family were sat comfortably in her room with enough food and weapons to survive for a long time. That didn't seem likely. The worst-case scenario ... well, with the dead walking, it's obvious what that was.

While the door was closed, hope remained alive. The moment it was opened, reality would become apparent. Nonetheless, no matter what outcome I desired, I had to open the door to answer any of my questions. I walked forward, mouth dry and hand trembling. For the second time that day, turning a door handle seemed to be the hardest decision of my life. I turned the handle, hands slick with sweat. The door swung open slowly, revealing what future I would be living in.

What I liked about Alice's room was that it was the perfect representation of everything she was. She was a lover of music and singing, and there were huge stacks of CDs for her favourite bands and musicals. These, however, were scattered across the floor. The cases lay broken and discs everywhere. Little knickknacks of things she liked, such as Disney princesses and Tinkerbell. I had bought her a charm bracelet once upon a time, and that also laid on the side.

Other bits of jewellery scattered on the floor, on her desk, on the shelf. Memorabilia from various events. Programmes from the theatre, gig tickets, graduation photos – things Alice wanted to remember. The cardboard box of goodies I had posted to her was sitting in the corner next to the bin. The contents were still in there. Good to know they had made it to her. The clothes cupboard wasn't tipped over as it had been in the other room, but the clothes were strewn over the floor.

On the ceiling, there were brown-stained smudges. I smiled briefly at that, the memory coming back to me vividly. Alice had bought a small chocolate milkshake for her five-hour drive home from Bristol. I never understood why since she didn't even like chocolate milkshake. She got home without drinking it and forgot about it. Apparently she lived like an animal, because she found it a week later. At that point, it was out of date and the bottle was bloated. Without a second thought, she threw it into the bin in her bedroom. Even later again, she heard a small rumbling from her bin. She said she had looked at it in confusion and worry … before rancid milkshake exploded onto her ceiling. When she told me about it, I couldn't stop laughing. Several times a year, Alice would say that she would repaint her ceiling, but she never got around to it. I guess she would never get around to it.

I moved away from the funny memory and continued to look around her room. Her bed was against the far wall, the furthest possible distance from the door, covered with a humped section of bedding. Part of me hoped Alice was hiding under it and all would be okay. I knew that wasn't the reality I was in, but I couldn't help but wait for Alice to poke her head out and say she loved me.

I pulled the bedding away expectantly, only to be met with disappointment. A disappointment I knew was coming but was still difficult to face. So what next? I simply didn't know what to do anymore. No sign of where anyone was or where they had gone. No sign of Alice. No sign of her family.

The undead still pounded on the door below, and I

wondered how long it would be before they finally broke in. I no longer cared if they did. What was the point in carrying on at that point? I had no leads. Nowhere left to go. Alice and her family were probably one of the many bodies or undead in the Great British countryside. My family was probably dead or undead also. I was lost and alone in a dead world. My situation? It was all my fault.

"What the hell now?!" I screamed to the heavens. "Just give me a sign! Just tell me what to do!"

No response. No God or sign to tell me all would be okay. My voice felt strained. A lump had formed in my throat.

"What do I do now?" I whispered to myself, begging. Desperation welled up inside me. I could feel tears creeping into the corners of my eyes. I suddenly felt weak. Tired and exhausted. Drained and empty. I so badly wanted to sleep.

I climbed on to Alice's bed, feeling numb, physically and emotionally. I propped myself up against the wall. I was ready to die. Life was just so … difficult, and I didn't think death could be harder. I faced the door. If I was going to die, I wanted to see it coming at least. Feeling how I did, being dead didn't sound so bad right about then. I pulled Alice's blanket over me, her smell engulfing me. I imagined she was here. I could smell the coconut shampoo she always used, the light touch of her perfume. I wrapped the blanket around me, only my head exposed. I just wanted a minute with her before I finally *slept.*

I just stared at the wall and door opposite. Moments passed. I felt it again. That tick that something was wrong. I furrowed my brow and thought about following that feeling. But I didn't. My expression softened. I didn't care anymore. So I closed my eyes, thought of happier times, and listened to the rhythmic sound of the pounding on the door downstairs.

It wouldn't be long …

CHAPTER 3

It was my and Alice's first date. Although, it wasn't really a date, yet it kind of was. We had been best friends for more than a year prior to our first kiss, and it was weird to go on a date. Not because it was an unfamiliar territory. Not because friends shouldn't do that. Not even because we were *mostly* dating anyway. It was weird because we already knew almost everything about each other. So why have a date? We didn't need to learn if we were compatible through awkward small talk. We already knew we were. We had spent all our time together being best friends. That's pretty damn compatible. Yet there we were, sitting on either side of a table in a pizzeria, not sure what to say.

"Well, this is awkward," I said. Alice laughed awkwardly at my observation. Why was this happening? Why was it so difficult? Was it an unspoken biological rule that once you began dating someone you both become idiots? It was frustrating. Here I was, soon to finish my university degree, and I couldn't speak to a girl I'd been speaking to for over a year! Don't fail me now brain!

But fail me my brain did. I was a very logical human, who always thought with my head and never my heart. Yet here I was letting my heart lead the way while my brain was on vacation.

We sat there, silent and just looking around the room. Then we began making small talk about the restaurant. How nice it looked and such, even though we had both been there before. Finally the pizza arrived. At least that would break the weirdness. I picked it up and began munching.

Wait! said a voice in my head. *This is a date dammit! Use your goddamn knife and fork! Be a gentleman!*

So I picked up my knife and fork and began to cut my pizza into smaller pieces. I was staring at my hands. Was I cutting my food right? I didn't remember how to use a knife and fork! Did my hands always look that weird? They were so veiny. I sighed and put the cutlery down. I looked at Alice eating her pizza, oblivious to my obvious moron-ism. She was eating with her hands, so should I? I picked up the first slice of pizza and bit a piece off. I hadn't been shunned out of the restaurant for bad manners. Alice hadn't thrown her glass of water in my face and stormed out. It was going fine! I took another bite. Was I crunching the crust too loudly? I looked at Alice's face. She didn't appear to notice. This is a lot easier than I thought! I laughed aloud.

"What?" Alice asked smiling. Her eyes twinkled. She looked amazing. I relaxed.

"Nothing," I replied, a smile continued to linger on my face. Then I thought about it. We had been friends for so long and I may as well tell her! I leaned forward and said, "Just laughing at why we are being so awkward."

"I know, it's so silly isn't it!" Alice laughed. We both smiled at each other, the awkwardness gone. We continued eating, and talking about rubbish. The same rubbish we would always talk about. We finished up our food and left for the cinema.

The cinema trip was less awkward and more fun. We

didn't have to talk, which I was thankful for. I don't remember what the film was, but I do remember that part way through the film, Alice grasped my hand and interlocked her fingers with mine. I was holding her hand! It was so simple but so nice.

I could get used to this, I thought, truly relaxed for the first time in a while. And get used to it I did get. Best friends becoming more than best friends definitely worked. We were happy together for such a long time.

CHAPTER 4

How long had I been in Alice's room? I became aware of my surroundings again and looked up. My head was groggy, eyes tired and moist. Had I been crying? I couldn't be sure. I looked around. Compared to when I got to the house, there was very little light pouring through the window. It was getting dark outside, and in a few more hours it would be nightfall. How much time had passed? I was pretty sure I hadn't fallen asleep, but I don't think I had been entirely awake either.

My body ached and clicked as I moved. My injured leg burned intensely. Had infection set in already? I looked down and there was fresh blood seeping out of the poorly wrapped wound. The wound wasn't going to heal by itself, and I didn't know how to deal with it. My back was tender and stiff from being pushed against the wall for so long. Nothing had changed in the room and I was still alive, which was a surprise.

I was vaguely aware that the undead had broken into the house sometime in the last few hours. I recalled hearing the door crumble as the dead finally fell through. I'd been expecting death's cold embrace the moment the door collapsed and for what felt like hours after that. I had hoped for it, yet it didn't come. The undead must have broken through the door and just forgot why they were trying to get in. One-track minded. They were probably still wandering around on the floor below or in a dormant-like state until they met another stimulus.

I wanted the death that I deserved, and I was impatient about it dammit! How dare I be kept waiting from what I wanted it. I wouldn't be denied the long sleep I craved. Rage surpassed the all-encompassing sadness momentarily, and I liked it. I was going to storm downstairs and face them head-on. If I died, so be it. If I lived? I would just have to find another encounter with the undead, and another and another. I would fight until I died! Just because I wanted to die didn't mean I would go out easily! A warrior's death.

I stood up, blanket still around me. I was reluctant to leave it behind so soon. My leg felt weak, and I stumbled. As I did, I knocked a photo frame off the bedside cabinet and it hit the floor with a clatter and smashed. Glass flew in every direction. I was annoyed. It was a nice frame after all. Then again, it didn't matter anymore. This disturbance would probably lure the undead to me, if my elephant sounding footsteps didn't.

I dropped the blanket and bent down to pick up the frame. It was face down and I wondered what photo was in it. Was it of me? I hoped so. I really hoped it was. I turned the photo frame over. No photo. My face contorted in confusion. Had it fallen out? I looked around the floor, looking to see if there were any photos on the ground. Nothing. Like it had just vanished. In fact, I hadn't seen a single photo in Alice's room.

I raised my head cautiously. There was normally a photo collage on the wall opposite Alice's bed, with pictures of her friends, her family and other pieces of her life. It was no longer there. Cogs began to turn in my head.

"Whoa, whoa," I said as I started connecting the loose threads of the situation. Had … had the photos been taken? I didn't think looters would've taken them. That wouldn't make sense. Why would looters want a photo collage? The only people who would take photos were … Alice's family or someone who knew the family. Had Alice's family got out in time? Surely, if they had time to pack photos they had made it?

I moved to the collage wall. There were marks from where wall putty had been used to stick the collage up. Definitely taken down intentionally. Hope began to rise within. I didn't want it to blossom because I found hope often lead to disappointment. There was only one way to tell, and the answer would be in the spare room. I raced there, leaping over the mess and shoving the bookshelf on the landing out of the way, not caring about the noise I was making. My leg made it difficult to manoeuvre, and I was sure I was leaving blood everywhere. I didn't even collect my machete from Alice's bed. I was being careless, but I suspected that most who had gone from suicidal intent to survival in the space of a few minutes would be the same.

I stood in the doorway and scanned the room. With the mess, I couldn't find what I was looking for. I stumbled into the room and then dived into the centre of it. I began throwing stuff around, checking under things, looking inside of other things. I even moved the drawer set out and checked down the back to see if *it* had fallen behind. I couldn't find *it*, and that filled me with relief!

They weren't here! If *they* weren't here, then the Kingsleys had gotten away! With that revelation, I grinned and couldn't stop. I could feel the dried blood caked on my face cracking and splitting as my grin spread ear to ear. I probably looked like some psychotic clown. Not that clowns didn't look psychotic to me anyway.

"They're not here!" I cheered. I looked around, desperately wanting to tell someone. Anyone. Even the undead would suffice. Joy rippled through me, chasing away the cold depression that had set in. I shouted, "They got out safely!"

I was so happy I could feel myself a few seconds away from dancing a little jig. But a lifetime of social anxiety and incidences of public embarrassment couldn't be set aside just because of something as silly as an apocalypse. I refrained from dancing and stayed as cool as someone who had probably already lost it could.

I probably seemed like a madman to anyone watching or listening. Completely crazy. Suffering from a severe case of insane-atosis. Gone off the … you get the point. And for all I knew, I may very well have lost it. I had never been the most levelheaded of people as it was. The world had fallen apart and there I was hooting and cheering. But my exclamations of joy were justified. What had put me into fits of such hysterical joy? The Bogs were missing, of course! How could it not have been so obvious before? That was what hadn't felt right. That's what seemed out of place and missing from the house. There were no photos. There were no soft toys. There were no personal touches which made a house a home. Most importantly, and the greatest clue of all, there were no Bogs!

CHAPTER 5

See, what you have to understand about the Bogs is that they're essentially members of the Kingsley family. So what are they? They're soft toy bears, but don't you dare call them *just* soft toys! They're the Bogs. Long-armed and legged teddy bears. They've been in the Kingsley family since Alice was young, and they've grown up with her. They all have a personality and their own way of thinking, voiced by all the family.

So what are they like? They like to dress up, eat chocolate, and they love to swear. In a household where swearing wasn't allowed, the Bogs could get away with anything. It was a way for all the Kingsleys to express thoughts and feelings in a way they wouldn't normally get away with. They wanted to express anger? The Bogs would voice it.

They were also a way for Alice to deal with fears she had as a child. There was Sparkle, the bear who chased away lightning. Thundy, the loud one who told thunder to go away. And there was Doggone, the one who protected young Alice from scary dogs. It was a unique and weird idea, but they weren't original when it came to naming them. Knowing how much the Bogs meant to the family, the Kingsleys wouldn't leave them behind, in the same way they wouldn't leave another family member behind.

The Kingsleys were the sort of family who would name possessions, including their cars. I found it strange, but it was something I had to deal with because I would have to live with it forever once Alice and I lived together. I would have to love the Bogs as much as they did. It was always hard to make people understand the Bog's significance to the Kingsleys, so I used a certain story from our relationship to explain it.

It was my first time meeting Alice's parents. We had travelled all the way from Bristol to Essex. It was a long journey, filled with a stress-induced bickering. I was wearing a shirt, jeans and new shoes for the occasion. I'm not a shoe man or a shirt man. In fact, I was barely a clothes man if I could get away with it. But I was most comfortable in a pair of old trainers, a video game t-shirt and faded jeans.

"Do I look okay?" I asked Alice for the thousandth time. She told me that I did, for the thousandth time.

I was nervous about meeting her parents, but it wasn't her parents I had to impress. It was the Bogs. If I was allowed to meet the Bogs and their crazy personalities, the parents would like me. If I wasn't even introduced to the Bogs, well, I probably wouldn't be welcomed back into their home, Alice had told me. I almost didn't believe her at first because it sounded like the words of a crazy person. Luckily, I did meet the Bogs and won them over easily. I handed them a packet of chocolate buttons and I was their buddy. All was well. I had played their game and showed them I could be weird too.

I came to realise that even though the Bogs were mostly Alice's, they definitely belonged to the whole family. And twenty-plus years later, the Bogs slept in Alice's bed to keep her safe at night. Even though the Bogs were all loved equally, Thundy was Alice's most prized possession. This was because, even as an adult, she was still afraid of thunder. Thundy wasn't allowed to leave the house in case he got lost, but they would never leave him to fend for himself should they have to abandon the family home.

With that tale told, you can see the importance of the Bogs not being in any of the rooms. No one would take the Bogs while looting. They held no value outside of the sentimental kind. So that left one option. The Kingsleys had escaped with enough time to take the Bogs and other non-essentials with them. They'd made it out in time, and I had to find them.

CHAPTER 6

I climbed out of the spare room, through the massive amounts of debris which had once made up the Kingsley's life, and ran straight for Alice's room. I ran like the hounds of hell were at my heels. I didn't have a direction, but I had a purpose again, and I would *not* be stopped before I'd finished my quest.

I snatched my machete off of Alice's bed and gripped it. The fire of intent flowed through my veins and arteries, filling me up with power and life. I felt unstoppable. I almost stomped out of Alice's room and down the stairs to fight, what I imagined to be, the hordes of undead waiting for me. But I stopped. Something peeking out from behind the door caught my eye. A little fluffy head. A head I recognised. I pulled the door away and saw Thundy hiding away, alone and terrified.

"Oh, Thundy," I picked him up, dusted him off, and held him close to my chest. "How could they leave you behind?"

He didn't reply, which was lucky because that would mean I was losing it big time. He was just a soft toy after all, but I wasn't going to leave him behind because of what he stood for. Alice's innocence and childhood.

Thundy was just as lost as me, and him being left behind brought tears to my eyes. Everything about this world was wrong. The dead were walking. I was alone. Alice was missing.

And Thundy wasn't with the other Bogs to take care of her. I needed to return Thundy to her. He would always keep her safe.

I decided that Thundy was coming with me on my journey. I would return him to Alice's arms, even if it meant walking through hell to do so. I tucked Thundy through a belt loop, with his head holding him in place and his body hanging loosely through the bottom part and bouncing against my leg when I walked. I felt overwhelmed. Overwhelmed by what to do. Overwhelmed by emotion. Overwhelmed by everything. Emotions that I had locked down began to leak through the barriers I'd built up since leaving home. I wanted to see my family. I had to try and find a way to contact them.

I remembered my smartphone, the one I almost left in my bag. The bag that now belonged to the *charismatic* General Harrington. My fists instinctually clenched at the mere thought of my sworn enemy. I took a deep breath and slowly let it out. He wasn't the problem at that moment. Contacting my family was.

I emptied out my pockets, pulling out the bullet I had reserved for Harrington's head and my phone. I held it up and saw it was dead. I didn't have time to wait for it to hit that crucial five per cent charge for it to work, so I slipped it back into my pocket and thought about my circumstance. It was then that my gaze fell on the house phone sitting on the desk in Alice's room. I picked it up and pressed it to my ear. I listened for a dial tone. No sound. The phone was connected to the wall, so that must mean the system was down! I had no doubt the television would be the same. I didn't have time to concern myself with that. I had to push myself forward and move on.

I placed my hand on my waist and checked for Thundy. He was still there. Gun was still in my waistband. I swished my machete through the air a few times, readying my slaughtering arm. My next steps would be to clear the downstairs of undead and then to find some clues on the Kingsleys whereabouts.

I prepared myself to go downstairs, bouncing up and down on the spot, psyching myself up to get ready for the conflict. I took a step forward, psychologically prepared to take on the entire population of Willamette if I had too, but I wasn't physically able. My leg buckled under my weight, my wound clearly getting worse. I winced. Fixing my leg would have to be my first step before I could try to take on a single zombie. I limped towards the bathroom, shut the door, and bolted the lock. I didn't think the lock could hold off the undead, but old habits die hard. I slumped onto the edge of the bath, not realising how much my leg truly hurt until I had taken all the weight off it in a moment of peace. I could feel it pulsing with each heartbeat. That couldn't be a good sign.

I didn't really know how to go about fixing my leg, but I knew I had to clean it first. I decided to plug the bath and turn on the water all the way up to scorching hot. I let the tub fill up. Not too much, but enough to be able to dip my leg in. I went searching through the bathroom cupboard under the sink. I was looking for an anti-bacterial cleaning agent, but there was nothing except bleach.

I stared at the bleach for a few moments. A bit uneasy about using it to clean a wound, but I vaguely recalled it being okay as long as it was mixed with water. Or was I remembering that right? Maybe it had said to never mix with water to clean a wound? I sighed and shrugged. I would die if I didn't treat my leg, so it would have to do. I unscrewed the cap, fumbling with the safety mechanism, before releasing it and pouring it into the bath. The thick, gloopy liquid streamed into the hot bath water, the chemical smell burning my nostrils.

I hated bleach. Hated everything about it. Screw the lack of colour. Screw the smell. Screw the viscosity of it. I think it linked back to being forced to do housework. Hated housework too. At least I would never have to do that again.

My focus snapped back to my current situation. I had to get it done as quickly as possible because I had to be prepared at all times. The undead could begin slamming against the door and break through at any moment.

I made sure the bleach was mixed into the water thoroughly before I continued. Next was the horrible job of removing the glass protruding from my leg. I didn't want to do it. It would hurt, and then there was the issue of evaluating the damage. It could be irreparable and, as much as my medical skills had advanced since preparing for my journey, I wouldn't be able to repair the damage. Yet the alternative was to bleed out or die later of infection. I needed to deal with it, so I re-evaluated what was in the cupboard. Bandages, medical tape, the watered down bleach which would have to do instead of hydrogen peroxide, and the white hand towel would have to be used for compression. There was also a pair of scissors on the side which would be useful to free my leg from my clothes.

I got to work, cutting up the length of my trouser leg until I was slightly above the wound. I then cut around my leg and removed the piece of blood-soaked material covered in mud and filth of unthinkable origins. I threw it to one side, and it slapped against the tiled floor. I stared at my exposed calf. It was red with wet and dried blood. The flesh around the glass was all puckered up around the wound, cut jaggedly by the foreign object. The skin was swollen and purple like a bruise. The blood leaking out was thicker than normal. Had infection set in already? All the more reason to get the filthy piece of glass out of me. What had I been thinking when I left it in there? The flash of being chased by undead came back to me. *Oh yeah.*

I wrapped the towel around my hand and gripped the glass. I would have to pull it out smoothly to avoid breaking any off inside me. I gritted my teeth, gripped the glass, and pulled slowly. It was strange seeing fresh blood flowing. I'd seen so much of the undead's coagulated blood that I had forgotten how blood was supposed to look.

The pain was excruciating. It hurt even more than when the shard had pierced me. My eyes welled up with tears and I ground my teeth as I pulled it out further. Blood began to flow more freely. The glass was coming out swiftly while cutting further into me. My vision began to go dark. I forced my eyes to stay open. I couldn't pass out. Not then.

With one last tug, I removed the glass from my leg. I blacked out momentarily before everything came spinning back and I pulled myself back from the edge of unconsciousness. I had to finish it while I could. I left the glass where it lay and threw my leg into the bath. Big mistake! The pain intensified! The bleach-laden water filled my wound, burning. I howled through gritted teeth in the most inhuman way imaginable. The pain didn't get better. I swished my leg around to make sure the water cleaned my entire wound.

Water lapped up over the side and onto the floor. I was making a mess, but the wound would be clean at least.

I pulled my leg out of the bath and dried it with the towel, wiping away the fresh and old blood. I cleaned up most of the water, too. I made sure to gently rub the area around the wound. I didn't want to hurt myself any more than I had to. It may have been the placebo effect but, even though it still hurt, it felt much better.

When I was sure that the wound was as clean and dry as it could be, I wrapped my leg tightly with the bandage, compressing it as I did so. Next, I wrapped it with many layers of the cream coloured medical tape. It held the bandage in place and added more compression to the wound. I was fairly certain the wound would be okay … hopefully. I knew I had antibiotics in my saddlebags, which I needed to get to. It would stop my wound from getting worse. If it wasn't too late anyway.

I stood up, leg still tender but pressure could be applied to it now. I looked at myself in the full-length mirror on the back of the door. I was extremely pale, sickly so, except for the blood caked all over the rest of me. My military clothes were a mess, and one trouser leg was missing. Stubble had started to grow back. I wanted to deal with that sooner than later, but it wasn't the time. I didn't feel safe having my fresh bandage as exposed as it was because it could get dirty so easily. I didn't have a change of clothes anywhere in Essex. But Alice had stuff that I could wrap around it. Exotic items such as scarves.

I left Alice's room, a multi-coloured scarf now covering my recently bandaged leg wound. It added to my madman appearance, yet I looked so *damn* fashionable. If only looks could kill. I was stood where I had been an hour earlier, psyching myself up again. The irony that I could have charged my phone in that time was not lost on me. Before it got too dark, I had to make a move. I patted Thundy's head and twirled my machete one more time before taking a step down the stairs.

CHAPTER 7

I hadn't even made it to the bottom step before the undead were on me. I descended the steps as carefully and quietly as I could for the element of surprise, but the ageing stairs were having none of it. I made it about halfway and spotted many undead before they were aware of me. They were rooted to the spot, swaying as if unable to maintain their balance, oblivious to my presence as I moved.

That all changed when my foot hit one particular stair. Whether the wood was warped or if it was as simple as the Universe hating me, the loudest creak sounded and elongated as the full weight of my foot pressed on it. My breath caught in my throat as several heads swivelled to look at me. Death howls and snarls emitted from the shambling corpses as they charged, the stimulus immediately setting them into action. Each was trying to climb over the other to get to me. But I had the advantage. It was as good as over for them since I had the high ground. The narrowness of the stairs combined with my position meant that only one zombie could come at me at a time. Much better than having to fight them all at once.

The first zombie reached me. I slammed my machete into its head before kicking it aside. All this happened in the time it took another zombie to clamber over its fallen comrade's body to get at me. I repeated the pattern. Adrenaline flowed through me as I lifted my machete again. I was beginning to recognise the moment adrenaline entered my body, creating the essential chemical reaction I needed to survive. I craved it.

There were so many undead in the house. I counted at least five in my peripheral, not including the four I killed in my bloodlust. It didn't matter, though. I felt I could keep it up forever.

"You're never gonna win!" I snarled as I kicked another bloodied corpse aside and pulled my machete from the front of its cranium while watching it tumble down the stairs. Almost as if they were responding to my taunt, a hand grabbed my ankle. I looked down to see a zombie had reached between the wooden bannister supports to grab me. It yanked at me hungrily and tried to pull itself between the supports, ignorant of physical limitations. As its face pressed against the wooden supports, the soft, rotten flesh began to slide away the harder it pushed. It was like watching a man's foreskin peel back. A disgusting, rotting, gory foreskin. The once-human face had split down the middle and peeled away to reveal a red gory and blackened mass of sinew below, but it still couldn't reach me.

I kicked another zombie backwards, down the stairs without killing it but used the excess time to swing my machete down onto the undead man's wrist. A clean slice. The zombie fell backwards and onto its backside. I ignored that the hand was still gripping my ankle and pushed forward with my attack, killing yet another zombie rushing up the stairs. That zombie was replaced by another and that one by another. Their ascent was getting slower and slower due to the corpses they had to climb over.

My arm ached and breathing grew heavy. It was exhausting. I may've been fit, but it was tiring work, and it was making me worse.

"How. Many. More. Are. There?" I could barely catch my breath, yet I continued swinging my machete, slaying more and more undead. The tide of undead seemed to be slowing. I couldn't see many more of the creatures downstairs, but that didn't mean more of them weren't waiting outside.

The flow of undead lessened even more, and I moved forward. I quickly clambered over the corpses in case there was any undead faking their death in the pile of re-dead. I paddled through the blood in the hallway, forgetting it was even there. But I wasn't so distanced that I didn't notice the blood splash up over my military boots, and I grimaced. I moved onwards. The front door was a mess. Splintered wood was exposed from under the paintwork. When the undead had finally busted the door down, it had been the woodwork that gave way first, as opposed to the lock.

I closed the door over as best as I could and pushed a small table in front of it. The table wouldn't stop anything. The door would open with the slightest bit of pressure, but it obscured the undead's view of me. I was aware that there were probably more in other rooms again, but I would deal with that when it came to it. For now, I had to look for clues as to where Alice and the rest of the Kingsleys had gone.

I moved into the front room, still clear of the undead, pulled the curtains to one side, and peeked out of the front window. There were zombies milling around nearby. None attempting to enter the house. I had an eerie sense of déjà vu as I looked out of the window. It felt like it had happened such a long time ago. I think it was a dream at some time or another, but I couldn't remember.

I continued to look around outside, my focus was the cars on the drive and not my chances of survival when I leave. As far as I could tell, all the family cars were there. Then again, I couldn't remember how many cars they had. I knew the parents had a car and so did Alice, plus a spare car they were planning to sell. Or did both parents have a car each and not just one between them? Did they still own the work van as well? Did they get around to selling the spare car? I couldn't remember. So all of the cars were there, or a couple were missing. That would hinder my search.

I let the curtain fall back across the window and left the front room to re-explore the downstairs. I splashed my way through the thickening blood, stepping over the corpses. I made my way into the kitchen, spotting the corpse I had left there earlier, and noticed a fresh trail of blood leading to the side dining room. I must've left the door open.

I silently crept to the open dining room and spotted the zombie. Unfortunately, the zombie spotted me first and was on me in a second. I barely had time to bring up my arm in defence before it charged into me. I managed to shove the zombie away, its gnashing jaws reflexively biting down as my arm got close to it.

The undead don't breathe. They're dead. But the impact of my shove pushed out whatever foetid air was still in its lungs, into my face. Its rotten stench filled my nostrils and lungs. Luckily, I had no food in me to sick out, but the heaving motion still came forward. I was retching, and my body convulsed as it tried to reject the death while I tried to keep the zombie at arm's length. With my other hand, I fumbled with my machete, trying to bring it up to attack. But every time I shifted my weight to bring the machete up, the zombie would gain an inch on me. A killing blow would be unlikely, and a major wound would do very little to something already dead.

I did notice that the frail creature would've probably been considered elderly when it was still alive. Hard to tell underneath the rot that had set in. That gave me an idea, though. I pushed my attack forward, which would leave me open briefly. I just hoped it wouldn't be enough for the creature to grasp me.

I leaned forward, causing the zombie to begin toppling. At that moment, I lifted my foot and slammed the heel of my boot into the side of the zombie's leg. It buckled inwards. Bone snapped and burst out of the rotten skin. Gore-covered bone was now exposed, snapped like wood. The zombie collapsed. That didn't stop it from coming, but it did give me a moment of respite to collect myself. I expelled the putrid air from my lungs and then pounced on the zombie. I stomped my boot into its chest to pin it down. Ribs cracked and snapped under the force of the impact. It laid there, trying to grab me and pull its mouth to the flesh of my leg. But I was stronger. I kept the zombie where it was and stared it in the face. I felt disgust and hatred for the creature in front of me. I no longer felt the sadness and remorse about the life it once had. I didn't even see it as human anymore.

I felt a sneer cross my face. Its empty eyes stared back at me. There was no hate. No fear. No sadness. Just an endless hunger.

"Fuck you," I snarled at the creature still reaching for me.

I placed my machete against the side of its head, much like a golfer would a golf club against a ball. I braced myself and let loose a full swing of my blade towards its head, arching it high like driver wedge. It crashed into the zombie's temple, splitting bone and destroying blackened grey matter. I had completely smashed the left side of its face. Eye socket crumpled under the blow. With that, it stopped moving. Stopped trying to eat me. Its one remaining eye still stared at me, just as empty as it had been moments earlier. Nothing human about the undead creatures, and I truly understood it at that moment.

I wiped my machete clean on the zombie's torn clothing before turning away. Awareness of my surroundings finally returned from the tunnelled vision of the fight. I calmed down, breathed more steadily, and focussed my mind on the present. I really needed to find clues to Alice's whereabouts.

CHAPTER 8

I quickly opened and closed drawers and cupboards in the kitchen. I was looking for something. *Anything.*

The Kingsleys had clearly made a move out of there. Sharp knives and other potential weapons were missing. Most of the food had been taken from the cupboards. Half a loaf of uncut bread was all that remained. I grabbed at it, took huge, hungry bites from it, not bothering to cut it into a manageable size. Didn't even care about the growing patches of mould. I was starving and couldn't remember the last time I had eaten. I swallowed the dry bread, washing it down with a mug of water. There were no clean glasses about. They were either dirty on the side or dirty in the dishwasher. A mug was all that was available. That probably meant they had to leave in a hurry. No time to clean up and leave the house presentable for their return. If they thought they would return.

I looked in the side room, which was used as storage. A couple of suitcases were missing. They had clearly packed some stuff but not all of it. Perhaps they'd been cut short? Had they been planning to leave for a while but had to push ahead with their plans sooner than anticipated? The question still remained, where did they go?

I carried on opening cupboards. Footwear was missing

also, specifically hiking boots. Smart thinking. I almost bypassed the last cupboard since it was just the keys cupboard. But I stopped to take a look. All the keys were there except Mark's keys. They were his work and leisure keys, yet his car was outside. That didn't help at all! I sighed in frustration. They were probably somewhere else in the house, and I'd just missed them. I hadn't been looking for them at the time. I had always liked his keys, mainly because it had the coolest key fob I'd ever seen. They were on a wooden buoy keychain. He said it was because he went sailing a lot and it was in case his keys ever fell overboard. I smiled. It was a nifty idea. Something simple, yet effective. I remembered seeing his boat at the docks, too. Nice little thing, but big enough to sail long distance if he wanted. I had never been on his boat, but I would have liked to. A boat would've been useful nowadays, I think. A boat … a boat would have …

For the second time that day, I had an explosive moment of realisation. How could I have been so stupid?! The boat keys were gone. The Kingsleys had more than likely headed towards the docks. They would've gone for the boat to get out of there as soon as possible. I didn't know how far behind them I was, but I sure as hell wasn't going to let them get any further.

I scoffed down the rest of the bread and drank my fill of water. I even emptied my bladder and rinsed my mouth with mouthwash. I wasn't giving up the clean-freak in me so easily. Before leaving the bathroom, I looked at my face. It was thinner than I remembered, almost shallow, with pronounced cheekbones. Facial hair was making rapid growth around my mouth. I didn't like having any resemblance of a beard. I felt I looked homeless with facial hair, but it would have to wait.

Many more important things were afoot.

I looked at myself one last time, eyes meeting their counterpart in the reflection. A haunted look resided in them. Eyes that had seen terrible things looked back at me. I continued staring at myself solemnly before a smile broke out. Enough with the poetics. Things to do, true loves to save. I walked away from my reflection. I didn't want to look at it anymore.

CHAPTER 9

I found myself upstairs again, this time looking out the window and surveying the surrounding area. My recent activities had definitely caused a stir for the local undead population. The commotion had drawn undead into the immediate area, making the planned heroic dash to my motorcycle difficult. They weren't actively seeking me out, yet I wouldn't take a car. I didn't have an option because there could be any number of roadblocks between the Kingsleys' home and the docks, so keeping the motorcycle was the only option.

I made my descent back down the stairs and towards the front door. I gripped it to leave. For a brief moment, the finality of leaving saddened me. The odds of me standing in that exact hallway, or the house regaining the warmth of a family home again, was slim. I would never see it again. I suppose it was the people who made a house a home, and not the building.

"Bye," I muttered to no one as I opened the door and left. None of the undead noticed me as I walked out the front door and quietly closed it. I didn't want anyone or anything going into the house while it was unoccupied. I was still holding onto the small hope that one day I could return, no matter how unlikely it seemed.

I viewed the undead's shuffling positions. There was no straight and direct route to my motorcycle, which now was on its side in the street, but I still had the element of surprise on my side. I took a few quick rapid breaths to quell my nerves and get myself pumped. I gripped my machete in one hand. The other instinctively touching Thundy. I sprinted. I wasn't heading for the gate leading out of the driveway, but instead for the knee-high wall which surrounded the rest of the garden. I kept my legs pumping, the noise of my boots slamming into the ground caused the undead to begin turning my way.

I reached my maximum running speed and jumped. With one foot, I pushed myself off the wall and propelled myself forward. I cleared the wall and felt as though I was soaring through the air. Everything seemed to slow down. Undead were starting to move towards me, their awkward and clumsy limbs unable to coordinate a swift running speed at such short notice. I felt free for the few moments I was in the air, before I came crashing back down to earth. I landed in a clumsy pile, rolling to spread the force of my landing. My leg gave way the moment the weight of my impact reached it! It was nothing like in the films where the hero got up out of the graceful roll. I, instead, pushed myself to my feet, wiping grit and blood off my face with the back of my hand, and looked to my left. A few undead were beginning to coordinate themselves and move much faster. It still wasn't a fearsome sprint, but worrying, nonetheless.

I ran for my bike, limping, my injured leg still not quite ready for the performance I needed. I could sense the undead gaining on me. Eerie thoughts of their dead fingertips swiping at my collar as they got closer passed through my head. No fingers grasped me though as I picked up my still-running motorbike. I had been in such a hurry to get into Alice's home that I hadn't even shut it off.

I straddled the bike, took one glance over my shoulder at the oncoming undead before pulling the throttle back and disappearing down the road. I didn't need to look back to know the undead were still chasing me, and I didn't need to be a genius to know that they'd probably carry on chasing me until they forgot about me – or easier prey came along. The roar and rumble of the motorcycle gave me confidence. I felt safe on the bike, probably because I could easily get away on it. I had planned to pull over somewhere and collect myself. Just to get myself into some sort of order. I still needed to take some antibiotics, which was essential to surviving in an undead world. Without any real medical care, something as simple as a leg injury could be fatal if not kept in check. But what prevented me from pulling over was the undead everywhere. I would turn a corner, only to be met with another street of carnage and the walking dead. I wasn't entirely sure where I was going or if I was going to the docks. I had a vague idea of where I was heading, but I needed to stop and prepare myself for the next leg of my journey.

I eventually found a small cul-de-sac where there was no undead in sight, but the street hadn't escaped the carnage. Blood and corpses littered the street, as well as bullet shells scattered amongst it all. This was the biggest sign of people fighting back. Not that it did them much good.

I hopped off my motorcycle and left it running. Doing so had saved me plenty of times, and it would be silly to change things. While doing one last visual check for the undead, I noticed an acrid smell in the air. I remembered the smoke I'd seen whilst entering Essex and noticed the cloud it formed was getting a lot bigger. Fire was spreading fast. I doubted there was anyone trying to fight the fire. The military was gone. Firefighters probably non-existent. Anyone else would be fighting to survive. The fire would just keep burning until it ran out of fuel. The Great Fire of Essex. That's what it would be called. I'm sure the fire would've started in the chaos, but no one would really know how. Hell, it was probably hundreds of smaller fires that had joined together. But with no emergency crews around, it wouldn't stop. Before long, it would gut the majority of Essex and leave it looking like a bombsight wasteland.

I checked through the saddlebags until I found the medication I was looking for – painkillers and antibiotics. I swallowed both with a swig of water from the canteen. The pain instantly decreased, and I smiled. Good-old placebo effect. Next, I had to find my way to the docks. Road signs weren't going to be much help if I was nowhere near it to begin with, and I no longer had a working phone to help me navigate with its GPS. But a GPS device was always an option. There were a couple of cars on the street. Perfect. I approached the first car, a black BMW probably worth more than my mother's house back in Bristol. It was in pristine condition except for a few flecks of blood splashed across it. I pressed my face up against the tinted windows and looked inside. Stuck to the front window was a small black box device. I smiled. It wasn't often I got lucky, let alone in the first instance and in a world where GPS devices were disappearing with the rise of smartphones. I tried the handle, and the alarm light flashed as a warning, but the door didn't budge. Now I had a chance to let my inner anarchist loose. I un-holstered my pistol and gripped it by the barrel. I quickly slammed it against the passenger side window, shattering it. A high-pitched alarm squealed, and I reached inside to pluck the GPS off the front window. The siren call of the alarm summoned the undead, and they began to shamble out of the open doors of the houses. They were drawn to the sound but weren't running yet. That would happen once they saw me.

As I walked back to my motorcycle, I turned on the GPS. It booted up quickly, and I began searching. I typed in the words *Essex* and *docks,* which brought up several results. I set the location for the closest one and clambered back onto my motorcycle. The undead began their sprint towards me. I pulled away and left them in my dust. I felt unstoppable.

CHAPTER 10

It didn't take long to find the docks, with the help of the GPS. I traversed the chaos-strewn streets, not seeing a single living person on the way. Plenty of undead, though. The docks were a glorified place to store boats. Not many boats sat on the water, but on transport frames so that they could be moved to the water by car.

I pulled up to the entrance and climbed off my motorcycle. I left it running. That had saved my life twice, so why fix something that's not broken? I walked to the entrance, stood just inside it, and stared at the area around me. There were rows and rows of small boats in storage. They stood tall up on huge metal stands at least another twelve feet above me. About ten rows of boats stretched in front of me, and many more rows wide. Probably a hundred boats in the yard. It occurred to me that a boatyard was a better name than a dock, considering the size and use.

My view was mostly obscured by the number of boats in front of me, and I couldn't see very far. Anything could be lurking around any one of these corners. To my right was the boathouse. I had been there once. It was an old-fashioned lodge which had been changed into a pub and restaurant for people who used the boatyard. It stood on wooden beams and slightly above ground level. A staircase led up to the old wooden building, which looked like it had been painted recently. The owners had always been proud of their lodge and kept it looking good. It appeared dark and uninhabited. No lights or activity. It was sad to see it so quiet. Although, I preferred the quiet rather than bustling with undead. I remembered where the Kingsley boat was. Vaguely, anyway. I would know which one it was if I saw it. So if I didn't see it, all was good.

A strong breeze blew in off the sea. The saltiness stung my nose, and it was bitterly cold on my face. But a refreshing change to the stench of the undead. Though, not as much of a comfort as I thought it would be. As bad as the undead smelled, it was beneficial to have around. A sufficient warning system if there were any nearby. Having the sea breeze would potentially eliminate that. Guess I couldn't even enjoy the small things anymore! I sighed. I didn't even enjoy the smell of the sea anyway. Not being able to have it is what frustrated me.

I walked further away from my motorcycle, the low rumble disappearing behind me. My machete in one hand and pistol in the other. I took quick but careful steps. Pretty much on the balls of my feet, ready to run if I needed to, moving silently. I couldn't see a single zombie as I crept past the rows and rows of boats. The further I walked, the more casual I became. Almost careless. My arms relaxed and my machete hung loosely in my hand, by my side. It was natural to relax. You could only maintain survival-induced terror for so long.

The sea breeze became stronger the closer to the waterfront I got. No boats to shield me from being buffeted by the wind and moisture spraying my face. It looked like there would be rain. The skies were grey and appeared as if the heavens were about to open and rain judgement down upon us. Perhaps there would be a flood of biblical proportions, ready to wash the tainted away for a new start. Maybe I was living in an apocalypse of the biblical kind. It made sense, even if I didn't believe in a god. Science couldn't even explain how the dead were being brought back to life, nor work out how they kept going as if they were alive. It was something straight out of a movie, so maybe the explanation would be straight out of a movie also.

"When there's no room in hell, the dead will walk the earth," I recited quietly. I didn't think that quote was in the Bible, as widespread as it was. There was quote in the bible to match it though, which I also said, "And the earth shall cast out the dead."

That seemed a lot more accurate for the current circumstance. I reflected on that and how a man of no religious inclination knew so much about the Bible. Curious. Perhaps the undead had … perhaps they … I stopped mid-thought, horrified at what I saw.

I had been walking on autopilot, just letting my feet guide me to where I needed to go while my thoughts ran wild. That was a mistake. I had absentmindedly turned a corner around one row of boats. I hadn't noticed the faint moaning or the slight stink of rot increasing in the air. After I turned around the edge of the boat, walking tightly to it instead of walking out further to get a better view on the situation, I walked straight into a congregation of undead. I stopped mid-stride, mouth agape at the size of the horde. There was probably a few hundred undead tightly packed there. All milling about, wandering aimlessly amongst themselves.

My heart leapt into my throat, and I froze in fear. I truly understood the phrase *deer in headlights* in that moment. I continued to stare at the shifting mass of undead, afraid to move. I went completely unnoticed by their glassy and lifeless eyes. Had I walked any further, I would have been among the dead. My motor functions snapped back to me in an instant, like a bungee cord at the moment when the jumper has reached maximum descent. I walked backward, remaining unnoticed by the undead. I kept walking backward, never taking my eyes off of them as they performed their meaningless functions. The occasional twitch as a burst of electrical energy spread through their nervous system, or a random snarl as something out of the ordinary caught its attention, only to be quickly forgotten.

They never would've noticed my retreat if I hadn't performed the ultimate horror movie faux pas. I forgot that each boat stand had a large black wheel sticking out of the side, should you wish to transport your boat via car. As a result of my lapse in awareness of my spatial surroundings, the heel of my foot caught on the wheel. I tripped and landed flat on my toned backside. An *oof* emitted at my meeting with the floor pushed all the air out of my lungs, winding me in the process. What was even worse than my clumsiness was the overly dramatically loud clang of the wheel rattling against its own frame. I was certain the folk in Kent, just over the water, would've heard it. Most importantly, the undead heard it. All at once, they turned to look at me. *This is where I die, you goddamn moron! You bloody well deserve it, too!* I cursed myself relentlessly as I attempted to push myself to my feet.

The undead had begun their slow but gradually faster shamble towards me. I still couldn't regain my breath as I pushed my dumb self to my feet. *You idiot!* I wheezed and choked as I pushed myself forward, stumbling. *All the films you watch!* I was on my feet. *This is how you decide to die!* I was running. *You should be ashamed!* I managed to swallow a huge ragged breath as my body finally gave way and allowed me to breathe again. *Now focus!* The undead was a fingers breadth away. I was swaying as I ran, body not fully recovered but getting there.

I felt cold fingers brush against the back of my neck. That was enough encouragement to push myself harder. My chest burned from the exertion forced on it. I could vaguely feel a warm trickle running down my leg. I hadn't emptied my bladder, so what was it? I risked a glance. The scarf I had wrapped my leg in was thick with blood! I must have torn the flesh that was trying to knit back together. The wound would never heal if I carried on as I was. I ignored my weakening leg and focussed on the ghastly howls of the undead behind me. They were so close! I wouldn't able to outrun them. They were tireless and couldn't be stopped easily. My brain rapidly snapped pieces of an unseen puzzle together until I realised how I could get away. My only chance was to use my natural advantages against the undead. I had to do something they couldn't. Climb.

Up ahead was another row of boats atop their metal stands. I pushed myself ahead for my target, giving me an extra inch on the undead. I would need every bit of distance I could get. My lungs and leg still burned. I felt like I was about to pass out from exhaustion. But, by some miracle of God, I managed to stay on feet!

I was rapidly approaching the boat, and I knew timing

would be everything. I sped closer and closer. It was only a matter of feet away. I tucked my machete and handgun into my waistband. Hands needed to be free for what I planned. In one swift motion, the foot of my uninjured leg hit the ground and I pushed off into a jump. I travelled through the air swiftly, but not the least bit graceful. I collided with the metal frame of the boat stand. Chest slammed into the cold metal support bar. I instinctively began to reach for my ribs but stopped myself. I had to climb.

The metal was icy cold and wet in my hands, causing me to slip at first. I readjusted my grip, knuckles going white as I held on for my life, and started to pull myself up. My calves were at the head height of the undead, which had rapidly gained on me. I started kicking wildly, doing my best to hold on. The heel of my boot hit one of the undead's nose. It crumbled and collapsed beneath the impact. Blackened blood leaked out from the facial wound. But that didn't stop it, not that I expected it to. Hands fumbled at my legs, trying to grab them to pull me back down into the swarming mass of bodies below. I thrashed and kicked and swiped at any zombies that managed to get close. I pulled myself up little by little. A smile of victory spread across my lips as I got further and further away from the undead. I climbed hand over hand further upwards. Soon I would be safe.

"You rotters," I huffed, with a smile as I climbed. Happiness flooded my brain. I was *nearly* safe! So close! Ever heard the warning about celebrating too early?

I was just pulling myself out of reach, when I felt an iron-tight hand wrap around my ankle. My hand was just moving up to the next wrung as it gripped me, and I could offer little resistance as it pulled me down towards it. It was my injured leg, so I could barely fight back from the intense pain. It had a tight grip on me, as if it were trying to squeeze all the blood out of me.

It continued to pull me down. I struggled and kicked. It was no good. Further and further down I went until I felt a sharp, blinding pain in the back of my calf. The pain of broken, rotten teeth breaking skin.

CHAPTER 11

I screamed. Agony ricocheted through my nervous system. I thrashed and kicked, but the zombie's teeth remained attached to me. I could feel every single shard of every single tooth piercing my skin. Every movement tore flesh. Every movement caused me to sink further. I tried to pull myself up, the pain reminding me that I wasn't going anywhere.

The zombie began to move away, chewing on my flesh. The flesh tore and ripped as it pulled away. Adrenaline and the wound on my leg were in a constant battle of dulling and renewing the pain. It would start to become numb, only for the simplest movement to set it off again.

Flesh, still in the zombie's mouth, fell away from me. Blood leaked down my leg. I could see the red dripping off of me and onto the undead. Their undead hands were still clambering for me, trying to get a piece for themselves. Any hands that did grab me, slipped away, slick with blood.

I pulled myself up in that moment of freedom, faster and faster. No undead could reach me. I was out of their grasp, and they showed no signs of being able to climb. Lucky for me. I climbed up to the lip of the boat, a tarp covering it. I gritted my teeth and stabbed my machete into the elastic cord which held the tarp in place. The tarp loosened and the wind took the rest of it away.

I rolled over the side of the boat and collapsed onto the floor of it. It was pristine white, plastic and painted. It even smelled new. I was ruining it. I had left splashes and trails of blood everywhere I touched. It had formed a puddle around me as my leg continued to bleed. I felt cold and clammy. I was shaking. Was it shock? Shock was setting in. I was exposed to the elements there also. I would freeze and die when the sunset and nightfall came, if shock didn't take me first. *It doesn't matter.* I tried to bat that thought away. The voice of cynicism was right, though. It didn't matter anymore. I would be dead soon. I had been bitten after all, and a bite meant only one thing. Death. Death followed by reanimation, followed by the killing of people I may or may not have known.

"Dammit," I sighed, then pushed myself up onto the box that probably contained fishing gear.

Up as high as I was, I could see a lot of things. I could see the decks of other boats. I could see the ocean. I could even see a random boat that appeared to be abandoned not far from the docks and out in the seas. It bobbed up and down on the water. My gaze finally fell on the dark windows of the boathouse. I smiled, remembering my meal there with Alice. A lovely meal in taste and atmosphere.

I took Thundy out of my belt loop and sat him next to me. I said to him, with a weak smile, "We had a good run, didn't we?"

"Not good enough," I replied, imitating Thundy's imagined voice.

"I just hope Alice can deal with the thunder without you," I croaked. A lump in my throat had formed. "I'm so sorry."

I didn't know who I was saying sorry to. Thundy? Alice? My family? Myself? Probably all of them. I was so, so sorry.

I could feel my insides clenching as thoughts of death and the dark abyss after came to the forefront of my mind. *I'm not ready to die!* I felt sick. Fear gripped me.

"Oh, God!" I sobbed. Tears ran down my face and blinded me. I would never see anyone again. No one would know what had happened to me. I would just be a faceless zombie, waiting to kill someone like me. Waiting to be killed by someone better than me.

Determination came over me. I would not become one of those things. It was better to take myself out of the equation. My face twisted into a snarl. Sadness and fear replaced by anger. I reached my shaky hands for my handgun and held it loosely. I stared at it. I could see blood pooling on the floor, out of the corner of my eyes. My blood. The gun felt so heavy. Heavier than the first time I'd touched one. For a fleeting moment, I wondered how the man who had given me my first gun was doing. Probably dead.

I stared at the finer details on the gun. The grooved handle for grip, the small screw. I knew what I needed to do. I raised the pistol up. I turned the barrel of the gun towards me and placed the end on the underside of my chin. It was cold. I could feel tears rolling down my face, tickling me. I didn't know if it was the coward's way out but I did know it was the better option. I didn't like the idea of my shambling corpse killing others. There was too much of that going on as it was. The world didn't need another. I would die on my feet, with my eyes open. I stood. I could see the undead's hands up and around the boat. They hadn't forgotten about me.

I would have many regrets. I regretted never saving Alice or returning Thundy to her. I regretted leaving my family. I definitely regretted being bitten and dying there on the boat. That was it, I suppose. I pushed the gun harder against the soft skin of my chin. I would fire the gun. The bullet would enter my mouth. The bullet would only be in there momentarily before exiting through the roof of my mouth. Every exit is an entrance. It would then tear through the hypothalamus. Up and up, destroying all brain tissue as it went. Everything I could be or had been would be nothing in a few moments. It would've been that way. But the human survival instinct is very strong.

I began to squeeze the trigger. Ever so slowly I applied pressure to it. I was ready to end it all, but I hesitated. There was a distant buzzing sound in my head. Blood rushing to my ears? Except it wasn't in my head. I turned around to find the source of the noise. What I saw was a complete surprise.

CHAPTER 12

A small, silhouetted object was moving towards me. I couldn't be sure, but it looked like a plane. Not a big one. A remote-controlled one perhaps? I looked to the boathouse, where the plane was moving from. I could see a figure standing in the doorway, looking towards me. I couldn't see the person in much detail, but I could tell that he was male, alive, and concentrating on the plane. There was a small box in his hands. The remote control?

I lowered my gun, curiosity overtaking my need to end my own life. The plane got closer and closer. It was definitely a remote-controlled plane, probably a hand-built model. It was white plastic-styled material with a red trim. Looked like a biplane. It flew low enough that I could've touched the underside of it. Then it began to circle overhead. The rotating buzzing made me feel a little motion sick. The plane did a few more wide rotations before continuing away from me and toward the boathouse.

I just stared in confusion, unsure of what the whole point of the display was. Then something amazing happened. One by one, the undead surrounding the boat turned and began following the direction of the plane. It was only a couple at first, staring at it above them and running awkwardly to follow it. And then more started to follow. They seemed to be chasing the other undead that had left. Perhaps they weren't following the plane but the others who had left? Mindless creatures just following whatever they saw.

Before long, there was only a couple of undead around the base of the boat, and they seemed to have forgotten what they were doing there. I marvelled at the use of a model plane being used as a distraction. This could change warfare against the undead in humanities favour!

"Run!" a voice bellowed. The man at the boathouse. I snapped my head to look at him and saw that he was waving me towards him. He used sweeping arm movements as if to emphasise his point to me across the distance. My glorious moment of self-sacrifice was forgotten as my survival instinct kicked in with a full fury. My leg was weak, as was the rest of me from blood loss. That wasn't going to stop me. I walked wearily over to the edge of the boat, stared below. Eyes blurred in and out of focus. Arms felt heavy, and my machete felt like a huge weight in my hand. I could feel myself swaying. I needed to get down. Then without thinking about it or meaning to, I pushed myself off the side of the boat.

I felt more like I was tumbling during the split second I was in the air than falling. Wasn't a smooth landing either. I collided with a zombie, whose rotten flesh softened my fall. We fell to the floor in a tangled pile. The force of my weight slammed the zombie into the ground. Its head slammed into the concrete floor with such force it bounced back up, with a snapping noise in its neck. I pushed myself onto my unsteady feet. I had lost my sense of direction. I began doing a serpentine-style run, more so through loss of my motor functions than strategy. My spinning head briefly caught sight of the boathouse. I quickly twisted myself in that direction and began sprinting. I say *sprinting*, but there was no fluidity to it. I had about as much coordination as one of the zombies. I began to worry that the man at the boathouse might think I was one of them.

"Alive!" I tried to shout, but it came out like a slur. I hoped it would at least alert him that I was *alive*. But I think it worsened my case. Exhaustion and blood loss were going to be the end of me.

I kept going, knees buckling under my sprint. Through sheer force of will, they didn't. I thought I felt fingers grasp at my neck. This snapped me back to reality and fuelled my adrenaline. The boathouse stairs approached quickly. How had I run that far? I turned my head up to the top of the stairs and saw two figures there. They were shouting something, but it just sounded like a blur of noises in my current state. I didn't slow down. I simply kept running. Legs pumped as they pushed me up the stairs.

I glanced at the man who'd saved me, but I couldn't stop. I ran through the doorway. I sprinted across the room. I slammed into one of the round tables and collapsed onto the floor. I didn't even attempt to get up. I couldn't.

"Thanks," I managed to mutter before the old-fashioned woodwork of the ceiling faded away to black and the darkness closed in on my vision.

CHAPTER 13

Once upon the time, I went for surgery. It wasn't a major surgery, just the removal of some kidney stones. The stones were the worst physical pain I had ever experienced. Worse than the time I broke my little finger playing basketball when an opposing player stamped on my hand. Worse even than the time I fell off a climbing frame as a kid, back first onto a wall, and thought I had broken my spine. The pain was even worse than the zombie that bit into my leg that day at the docks. I digress.

I went into surgery. I remember being laid down on the bed as I was prepped for the anaesthesia. My heart was going at five hundred beats a minute as the nervousness wracked my body. It was all a blur. None of what was happening would register in my head. The clinicians spoke to me, but none of what they said made sense. It was all technical jargon.

"What is it like being under?" I managed to ask.

"It's nothingness," one of the clinicians replied after a couple of seconds thought.

"It's like sleep," another clinician reassured. Although his mouth was covered by the surgical mask, I could see that he smiled as his eyes lit up.

"I'm scared, Dave, will I dream?" I asked in an attempt at humour. The questions were giving me the focus I needed to steady my nerves. The humour was used to cover my nervousness. No one caught my reference.

"No, it will be nothing," the first clinician replied, confused by the name I'd called him. Then added, "My name is Mohammed."

I was about to ask another question, and then darkness hit me. The doctor hadn't lied. It was nothingness. Yet he hadn't entirely told the truth. Maybe it is different for everyone, but I did dream. Not the fantastical stuff of a regular night's sleep. There were little flashes of images. Little splashes of dreams. It was like being dragged through water, a sudden blast of feeling and emotion, before tumbling into another scenario. I don't think any momentary image lasted for more than a few seconds. It didn't make any sense or link up. Yet I dreamed.

The reason I say that is, even though I fell to the darkest recesses of my mind through the chemical cocktail they'd pumped into me, I still dreamed. That day I got bit, made it into the boathouse, and passed out, I fell into the darkest and deepest parts of my mind. It was utter darkness. No dreams. No reassuring thoughts. Pure nothingness. It was unexplainable and unimaginable. One moment I existed, the other I didn't. No way to comprehend it. It was like trying to comprehend the idea of infinite. Something like that is inconceivable. There's no way to comprehend nothingness. I wouldn't be able to even explain it had I not been able to reflect on it later.

Was that what death was like? It was terrifying. I didn't want to die.

CHAPTER 14

I awoke. Not a sudden awakening as I was used to, but a systematic awakening. I could feel my body slowly coming back to life and start to twitch. Electrical impulses had started to spread to my limbs. Then I realised that I was actually aware of these things happening. My eyes gradually opened, crustiness in the corners fell away. Grogginess filled my vision and thoughts. The room was blurry.

I tried to lift my right hand to my face, but it met resistance. Panic began to flood me as thoughts of a stroke arose. This was dispersed as I pulled again and heard a metal on metal rattle. I turned my head to look. It hurt, like all the blood had rushed to it in that movement. I saw that my hand had been handcuffed to the rail of the hospital-styled bed I was in. My other arm was completely free and I saw that within arm's reach, on a bedside table was a bottle of water, my mobile phone, the bullet for Harrington, Thundy, and a note with a silver key taped to it. The handcuff key!

I reached over with my spare hand. My hand flailed about as if the motion was foreign to me. I focussed with great difficulty and steadied my hand. I gingerly clasped the piece of paper with the key on it and carefully and brought it over. My hand shook as I tried to hold the note to read it. My vision focussed and so did the words.

Just come and say hi. Night or day.

There was a smiley face at the end of the note, or an emoticon, or an emoji. Whatever the kids were calling it nowadays. I crinkled my nose at it. Too friendly for my liking. I didn't want to complain since whoever it was had saved my life. Saved … my life? I suddenly remembered how I'd gotten there and that I had been bitten!

I detached the key from the note and slid it into the small lock. Wasn't easy with one hand. The handcuffs clicked it open, fell away from my wrist, and clattered against the bed. I threw the thin hospital sheet off of me. I wasn't bothered by being naked, even if it meant someone had undressed me. I was more worried about my leg.

I saw that my leg was bandaged. Dressing seemed fresh. I unwound the bandages as fast as I could. It was like a macabre version of Pass the Parcel as I desperately tried to get to the centre. I managed to fumble away the last of the layers and threw it to one side. The wounds on my leg from the motorcycle crash and the bite were … fine. As fine as it could be, anyway. The skin was uneven and damaged. It was fleshy and pink, a combination of healing and scarred tissue. I could see the stitching on both wounds. The bite wound looked a lot worse, like someone had wrapped string around raw chicken. The flesh looked a mess. I rubbed my hand over the skin. It was tender, but it didn't hurt. Looking at the twisted mass of flesh, I came to the realisation that I wasn't going to follow in the footsteps of my grandmother and become a leg model. *The sacrifices I had to make.* I smiled with relief. Assuming the people in the boathouse had fixed me up, they had done a good job.

Impressive. I slapped the old wounds, sending a slight sting through my leg. It was satisfying not to have crippling pain.

Then something occurred to me. I had been bitten. By a zombie. A zombie had pierced my flesh, drawn blood, and I hadn't turned? I was shocked. Why wasn't I a zombie? Is that not how it worked? Everyone had been so sure of how it worked on the internet. You get bit, the fever hits, and that's it. So why had I survived? Perhaps, movie clichés aside, the infection was not in the bite. It wouldn't be the first time the Internet had been wrong. Maybe it was the bite that killed. Maybe it wasn't. I didn't know, but that wasn't a problem now. I had to focus on surviving and continuing to survive. I would just be thankful for that small miracle.

With that issue aside, I turned my attention to the bottle of water. I was so thirsty. Felt like I had been swallowing sand for weeks. I opened the water and downed it in one go. I was still thirsty. Thirsty and hungry. How long had I been there? I would find out soon enough.

I looked down at my body in all its nudity. No socks, no boxers, nothing. I finally felt the flush of embarrassment shade my face red. Someone had seen my bare bottom and exposed genitalia. I felt mortified! I was going to have to confront whoever had seen me nude. I wasn't happy about that in the slightest. But I needed to push my shame aside and go greet my hosts. The note had invited me at any time, after all.

I pushed myself to my feet, nearly collapsing. Legs were weak. That was a sign I had spent an extended period of time laying down. I held onto the edge of the hospital bed and looked around. Before I moved away, I realised that I needed to be aware of where I was.

The room was small and looked like a bedroom. There were photos and other personal knickknacks on shelves. I noticed an armchair in the corner, with a turned-off plug-in heater by it. The entire room gave the impression of an elderly woman, and the hospital bed suggested a sick one at that. Laid over the chair was some sort of clothing. I stumbled over to it, pushing myself off the walls and furniture for support. I collapsed into the chair and pulled up the item of clothing in front of me. It was an all-in-one, dark grey boiler suit. It didn't look like something I would wear at any point in my life pre-apocalypse, but there were no signs of any other clothing. I would have to wear it. I gave it a cautious sniff and was relieved to find that it was clean, or smelled clean at least. I didn't know what was worse, walking around nude or in another man's dirty clothes.

I climbed into the boiler suit, which was about two sizes too big. It was surprisingly comfortable though, especially with the lack of underwear. It was freeing, and it felt a little taboo. I dropped my phone and bullet into one of the many pockets, and Thundy got his own pocket. I looked at my surroundings again, noticing there were no windows and only one door. That's the door I would be leaving through. I felt naked without my weapons. Even more naked than being nude in a boiler suit. My weapons were nowhere in sight. I could only hope that since these people had saved my life, took care of me, and left me a friendly message, they were looking after my best interests and I was amongst friends.

I stumbled out of the door, swaying madly. Head rushes and weak legs the sole cause. I walked down a couple steps only to realise I was in the bar of the boathouse. The one I had drank and eaten in many years ago. The same one I had passed out in on my arrival, whenever that was.

It was dimly lit, the only light coming from a glow around the corner. I followed it uneasily, holding onto the bar. I rounded the corner, stumbled into the dining area, and saw two people at a round table, eating food by candlelight. They seemed unaware of my presence and ate in silence.

The man was a huge guy, more muscles than fat. Probably his boiler suit I was wearing. He had a shaved head and had black skin. Looked middle-aged. Middle-aged as in older, not middle-aged as in medieval. The woman was petite and ginger. I couldn't tell how old she was. Had one of those faces that could look twenty-five in one light and fifty in another.

"Uh, hi?" I said. The two at the table jumped, and the man reached for something. A gun, perhaps? After they saw it was me, they looked at each other, silently communicating the way only couples could. There was an awkward silence.

The woman finally broke it with a soft voice, "Why don't you join us?"

CHAPTER 15

It was awkward at first. I shuffled uneasily into one of the extra seats at the table. A relief to be off my feet, even though I hadn't been on them for long. There were a few more moments of silence before the man, who I recognised as the one who saved me, broke it.

"Hungry?" he asked between mouthfuls of food. Their meal looked like a basic roast dinner. Chicken, potatoes, peas, carrots, and gravy. It looked and smelled fantastic. I nodded dumbly, not able to bring any words to my mouth. With that, the woman got up and walked in, what I assumed was, the direction of the kitchen.

"I'm Gary," the man said after a further silence. He clasped his hands and elbows on the table, and rested his chin on his hands. His brow was furrowed, and he stared at me intensely, like he was sizing me up.

"Sam," I said. "Thanks for, uh, saving me back there."

"Wouldn't have been very Christian of me not to," he replied, the corner of his mouth twisting into a small smile. "The lady, she's my gorgeous wife. Her name is Tracey."

"Thank you again," I nodded.

I was pleased to have been rescued and given a place at their table. Yet I couldn't see why they had saved me.

I must've looked puzzled because Gary cocked his head

and asked, "What's up?"

"How did you know you could trust me?" I decided to go for the blunt approach. "I mean, I don't look like the most trustworthy of people as it is, plus I'd been bitten. How'd you know I wouldn't turn?"

"You look perfectly trustworthy to me," Gary smiled, then added, "and what does being bit have to do with turning?"

"Huh?" I was taken aback.

"Being bit. Turning into one of those things. What's the relationship?" Gary asked, clearly confused. He took a swig of his pint of, possibly, cider. When I didn't answer, he said, "I assume turning into one of those things is what you meant."

"I … uh," I paused to compose my thoughts. "The bite carries the infection, brings you back as a zombie. You know, like in the films."

"We're not much of a film-watching couple, sorry," Gary sat back in his chair, looking embarrassed. "Zombies?"

"Wait. What? Who hasn't watched a zombie film?" I was a little lost on how to approach the subject. Something so deeply ingrained in my upbringing. "Zombies. You know, as in the … like, reanimated corpses? The dead that walk and all that."

"I got that. We've seen them. Smelled them, too," Gary said dryly. "Heard the word zombie before, too. Never really knew what it meant. Besides, I don't think it's just the bite that spreads infection. If at all."

"Why'd you say that?" I was genuinely curious about what made him the expert, especially since he hadn't even seen any films. Now *that* was insanity.

"You noticed you were handcuffed in a hospital bed, yeah?" Gary said. I nodded, resisting the urge to give a sarcastic answer. He opened his mouth to speak, shut it, and then opened it again. "Do you want the long version or the short version?"

"I'm not going anywhere. Give me the long version," I laughed. He didn't smile. Luckily, I was saved from the awkward situation. Tracey came back in with a plate full of food. A roast dinner. I smiled gratefully taking the food. "Cheers."

"No worries, hun," she said in a soft and kind voice. "I'm Tracey."

"Sam," I replied, "Nice to meet you both."

Tracey smiled, but Gary looked grim, set to finish his story.

"I'm just telling the story about Mama," he told Tracey, taking her hand and gently squeezing it. There was instant recognition in her eyes. Sadness as well. I didn't know if I wanted to hear this tale.

"Okay," she said softly, squeezing his hand back.

"I'm sorry to say this but, for this story to make sense, you need to hear how we met," Gary said, with a short bark of laughter. Tracey rolled her eyes.

"I love hearing people's stories," I said, with a smile. I wasn't entirely telling the truth.

"Well, you may be disappointed. There's nothing romantic about this one," Gary smiled. "My Mama got very ill a time ago and ended up being in and out of the hospital for a while. It got to a point where she spent more time in the hospital bed than her own. It was gut-wrenching to see. She was always a very proud and strong woman. The doctors said she would have to go into a care home. I couldn't have that. I arranged it so that she would be at home with me. I bought all the necessary stuff, like the bed and medical equipment. Cost me a pretty penny or two. I hired a care assistant from an agency to take care of her, and Tracey turned up. She cost me a fair few pretty pennies as well!"

"Shush, you," Tracey smiled, and Gary winked at her.

Still smiling, he continued, "We got to chatting over time. She treated Mama wonderfully, and we started to date. We married many years later. Eventually, we had to hire another care worker. It would've been strange if she carried on looking after Mama while we were married."

I nodded.

"Mama was tenacious and lived a lot longer than any doctors expected. A couple weeks ago, she died. She got a real nasty flu bug, and that was it," Gary said. By his tone, I could tell that he was building to the climax of his tale. "We had been expecting it. She'd been going downhill the preceding weeks. We called for someone to come and pick her up, just to move her. There were delays due to the goings-on in the city. The, uh, zombies. I went to pay my final respects to her, say one last goodbye. I nearly collapsed when I saw her. She was sat up in bed, something she hadn't been able to do for so long! I was so happy, so relieved. I called out to her and went to hug her. Except … she threw herself out of the bed, at me. She hit the floor hard, and I saw her arm snap. It twisted away from her in the most horrible way imaginable. She didn't even seem to notice! No cry of pain or anything. She kept coming towards me. I ran over to help her. I grabbed her arm, but – but she was so cold!"

A sob escaped. He stopped for a moment, took a deep breath, and wiped his eyes before carrying on.

"I tried to pull her up, but she bit me. Or she tried to, at least. She didn't have her false teeth in, luckily. I tried to restrain her, but she didn't stop thrashing. She caught my

Tracey around the eye with a fist," Gary said and stroked Tracey's face.

"It wasn't her," Tracey said to Gary, sympathetically.

"I knew this wasn't Mama anymore," he said firmly. "I'd seen the news. I wasn't stupid. We had both checked her, seen her heart monitor ourselves. She was dead, no doubt about it."

"What did you do?" I asked. I hadn't been aware of it, but I realised I'd been holding my breath.

When he didn't answer, I was worried I had offended him. But that wasn't the case. He was simply deep in thought. Tracey answered for him.

"Neither of us could bring ourselves to end her life. She hadn't done anything wrong," Tracey said quietly. It was hard to hear her, but I believe she was just a soft-spoken woman. "We ended up tying her arms and legs with duct tape. Wrapped her in a tarp and locked her in one of the back rooms."

My body went into survival mode. There was a zombie in the same building as me, and they were okay with it?! How did they sleep at night? I had seen the films. It wasn't going to end well. She would break out, slip in when we were at our weakest, and … no. I couldn't think like that. I had been wrong before, and so had the films. I couldn't kill the zombie that used to be his mother. I was a guest in their home after all, but I was sure as hell going to be prepared.

"Your food is getting cold," Gary interrupted my thoughts. "Eat up. I can continue the story when you're finished."

"Uh, thanks," I said, mouth watering at the thought of food again. I picked up the fork and dug in. Then nodded approvingly at the tender chicken. It was definitely good food. I almost cried.

CHAPTER 16

I finished the food and would have asked for second helpings if I hadn't felt like I was imposing. I offered to help clear up but was firmly told that I was a guest in their home and they would clear up. I didn't mind at all. I hated clearing the table and doubted I would be of much use, but I still felt bad.

I was shown the way to a lounge area, which looked as though it was the social area of the boathouse. There were four two-seat sofas set in a square, facing each other. People would probably sit there after a meal and chat over a pint. I slumped down onto a sofa and looked at the area around me. There were paintings all over the walls. Odd bits and pieces, too. A steering wheel from an old ship hung on the wall. Rigging all over the ceiling. If a pirate ship and a pub decided to do the dirty, its offspring would probably look like the boathouse.

I felt hyper-vigilant the entire time I was there, my moments alone causing wild thoughts. I was in constant fear of Gary's mother breaking out and sneaking up on me. Although, the undead didn't seem to do much sneaking. Pain was starting to become apparent in my leg again. Did I need painkillers? I hoped not. I hated the feeling of it. But what I wanted and what I needed were often two different things.

The longer I was left alone, the more my attention wandered. I noticed things in my surroundings, like all the windows had thick sheets over them, probably to block out light from leaving, like towns throughout Britain did during the Blitz. At least the undead's attention wouldn't be drawn to our location.

A cluttering of cutlery behind me made me jump. My thoughts going to Mama having escaped. I jerked around and saw Gary and Tracey walking towards me. She carried a mug, Gary two.

"We didn't know if you liked tea, but there isn't any coffee. So we brought you one just in case," Tracey said, with a shy smile.

"Love tea," I took the mug and sipped the bitter, hot liquid. I accidentally let out an, "Ahh."

"We have sugar if you want," Gary nodded towards the bowl of sugar cubes.

"I'm good, thanks," I shook my head.

I waited for a few moments, all of us deep in thought, before pushing forward with the subject on hand, "So what happened next?"

"By the time we tied her up," Gary said, no context needed as it was the only thing on his mind, "things had already started to go bad here. The news wasn't saying anything, but no one can stop people on the radio. Reports were coming in from all over Essex. Those creatures were everywhere. The place had essentially fallen. We didn't have time to leave, so we bunkered down and decided to wait it out."

He shrugged and sipped more of his tea.

"You won't be able to wait it out here forever," I said.

"Why not?" he sat up straight, annoyed by my accusation. "We have food, fresh water, and electricity. We can wait this out until we're rescued!"

"This isn't something you can just wait out," I shook my head. "I came all the way from Bristol and saw nothing but the dead all the way. London has fallen. Bristol has fallen. Essex is no different. The British Army has disbanded. It's every man for himself now. There's no one coming."

"Then we'll survive here!" Gary shouted. He acted as if I was reminding him of his own mortality, and he had to defend himself.

"You can survive here, but you need to be prepared to leave. The electricity won't run forever. It'll turn off soon, and so will the water. What then? The food won't last. You're lucky we're currently at the ass end of winter, but still … winter is coming. What then? What about heat? I'm not saying this to be mean, but you need to think ahead," I said, with more sympathy this time. Perhaps I had been harsh to begin with. I placed a hand on his shoulder. That seemed to do the trick. He relaxed and slumped down.

"Shit," he sighed.

Shit, indeed. I said, "You never explained how you knew the bite wouldn't turn me into one of them."

"Oh, yeah," he said. "Mama was never bit. She died of the flu and then came back. It must be in the air or something. That's why we handcuffed you. We weren't worried about you coming back from the bite. We were worried about you dying from your wounds and coming back in the night. Tracey did what she could to help you, with what we had. We honestly didn't think you would pull through. Fever was tearing you apart. You were dehydrated and starving. Yet here you are. My Tracey is a pretty nifty nurse."

He slapped her leg, and they leaned in for a kiss. My heart seized up and pangs of pain tore through my chest as thoughts went to Alice. Their kiss didn't last long, but my pain did.

I waited for the loving look between them to finish before I said, "I can never thank you enough for saving me. I don't think I'll ever be able to repay you."

"You don't need to," Gary put his hand on my shoulder. "Helping others is its own reward. I'm sure you'll help us without ever realising it. You don't have anything to repay."

"Cheers," I smiled and looked at them both in the eyes. These were genuinely nice people, and I would miss them when I left. I said, "It was lucky you had handcuffs. Where did you find them?"

Tracey immediately flushed red and looked away.

Gary stumbled over his words before saying, "We, uh, had them, uh, lying around. Just had them."

I looked back and forward between them before a massive grin spread over my face with realisation. The naughty buggers.

"Well, I definitely don't have any more questions," I stifled a laugh.

"We have our own share of questions for you," Gary said after the embarrassed silence that followed the awkwardly hilarious moment. "We need to know a lot more. But for now, we all need rest. It's late, and you're still recovering."

"You can sleep here on the sofa, or back in Mama's old bed. The choice is yours," Tracey stood and stretched.

"I'd rather sleep here, thank you," the thought of Mama's bed suddenly creeping me out. I didn't want to sleep so close to windows with undead on the other side, but I was happier on the sofa than on a deathbed.

"Okay, brilliant," Tracey said. "I'll bring you some blankets. I have some antibiotics and painkillers for you. You need to carry on fighting the infection, and you'll still be in quite a bit of pain for a while. We have the pills to keep that at bay. Try not to sleep for more than four days this time, okay?"

"What?" I asked, stunned. Had I been out for four days? She began to answer but I shook away her response. I'd heard.

"It's okay. We can discuss it tomorrow," she replied and walked away. She became a lot stronger of a person when discussing nursing. That's where she was confident. That's when something started to become clear.

"Was I being given antibiotics while I was passed out?" I asked her.

"Yeah, you were," she replied. I nodded my thanks, and she left. That may explain why the bite didn't kill me. The antibiotics in my system fought off any foreign bacteria. So since the bite didn't infect you with the Daisy virus, maybe it infected you with bacteria that killed you? *Daisy* being the colloquial term for the micro-organism that caused the dead to rise. I'm sure the rotten mouths of the undead were a breeding ground for horrific diseases. That would be what killed you. At least the bite of the undead was something to be feared less. Potentially, anyway. A bite was still a bite. It was definitely food for thought. I needed some paper to map out what I knew about the undead.

Before long, Tracey returned with bedding, some pills, and had still managed to carry a glass of water to me. I took them and thanked her. I swallowed the pills and the water. I then crashed onto the sofa, with bedding wrapped around me. As far as my drug-addled mind was concerned, my cocoon of bedding was the safest place in the world.

CHAPTER 17

"Uh," I groaned as I crawled out of bed. No, not a bed, a sofa. I hated the comedown from painkillers. The next morning was always horrendous and blurred. I couldn't live like that.

I gazed around the room, searching for a timepiece. Weirdly, there were no clocks. Why did I need to know the time anyway? I didn't have anywhere to be, nor did it matter what time I woke up. Being a time-obsessed species was a problem when the time was no longer an issue. *Time is always a problem. Time is always running out.*

I tried to remember the night before. Knew I'd been in and out of consciousness all night. Remembered wandering the boathouse, but also remembered sprinting outside in the scorching sun, with my phone, trying to catch 'em all. Wasn't sure what was real or what wasn't. I remembered scribbling down notes about the undead, so I looked around and found evidence of that – a piece of paper acquired at some point in the night. I read over what could only be described as the writing of a madman.

It's not the bite that infects. We're already infected. It's the bite that kills! Once we're dead from our wounds, we rise as zombies. Anyone is a ticking time bomb now. A death equals a new enemy. Cancer? Zombie.

Gunshot to the chest? Zombie. Blissfully dying of old age? A damn zombie.

There's no cure yet, not for the zombies. There's no cure for death after all. Does that mean everyone is infected globally? Only certain people? I had to treat every death, apart from a shot to the head, as an active threat. There are preventative methods to stop the infection from killing us. But a bullet to the head is still the only proper cure.

There are no undead animals. Still raises the question of whether they can carry the virus for those who aren't infected. Not that it mattered.

No special infected. They're all just your run-of-the-mill movie zombies. No climbers, or screamers, or anything like that. A zombie is a zombie is a zombie. No special abilities. No variations. No mutations. A pleasant surprise.

The undead are dumb, with no sign of learning. They do respond to noises. Dumb doesn't mean not-dangerous, though. Don't know if they'll starve to death or rot away. Just need to wait and see, I suppose.

Prognosis for humanity? Poor.

No cure, no problem.

Definitely the rantings of a drug-addled mind, but it did raise some good points. I tossed the paper down and looked around. I noticed my belongings were on the table. Gun, machete, clean military uniform, and Thundy. I must've placed him on the table during the night. Or Gary and Tracey did.

"I thought I heard you," I said to Thundy, attributing my negative thoughts to him. "Miserable git, aren't you?"

"*Says you,*" I imagined Thundy saying.

"Just shush," I said as I climbed to my feet and stretched,

slowly working the tightness out of my leg.

I hoped that wouldn't be an everyday thing. Decided I was going to keep the boiler suit, as opposed to the military fatigues. They were a part of my life I didn't want to remember. On top of that, they came with certain implications I didn't want to be associated with. Just hoped a shower would also be an option.

I limped my way around the boathouse, Thundy in one zip-up pocket, machete and pistol where I found them. I wanted to move quietly, not just because I didn't want to alert any undead, but because Gary and Tracey could still be sleeping. I moved around the bar, which was the central piece of the building, the rest of pub seemed to circle it, with the bar like the hole in a doughnut. I carried on hobbling, my limp easing up but still present. Opposite the bar was the couple sitting at a table.

"Good morning," Gary said, through a mouthful of food. He was eating a bowl of what appeared to be regurgitated food. Probably muesli.

"Hi," I said. There was a bowl set at the table, with boxes of cereal nearby and a jug of milk. They had set the table for me.

"Come and sit," Tracey was happy to see me. "What do you want?"

"Chocolate hoops?" I pointed to one of the boxes on the table. I didn't like being waited on.

"Of course," she poured my cereal and milk. "Tea?"

I nodded and slumped into the chair.

"Sleep well?" Gary wiped the dried food from his facial stubble.

"Not too bad thanks," I yawned and stretched again. I

was so tired, but I had slept so much. "What's the time?"

"No idea," Tracey handed me some tea. "Clock stopped days ago. We've just been sleeping and rising when we need to. Didn't see any point in changing the battery."

A world without time. Truly a hard concept to get your head around. Imagine a world where time didn't matter anymore. The only reason we needed time pre-apocalypse was to follow daily routines. The needs set forward by someone else, such as work. I mean, a world without a need to work for a living is a world that doesn't need time. In a post-apocalypse world, you only needed to be awake to survive. You could sleep in, as long as you were safe. You would go to bed when it started to get dark, like returning to the caves of our prehistoric days.

There are worse predators than man in the post-apocalyptic world, especially since we were no longer the rulers of the night. I suppose people would go to sleep earlier and wake earlier, rising and falling with the sun. Before, we could only stay up so late because we controlled our environments, through heating, lighting, and a roof over our heads. Without those things, we would revert back to the way Mother Nature intended. It was a scary thought. I needed to know the time.

Breakfast was a lot less awkward than the meal the night previously. It was mostly eaten in silence, but not an awkward who's-going-to-murder-who-first silence. Nonetheless, I finished up, as did Tracey and Gary, before Tracey disappeared with the bowls and returned with glasses of orange juice. I realised that, even though the couple weren't elderly, they were old-fashioned in the sense that the woman did everything related to the kitchen. Then again, I never saw them in a normal situation, so I couldn't judge. Besides, they were both so lovely. In the normal world, I would never have met either of them or got along with them. Yet when everyone struggled with the same problems, it bound us together. We all became family.

Gary broke my philosophical train of thought, "So we need to get down to business. I answered your questions. You need to answer some of mine now."

"I'm not going to murder you, don't worry," I laughed awkwardly. I meant it as witty and playful, but it came out more like a veiled threat. *Dammit.*

"I'm sure you won't," Gary said calmly. "But a military man stumbling around, covered in blood still raises a few questions."

"Military man …" I said slowly. It took a moment for the cogs to begin turning before it clicked into place. "Because of the uniform?"

He nodded as if I was dumb, "You said the military isn't coming, and you were wearing one of their uniforms. Aren't you military?"

"No," I replied. And there was the implication.

Thoughts of James came to mind, my friend who was killed by Harrington. I didn't want to go into it.

"So …" Gary said, prompting me to expand on what I said.

"I don't want to go into this," I said simply. "Can I just keep it basic?"

"Sure," Gary nodded again. He was definitely an empathetic man.

"Long story short, a military group took me in, took care of me, and betrayed me. Shortly after the military officially disbanded via radio broadcast and decided to bomb London into the ground. I got out, and those clothes are the remains of what I had," I spat.

Gary stopped me to ask a question, "And why are you here? You sound as though you're from the southwest. You're a long way from home."

I couldn't help but smile. My accent seemed to be known far and wide.

"Bristolian, born and raised," I said in my thickest Bristolian accent. That of a farmer and pirate mixed together. "As for why I'm here, do you have enough time?"

"All the time in the world," Gary smiled.

"Well, I'm searching for someone," I replied anti-climatically. We both sat back in our chairs. This was going to be a long tale.

CHAPTER 18

I hadn't decided how much I was going to tell Gary when I started out. I planned to censor my story. There was nothing wrong with portraying myself in a favourable light, right? Everything I'd done was for the greater good, but when I explained it, it may not have come across like that. So censoring was definitely the best thing for both parties. Why raise unnecessary suspicions?

I went into detail about my journey through London and the way the military behaved towards civilians. I told them how the undead had taken London. The dispersion of the British Army through the radio broadcast. Operation Guy Fawkes. General Harrington. I didn't mention James. Couldn't bear it. I told them about heading to my current location, and that brought me up to date.

"That is … insightful," Gary said. "You still haven't actually told me why you left to begin with."

I thought back to the conversation. I hadn't mentioned Alice once. I spoke about everything that had happened and that I needed to get to Essex, but never said why I had to. Never who I was looking for.

"I came looking for the love of my life," I said as if it was the most normal thing in the world. "I have reason to believe

Alice and her family came here to get their boat and head out."

Gary was silent for a moment, a contemplative look on his face, before saying, "Don't suppose there were three of them?"

I did a quick mental calculation of the family members, excitement rising up inside me. "Yes? Definitely should've been three."

"I don't want to get your hopes up, but was their boat on the upper left section of the boatyard, close to the waterfront?" Gary asked calmly.

"I think so!" I shouted, a grin spreading across my face.

"I need you to see something. It may answer your question," Gary stood. Even though I hadn't asked a question, I knew what he was referring to. Had Alice made it out? Gary led me over to a window and moved aside the bed sheet that hung over it to shield our presence from the undead.

"Look to where their boat should be," Gary handed me a set of binoculars.

I did just that after steadying my hands. There seemed to be a lot more undead hanging around, maybe attracted by the commotion the day before, but they still ambled about aimlessly. Getting out of there was going to be a pain in the backside. I returned my attention to hunting for the Kingsley family boat. I remembered where their boat was kept, mainly because the boat next to theirs was so goddamn awesome. It had a dragon-styled paint job and stood out from the rest of the monotonously coloured boats. Another reason was that it was so much easier to work out where everything was when viewing from higher up. On the ground, it felt like a maze.

After some cautious and steady wandering, I found the dragon boat and settled on their allotted space.

"Their boat is gone …" I said, letting the statement hang in the air. Excitement was getting ready to explode from me, but I dampened it down as a precaution.

Gary sighed with relief. "So it was their boat, then."

I let the bed sheet fall back across the window and handed the binoculars back to Gary.

"Did they all make it out?" I asked.

"Looked like it. It was before the whole county looked like this," he made a sweeping motion with his hand. "There weren't many of those … zombies about at the time."

Gary seemed uncomfortable saying the Z-word, like he had been chewing on something bitter. But something other than his discomfort caught my attention.

"At the time?" I repeated. "How long ago was this?"

"I reckon about … two weeks at least. About three weeks after the first major outbreak in Essex. So it's been about five weeks since then. Don't get me wrong, there were still some cropping up here and there, but they were normally contained," Gary explained.

So Alice and her family had waited three weeks to leave Essex, and I had missed them by two. I was two weeks behind them. How far could they have gotten in two weeks? Far enough that I was lagging behind. I cursed. Still playing catch up. I needed to find her.

"I'm going after her," I started limping back towards the sofa to pick up my travel goods. I needed to leave immediately. But I was moving at such a slow pace. To match my twenty hobbled steps, Gary caught up with me in three.

"You can't leave yet. You're injured. You'll be torn apart the moment you step outside. It wouldn't be right for me to let you leave," Gary said with concern.

"Well, I doubt you can stop me," I said coolly while

struggling to put one leg in front of the other. I don't know if what I said triggered him to react, or from watching me struggle, but he placed one hand on my shoulder before shoving my face down into the chair. I turned my face to Gary, pure rage masking my features. I think I may have scared Gary a little, as he took a step back.

I snarled, "What the fu–"

"Look how easily I stopped you, and I wasn't even trying," Gary interrupted. I tried to stand up again but Gary pushed me back down with minimal effort. "Now we can do this all day. I have nowhere else to be, and I'm pretty sure you'll tire before I do. Even if I did, the missus is here to take over for me. If we don't want you to go, then you won't leave. Now I can let you go, but you and I both know you'll be dead in seconds. You won't find Alice and it'll be your fault. So how about you stay and get your strength back. The missus will treat your wounds, and when you're fighting fit, we'll let you go. Deal?"

I nodded grudgingly. I knew he was right, but that didn't mean I liked it. I was too busy thinking with emotion and not intellect.

"I'm bored," I muttered after a few seconds of an intense standoff, and relaxed back into the chair.

Gary smiled with relief, "Now let's take a look at that leg."

He peeled away the bandages that hid my wound and grimaced.

"What is it?" I asked, panic setting in.

Were we wrong and the bite had transferred Daisy? Even if that wasn't the case, did the bacteria the undead carried in their rotten maws spread other diseases? Was gangrene setting in? Or something worse? Was there anything worse than gangrene? I could feel the dread in my gut and the fear in my head merging over my lungs to create an anxiety attack.

"You tore your stitches. They're gonna need redoing," Gary was still grimacing. Those simple words with their simple explanation made my fear evaporate. That was all it was! I laid back, grinning like a madman.

"Something funny?" Gary grunted as he got to work preparing the area.

"Not particularly. Just the whole situation," I was still smiling.

"Well, I would keep smiling if I were you. Redoing these stitches will hurt. A lot," he said dismissively as his concentrated.

"I'm sure I'll be fine," I said confidently. Gary smiled, not maliciously but knowingly. He had clearly done this kind of thing before.

I watched with fascination as he produced something that looked like a fishing hook. A small and narrow silver hook in a sealed packet. I could only hope that meant it was sterilised. Next came some tiny thread-like stuff he attached to the hook. I had an odd fascination with the hook and thread until the realisation hit that it would be piercing my flesh.

"You may want to look away," Gary said, noticing my grimace.

"Nah," I said through gritted teeth. "I need to learn how to do it."

And learn I did. I watched as his large hands made quick work of my damaged leg. The hook dipped in and out of my flesh, the thread tightening and pulling my skin together. Definitely more skilled than the barbaric work I'd made of it previously. Also a lack of pain, surprisingly.

Perhaps it was finally beginning to heal? Or perhaps I had destroyed all the nerve endings? What would happen to my leg with the best care available? If it was pre-apocalypse, I would probably have a skilled surgeon to repair the damage and cosmetic surgery to hide the scars, with a follow-up of months of physiotherapy. Even with all that, it still wouldn't be perfect. And I wasn't going to get close to that type of care. All I had was stitching with a fish hook, in a boathouse. Perfect apocalyptic healthcare.

CHAPTER 19

When Gary finished his handiwork, he told me to rest and to avoid doing anything strenuous. I begrudgingly listened to him that time. Didn't want to reopen my wound. But I couldn't help but keep thinking about how much further behind Alice I was. I didn't want to sit around forever.

"So what is there to do around here?" I sighed, knowing I was confined to the boathouse for the time being.

"There's a ton to do around here!" Gary clapped his hands for emphasis. "We have books, some old VHS tapes, and a radio. Although I doubt there's much happening on said radio anymore. There are even a couple of board games, if that's your thing."

"A radio," I repeated.

"Yeah, should be around here somewhere," Gary nodded and walked away. I was deep in thought about the radio. Places like docks tended to have two-way receivers, didn't they? I could potentially send messages and communicate with the outside world. Maybe Alice would hear the message!

My excitement was burst when Gary plonked an ancient radio down in front of me.

"Here you go," Gary smiled. "It was my pa's. Bit old but works fine as long as you move the aerial right. Let me show you."

As old as the radio looked, more replacement parts than original components, Gary was right. The radio worked fine. He explained about turning the dials to tune it in and adjusting the aerial to find a good signal. The radio occasionally became untuned, and readjustments to the dials had to be made, but it worked.

Once Gary was sure I was all good to go with the radio, he helped me to my room and left me to my own devices with it. Although retreating to my room was my idea, I still felt awkward. Not just because I was returning to Mama's room. Something else. Neither Gary or Tracey had made any indication I was unwelcome, but I just felt like a burden. I felt like I was in the way and encroaching on the lovely couple's privacy. So I decided I would rather be anti-social than an elephant in the room.

****

Gary

Gary gave Sam, who was staring intently at the radio, one last glance before shutting the door. He walked away, back to his wife, deep in thought. Tracey looked at him with concern. After all the years together, she knew when something wasn't right with her husband.

"Everything okay, hun?" Tracey asked when Gary sat opposite her without saying a word.

"I guess so …" Gary stared at his knuckles, massaging them. Something he did when deep in thought.

"Gary," Tracey replied sternly. He would feel much better once he started talking.

"I … with Sam. No," Gary began, trying to compose his

thoughts into a logical sentence. "This may sound crazy, but does Sam sometimes seem like two different people?"

"Go on," Tracey didn't know where he was going with it.

"He's very hopeful and determined, strong-willed, a bit rough around the edges. He swears a lot. All that, I like that about him. It's like he brings hope with him. He's a genuinely likeable guy. Now, the Sam sat in that other room is not the same Sam we've had at our dinner table. He's obsessive, distant, and vacant. He's still just as determined, but … I don't know," Gary said, trying to explain what he briefly saw in Sam moments earlier. He looked at Tracey, who was staring at him. He sighed and smiled, "I'm not saying I don't like the guy, it just feels hard to trust him at times. Like, he's suffering inside. I'm just tired, ignore me."

"Gary, I agree with you. I've seen something in Sam I haven't been able to explain," Tracey stroked Gary's hand. "I've always trusted your instincts, and I don't want you to think I'm belittling them, but he has his reasons. Think of the things he's seen out there. The things he's probably had to do. Added with, he's on a fool's quest. He's chasing after a girl who, from what he said, is more than likely dead. H's only lying to himself. If anyone is entitled to disappear to a dark place every so often, I think he is. He isn't a threat. He's just lost."

"You're probably right," Gary leaned back, rubbing his eyes. He smiled at Tracey again, "You're always right. I just wish he wouldn't talk to himself so much."

"He deals in his own way, and that old teddy he has with him is the only one who'll truly listen. I understand it, I really do. It doesn't make it any less strange, but it's harmless," Tracey shrugged.

She had seen people deal with loss in a lot more

destructive ways than how Sam was. Besides, there were more pressing concerns than the coping mechanism of some young man. Supplies were slowly running out. Something needed to be done.

****

Sam

The quiet moment alone gave me the chance to reflect on the couple whose home I was in. As anyone who knows me will say I always see the worst in people. I've always thought that the worst tended to find me because of my attitude. Yet in all the chaos of the world outside, I had managed to find the one bastion of good. The two who had taken me in were just plain good people. That amazed me.

I thought about what I would have done in their situation. Certainly wouldn't have done the same. Not only would I not have let someone into my home and place of safety, I wouldn't have even let them know of my existence. Hell, I would've pilfered their corpse for supplies the first chance I had. Somehow though, I still wouldn't class myself as a bad person. I was just trying to survive. Surely everyone would be like that? But sitting in the next room was a couple who had risked everything to help a stranger, in the most altruistic move I'd ever seen. Perhaps it was the veil of pain medication, but their very simple act shook what I believed about human behaviour.

I don't know how much time had passed, but I found myself smiling at my self-punishing and revelatory thought pattern. I looked down at the radio in hand and decided it was time to see what was happening in the outside world.

"I'm feeling lucky," I spun the tuning dial to a random

frequency.

Over the weeks I was stuck recovering, I listened to radio broadcasts. There were a few recurring folks I enjoyed listening to. Not because they were funny or smart or anything necessarily, but because they were living. They breathed life, with their inane and everyday conversations, into a dead world. It was beautiful.

There were plenty of radio broadcasts, mostly live ones of people communicating. There were, of course, a few repeated radio broadcasts, too. There was the usual military safe zone nonsense, which was redundant. A BBC message for people to stay in their homes. Also the ramblings of a madman leading a cult, naturally. Listening to the same people, I felt as though I knew personally. I felt like I was their friend, not in an obsessive way, but when you hear so much about someone's life, you can't help but feel like you know them.

A news reader called Tony would tune in every other day. He seemed conspiratorial with his statements while also providing news reports about happenings around the UK – something the government and mainstream media had long since stopped doing. He was annoying, yet something drew me back to listening to him. He reminded me of Bill Cooper. One broadcast really stood out amongst all his other rubbish. Some of the broadcasts I heard weren't even in English, but the language barrier didn't stop their fear and sadness from coming across.

I listened to everyone I came across, for that piece of connection. With time, I heard that people I considered friends disappear, and knowing I would never hear them again hurt me. I missed them. I never knew what they looked like, but I knew them.

Broadcast One: Shaun, Frank, and Barbara 1

Shaun: Every day I wake up and can't believe there are fricking zombies! Who else is with me on this one?

Frank: These clearly aren't zombies, you idiot. These are something else.

Shaun: Of course they're zombies! They rise from the dead and eat the flesh of the living. About as zombie as you can get.

Frank: Oh, you're one of those, aren't you? How old are you? Fifteen?

Shaun: Seventeen, actually. What do you mean, *one of those*?

Frank: You've never experienced any of the classic zombie films, have you? You're one of those post-nineties zombie lovers.

Shaun: Anything before 2000 isn't worth watching. Besides, I'm living the Z-apocalypse now!

Frank: These aren't goddamn zombies! Zombies only go for the brain. Where do you think the classic line *braaaaains* came from? These eat everything. Flesh, brain, sinew. These would be classed as *infected* since we're using movie terms.

Shaun: Grow with the times, man. Zombies changed and so should you.

Barbara: For God's sake. The goddamn apocalypse is happening outside and you're arguing pedantics.

Frank: It's semantics.

Barbara: What?

Frank: We're arguing semantics, not pedantics. Besides, arguing semantics is stupid. It's like beating a child at an IQ test. Sure, you look smarter, but you're also an asshole.

Shaun: Ha-ha. You tell her, dude!

Barbara: The hell? You're lucky I don't know where you live.

Frank: Here's a hint. It's the only house in the Southend with the door still closed. Besides, with the lovely voice you have, you sound like a very attractive lady. I look forward to seeing you.

Barbara: You're hilarious Frank. I *really* hope you don't get eaten.

CHAPTER 20

Gary

It was about 3:00 a.m. when Gary awoke to the sound of a hushed argument. He immediately thought of Sam and Tracey. Had Sam gone over the edge? He groggily felt the bed to find Tracey still in it. That was odd. It was then that Gary remembered Tracey's statement about Sam's way of coping. He considered going back to sleep, but curiosity was getting the better of him and he wanted to investigate the situation. It wasn't the first time one of them had been awakened by Sam in the night, whether from radio static, which Sam seemed to enjoy, or him pacing around the building. But it was the first time one of them had awakened to Sam arguing.

Gary got out of bed, pulled on some joggers, and crept along to investigate. He'd been there long enough to know when and where the floor creaked and avoided those areas even though he was blind in the darkness. When he approached Sam's room, the door was ajar and the bedside lamp was on, illuminating Sam.

"I don't blame myself," Sam hissed, pointing at the teddy he took everywhere. "No. You're wrong. He died because of him. Yes, I know I had a part in it, but he was my friend. That wasn't my fault either. I'm gonna keep looking and return you to her. Of course I'm capable."

Poor kid, Gary thought. Sam seemed so broken. He was having a conversation with a stuffed animal. He wondered if Sam even realised he was doing it. He turned away, shaking his head. Sam was maybe a threat to himself, but not to anyone else.

Gary climbed back into bed, no longer weary from being awakened.

"Everything okay?" Tracey yawned, rolling over to look at Gary.

"Yeah," Gary nodded. "Just … just went for a pee."

"Okay, hun," Tracey rolled back over. "Sam okay?"

He looked at Tracey, who had already fallen back to sleep. "No, I don't think so."

Gary laid back, listening to the gentle snoring of his wife and the wild ranting of Sam. He hated being left alone at night, with his thoughts. The eerie whispers of doubt started to worm their way to the surface. What were they going to do about food? What about water? Those things wouldn't last forever. Sam was right. People weren't coming to save them. Plus, there was the other issue. They needed to think about leaving.

****

Sam

I had a vague sense that someone was watching me. My skin crawled and hairs stood on end. I turned to my door, which had been left ajar. Was that me? There wasn't anyone there. My adrenaline peaked and dropped in the same second. Zombies don't sneak about, and the only other thing it could've been was Gary and Tracey, and they weren't any threat. I relaxed and turned back to my room, confused. What time was it? Why was I still up? I felt exhausted.

I looked around and saw Thundy sitting on a chair, facing the bed.

"Well, that's creepy," I didn't remember putting him there, and I was certain he hadn't sat himself there. I bent to the stuffed animal's eye level and whispered, "Thundy, level with me, you're not secretly alive are you?"

Thundy continued to sit there, as inanimate as ever. He was a really good actor if he was alive. I laughed again. There I was, talking to a stuffed animal, in the middle of the night.

"Get a grip," I slapped my face. I was definitely awake. "Screw it."

I climbed into bed. My body felt as though it had run miles. I checked my leg, as I did every night before sleeping. The wound was healing well. I could probably take the stitching out soon. But my leg still ached and I couldn't overdo it or risk re-injury. I marvelled at how I had survived a bad leg injury and a bite from a zombie on the same leg. Best case scenario, I expected to lose the leg if I ever wanted to live. Worst case scenario would've been death. I had transcended that and come out the other side with both legs intact and wiser from the experience. How wrong all the zombie media had been after countless films, books, and games. I laughed. Things may have been bad, but they could've been worse.

CHAPTER 21

Another day passed, and another, and nothing had occurred. I had listened to the radio most of the days and was surprised by the amount of activity out there. It was like listening to a radio play, which made it easy to forget the end of the world was outside. I was happy but impatient. Wanted to leave but knew I couldn't. And as the time passed, Gary became tenser. He would skip meals and drinks. He even started to forgo his morning cup of tea. I didn't take much notice at first, but when Tracey asked for a private conversation with me while Gary slept, it became apparent.

"Hi, Sam, do you mind me having a quick word?" Tracey stuck her head through the door, in the early hours.

"Not at all," I lied. She couldn't have come at a worst time. I was still in bed and pitching a tent.

She came over and sat on the end of the bed. "I'm worried about Gary …"

I sat up. "How so? Is everything okay?"

"He … hasn't been right. He spends hours writing down notes and hiding them from me. He's been skipping meals. I've never known him to skip a meal," Tracey added with concern.

"Do you think it's because of me?" I said. Was I the one putting strain on their relationship?

"Not at all! Gary has taken a shine to you," Tracey

explained. The old Samuel charm.

"So what do you think it is, then?" I asked her directly.

"I don't know, but I think you might be able to help," Tracey continued mysteriously. Inwardly, I sighed. I hated being asked favours of, no matter how much I owed them.

"What can I do?" I smiled.

"Just talk to him. Whatever's bothering him, he isn't telling me to keep me from worrying, but I think he may tell you. You're both men. Do something manly together or something," Tracey said, clearly grasping at straws.

"Of course. I'll try my best," I patted her on the back. "I'll be as subtle as possible."

I felt so awkward. She thanked me and left. I laid there for a few moments, thinking about what I could do that would be classed as manly. I'm pretty sure playing video games while drunk wouldn't constitute as something manly for Gary or Tracey. Time to leave my comfort zone and think of something else. First things first, I would just try to talk to him. That normally worked.

An hour passed, and in that time I did the three S's – shi … sit on the toilet, shave, and shower. I was in my oversized boiler suit and ready for action. Sam would solve the mystery of the depressed Gary, unless that was the reason – depression. I couldn't fix depression. No one could. A manly talk and a cup of tea wouldn't fix it.

I went hunting for Gary, which wasn't hard when we were confined to a single building. Gary stood, staring out of the window. He didn't appear to be looking at anything in particular, just at the massive expanse beyond. I approached him from behind.

"Gary," he didn't reply, so I said his name again. "Gary!"

"Hmm?" he finally replied, snapping back to reality. "What's up?"

"Well, we need a chat," I said, as diplomatically as possible.

"What about?" he finally asked.

"Can we just sit and chat. My leg is killing me, and I wonder if you could take a look at it, please," I lied poorly. He nodded, and I limped more exaggeratedly than I needed to, towards the sofa. I pulled my boiler suit leg up and exposed the wound. Gary twisted my leg back and forth, inspecting the healing wound closely.

"There's some minor swelling," he murmured to himself, then looked up with a smile. "Nothing to worry about."

"Cheers," I smiled also. Now to broach a subject I wasn't equipped for. "Look, I may as well just come right out with it. Tracey is worried about you. She thinks there's something up."

"She was always a worrier," Gary stood up. I grabbed his arm to stop him from leaving.

"Maybe so," I shrugged, "but I've noticed it as well. Lack of eating, lack of drinking. Other things as well. Look, I'm not an expert on this, but if you're feeling low, like there's no way to continue, then that's okay. It's a normal feeling. Depression isn't anything to be ashamed of. Hell, a couple of years back I was–"

"I'm not depressed," Gary interrupted sourly.

I persisted. "That's fair enough if you think that. But, and be truthful, do you ever find it difficult to find a reason to get up in the morning? I'm not saying you would want to end it, but–"

"We're running out of food," he held up his hands to silence me.

"How?" I had seen the massive amounts of food they

had. We couldn't have burned through it already.

"Come and look," Gary led me to their stock room.

It was filled with stacks of cardboard boxes, a chest freezer, and a huge fridge.

"I don't see the problem," I looked at the large amount of potential food.

"Perishables are mostly gone," he opened the fridge to show that it was almost empty. "The freezer is about half full. What can I say? We didn't ration very well."

"And the boxes?" I nodded to the stacks of them.

"Mostly empty. I've been rotating them bit by bit so Tracey wouldn't notice," Gary explained. "And there's something else."

"What?" I asked, trying to grasp how dire the situation truly was.

"We've had rats. I don't know if it's because of those things outside driving them inside, but I found droppings in a lot of the boxes. Some packaging was chewed clean through. Others looked damaged, and I couldn't tell if the rats had been at them," Gary explained sadly. He then pulled the chest freezer out to show me a hole behind it, next to the plug socket. "Lousy electrical fittings is where they got in. I filled it with foam and we haven't had an issue since. The food, though … I had to get rid of it."

"So," I ran my hand through my hair, "how much longer do you think we can stay here?"

"I don't know," Gary shook his head. "By my estimation, another two or three weeks if we ration well."

I had a sudden revelation about the situation, "That's why you haven't been eating, isn't it?"

Gary nodded.

"Damn, man, you do realise you're gonna be too weak to

help anyone if you need to. You're not doing us any favours by skipping meals," I replied angrily. "We need to make a plan. We can discuss it over dinner tonight."

He smiled. "Just don't mention it to Tracey in the meantime. Okay?"

"Sure, man," I nodded, leaving Gary with his thoughts. It was clearly a huge weight lifted from his shoulders, one I wasn't so keen to share.

I needed time to prepare myself mentally and physically. I was angry at Gary, probably more than I should've been. He was trying to protect Tracey from being scared and worried. But in doing so, he had endangered her, himself, and me. How much longer would he have kept us in the boathouse while he slowly starved to death? And sure, he was trying to protect her, but Tracey was a strong person. She could deal with adversity. Hell, she probably kept Gary together after his Mama died. It could all wait until that night, anyway. We would sort something out.

Waiting for the day to hurry up and end was painful. I paced the boathouse. Every time I saw Tracey, she tried to ask me about Gary.

Every time I only replied, "Later."

But that didn't stop her trying to approach the subject every so often. There was nothing to distract me when I desperately needed it. Seemed to be nothing of interest on the radio. No conversations or anything else, apart from the repeating broadcasts. I took to scouting the area through the window via binoculars. Nothing to see outside. I read the names printed on boats, trying to find one that stood out. Most owners had the same kind of humour – puns or a play-on-words. *Story of a Coy. Carp Diem. The Pacifisht.* Goddamn nautical jokes.

My gaze eventually fell on my abandoned motorbike. The rain and wind clearly had its way with it. It laid on its side, pieces of the body broken off. The undead had gathered around it. Whether it was because of the noise it once made or remnants of some distant memory, I didn't know. The motorbike was lost, and I had to accept that.

CHAPTER 22

Nightfall came, and we were seated for our evening meal. Gary had asked for a larger than normal portion due to our conversation earlier. He looked at me and smiled. Yes, I was the reason he was doing that, but why did he have to make it so weird?

"Eat up, there's plenty to go around," Tracey brought out several plates of food. Leek soup for starters. She looked so happy now that Gary was eating again.

We all tucked in after they said grace, which I sat awkwardly through. Before long, we were full and sleepy. Gary kept making intense eye contact with me. Guess it was time for our chat, and I had somehow been made designated speaker.

"So Tracey, it's time we spoke about what you asked earlier," I said. Her eyes went wide and she looked between Gary and me.

I smiled. "It's okay, Gary knows, and we all need to discuss something important. It's about Gary's strange behaviour and our current situation."

I brought Tracey up to speed about the food situation and that we probably had a couple of weeks' worth of food. She was angry at Gary for keeping it a secret and for skipping meals. They made up and were happy, though. Whatever they faced, they would do it together. Gary proceeded to list everything we had, including food, ammunition, and drinks. I was surprised by that they had ammunition, and Gary assured me they had the gun to go with it. A double barrel shotgun. A happy surprise.

I asked them about other supplies, including first aid items, other weapons, and useful materials. We compiled a written list and agreed to cross off anything that gets used. I suggested that we should leave sooner rather than later. We needed some food to take with us on our journey. Unfortunately, Gary and Tracey thought it was best to wait until all the freezer food had been used, taking us extremely close to the two-week deadline. I wasn't happy about that, but it was their house and their decision. I was just there for the ride.

Speaking of ride, we had discussed our plan of action. Gary actually owned a car. Didn't seem like the sort to me. He had it parked offsite in a rented garage. He said it was about a ten-minute walk, but we decided against it considering the amount of undead roaming outside. A number that seemed to increase each day. The next idea was Gary's boat, which was in the boatyard. This idea was also cut short, because we had neither the time or equipment to lower it into the water.

Finally, I suggested the boat out in the water. I had checked earlier in the day and saw that it was still there. It must've been anchored or something. Despite the difficulty of getting to it, the general consensus was that this was the right move to make. Issues with fuel? Gary had extra in the boathouse. Getting to it? Gary believed he could swim to it. We formulated a plan and convinced ourselves it was a great idea. Then again, when you're cornered by flesh-eating monsters and have limited supplies, you can convince yourself that anything is a great idea.

That night, we found some large holdalls and backpacks. Perfect for carrying our supplies. We could get there with everything, no problem. For the first time, things were going well. I just wanted to speed up the timeline for leaving.

Once we were happy with our plan, we all said our goodnights and went our separate ways. I would need to think of a way to move things along. I couldn't wait in the safety of a glorified pub while the love of my life was out there somewhere, probably fighting for survival.

****

Gary

Lying in bed, Gary recapped the day's events. He liked the plan they'd formed, and even though they all hadn't agreed on the timeframe, they were a team now and they could conquer any adversity the outside world threw at them.

A loud creek snapped Gary from his thoughts. He saw Sam slowly walk by the ajar door. Gary sighed. Sam was sleepwalking again. He waited a few more moments, knowing what was coming next. Sam would eventually saunter back past the door after waking up to find himself out of bed. And that's exactly what he did. If he wasn't arguing with a stuffed toy, he was sleepwalking. Gary smiled and tried to go to sleep once he heard Sam's door close for good.

****

Sam

I sat on the edge of my bed, panting, adrenaline pumping through my body. I couldn't believe Gary hadn't come to investigate after the noise I'd made. It didn't matter whether he'd heard me or not, though. I doubt he would put two and two together, and even if he did, there wouldn't be anything he could do at that point. I settled into bed, heart still racing, and attempted to sleep.

CHAPTER 23

"For God's sake!" Gary screamed, waking me. A few moments of silence before he said, "No, Tracey. I'm a damn idiot!"

I winced. Gary was really angry, but could I blame him? I got out of bed, dressed, and went to see the commotion.

"Just try to calm down," Tracey said calmly. "It was an accident."

"But it's ruined everything!" Gary screamed before breaking into a sob.

As I came round the corner, into the stock room, I saw Gary hunched over on the floor, with Tracey rubbing his back.

"What's up?" I asked. "More rats?"

"No!" Gary shouted. "Just me being useless!"

Tracey stepped between us and whispered. "All the frozen food became defrosted overnight."

"It didn't *become* defrosted. It was my stupidity!" Gary yelled.

"Well … what happened?" I asked.

"I must've knocked the plug out yesterday when I pulled the freezer out!" Gary sobbed again. He was caught between rage and tears. He then showed me the plug which had *accidentally* become disconnected.

"You didn't do it on purpose," I said, trying to soothe

him.

"But now I've put us all in danger!" Gary said, wiping tears away.

"It's okay," I put my hand on his shoulder. "We're in no different a position than we were yesterday. The only difference is that we need to do things earlier than we had originally planned."

"Listen to him, Gary. He's right. Accidents happen, it's okay," Tracey moved in to hug her husband. Gary, still crying, stared at me for the briefest of moments. I thought he was going to express doubts over the freezer incident, but he just closed his eyes and cried freely. I, on the other hand, turned and left. I had preparations to make.

That evening, we collected our supplies, in preparation to leave in a few days. We cooked up what we couldn't take with us and then prepared the stuff we would take. Gary was in a glum mood, and that was putting it lightly. Tracey echoed her husband. I was the only one excited to be leaving, and I had to curb my enthusiasm so it didn't rub the others the wrong way.

CHAPTER 24

When I checked on the supplies Gary and Tracey were packing, I was saddened. Amongst the food, water, and other necessities, there were discarded bits and pieces. Odd ornaments which had been put in a bag and then removed to make room for other items. An old knife and fork set had been cast to one side as well. The only personal item they managed to squeeze into the many bags of supplies was their wedding photo – without the ornate frame it once sat in. These people were literally leaving behind the only life they ever knew and nearly everything they owned that reminded them of it. It was sad but needed to be done.

I gave myself the job of waterproofing everything. I found reels of plastic wrap in the stock room, to wrap all the bags in. If we were travelling by boat and on water, then we needed to take the precaution to secure it all.

I considered putting Thundy, my phone, and Harrington's bullet in one of the bags but decided against it. Three of my most valuable possessions, after my machete and gun. I wouldn't leave their fate up to someone else. Instead, I covered them in plastic wrap and put them in one of my pockets. I was ready to leave, and so was most of the supplies. I just had to wait for Gary and Tracey to say their goodbyes.

I wandered aimlessly for my remaining time there. The boathouse didn't hold a special place in my heart the same way it did for my hosts. They would break down crying when a different object sparked another memory and, with it, an emotion.

I felt awkward walking in on Tracey while she cried, looking through a photo album. I felt even more awkward when I found Gary in the previously locked room where Mama was, and instantly assumed the worst. I pulled out my machete, ready to strike them both down. How would I reason with him that we couldn't bring her? What if he had been killed? But I found none of that. What I found was a broken man, crying over the reanimated corpse of his mother. He wasn't trying to free her or bring her with him. He was saying his goodbyes. He told her he missed her and that maybe they would be back one day. I doubted we would ever come back.

When he was done, he left the room, stench and all, and continued preparing to leave. He was a strong man. Before we left, Gary gave my wound one last look over. He was happy with the progress it had made and helped me to cover it to avoid any transmission of bacteria. Then we all laid out our appropriate clothes and prepared in our own ways for the coming time.

Broadcast Two: Church of the Midnight Sun

"Hello, this is the father and leader of the Church of the Midnight Sun. We were well aware of this day and waited behind barred walls for the eventual end of times. We knew the dead would rise. The evidence has been spread throughout history. Just read any of the historical tomes of the great Abrahamic religions. It's all there.

"We paid heed to these warnings, and through our ark, we've ensured the salvation of the untainted. All are welcome and will be provided with a safe home. Of course, the sanctuary will only be provided on the condition that you're not tainted by the evils of the old world or the new. After all … this flood, much like that of Noah's, was sent by powers greater than our own. But this flood wasn't sent by our divine creator who only deals with purifying the world with cleansing waters. This flood of the dead wasn't sent as punishment by an unjust god. No. This is the work of The Dark One, who commands the dead once the souls have returned to the creator.

"Some of you may call him Satan, others Iblīs. It does not matter the name you give him, for The Dark One still commands this unholy flood. This undead horror was cast upon us to turn all who are pure into unclean ones. A mockery of the creator's flood, which washed away the impure.

"Remember these words, pure and impure ones, for there is an appropriate and just end for you, regardless of your path."

CHAPTER 25

"Are you ready?" I whispered to Gary and Tracey, one hand on the door handle and the other clutched the newly sharpened machete. They nodded. Gary had all the bagged supplies slung over his shoulders. What he couldn't carry, he held in his hands. As our packhorse, he was defenceless. It was up to me and Tracey to protect him once we got outside. That was the plan, anyway. Tracey had the shotgun clutched against her chest as if it were a safety blanket. Her various pockets bulged from the shotgun shells that filled them.

I looked back at Gary straining under the sheer weight of the bags. If encumbered had a facial expression, Gary was making it. I had a momentary pang of guilt that I couldn't help him but, with my injured leg, I was better off defending him than being the mule, and his wife was too small to carry anything effectively. We were his armed escorts. I wouldn't have minded so much except Gary was the only one who knew how to sail, so we had to keep him alive … not that I wouldn't have protected him anyway, but now his survival meant mine.

I mouthed a countdown, "*Three … two … one …*"

I pulled the door open.

Tracey charged out first onto the walkway, with the shotgun levelled. Gary stumbled out next. I limped out at the rear, pulled the revolver out of my pocket, and thumbed back the hammer. Necessary? Probably not. Fun? Definitely.

Gary's wife and I guided him to the bottom of the steps, unimpeded. A couple of undead had started to wander into view, the noise of our heavy footsteps piquing their curiosity. Once they saw us, they started running, moaning excitedly.

"Get behind us," I told Gary, forcing his back to the boathouse. Tracey aimed the shotgun towards the undead.

I whispered, "No shots. Not yet. You two keep moving, but slowly. Don't get too far."

A look of relief flooded her face. She wasn't confident with the shotgun or with killing the undead. Lack of confidence would get her killed.

I hobbled towards the undead, which were in full sprint, and stood a comfortable distance from Gary and his wife. I needed to be able to swing without fear of them getting in the way. In my head, my attack would be swift and fluid, like the slow-motion fight scenes of modern thrillers, but the sagging weight of my leg reminded me that wouldn't be the case.

I clenched the machete in anticipation of the first zombie, who was coming straight for me and didn't slow down as it neared. Its plan for stopping was to crash into me. I wouldn't allow that to happen. At the last second, I sidestepped, arching the machete through its skull. The top half of its head fell away, hitting the floor like a half-eaten watermelon – a rotten watermelon. Black brain matter splashed, but the zombie carried on running past me. The signal from its non-existent brain not reaching the rest of its body to tell it to stop. It continued a few more paces and then toppled to the floor as its limbs lost what little coordination they had.

The undead seemed so simplistic it was almost amusing to watch. I could feel myself smiling dumbly, until the gravity of the situation crashed back down around me. I was fighting a war for my own survival. I snapped back to reality as the sound of pounding footsteps reached me. I spun back towards them, forgetting the corpse I'd just dispatched. The two zombies were bearing down on me, and I wouldn't be able to deal with them separately. I attempted a hobbled run towards them, my bad leg lagging behind. The first zombie was in grabbing distance when I swooped low and swung my machete through its leg. Its shin split and broke apart as splinters of bone pulled away. I tried to ignore the gory tendons attempting to hold the severed leg in place.

I dodged out of the way of the downed zombie's grasp and stumbled towards the second zombie. I only just managed to pull the machete up in time to stop it from biting me. My machete was between me and the creature, pressing against the zombies face. The blade cut a line from chin to forehead. The zombie didn't care. If anything, it seemed more excited for having prey so close, and tried to push against the blade to get to me. Chin and lips split as the machete sliced through the flesh. Broken and carrion-stained teeth exposed themselves as the zombie snarled, tearing its face along the slash. The meat of its lower face sloughed away from the frame of its skull, exposing the tendons as they expanded and contracted with each jaw movement. I didn't have enough room to pull the machete back without giving the zombie room to get at me, nor did I have enough room for a strong enough swing to cut through bone. Instinct took over, and I did the only thing I thought to do. Punch the blunt side of the machete.

I heard bone crack and break, partly from the machete

embedding in the skull bone and partly from my fingers breaking. Adrenaline kept the pain from flooding my system as I swept out the zombie's feet when it stumbled back. It collapsed to the floor, machete still lining its face. I lifted my foot and smashed it down onto the zombie's face. The machete forced its way through the rest of the skull, putting an end to the monster for good and cleaving its head in two. I stood tall, panting. More zombies were running towards our location. Tracey just stood there, shotgun in hand.

"Run!" I bellowed, all intention of keeping quiet gone. I grabbed the machete, spun on my heel and sprinted towards the water's edge. I made sure Gary and Tracey stayed in front of me. I was the first and, as far as I was concerned, the last line of defence.

The one thing I remember most from that moment at the boatyard was the noise. A cacophony of sounds. My boots as they hit the uneven ground, sending gravel skittering like small explosions. The pounding of blood in my ears as my heart rate accelerated. The explosive discharge of the shotgun, where Tracey had forgotten to remove her finger from the trigger. The slap of rotten flesh on the cold floor as the undead neared. The icy grasp of death was getting closer and closer, metaphorically and literally.

Gary, who was at the front of our little marching band, dropped the bags and dived into the unclean water in one swift motion, leaving the mark of white foam where he vanished. Tracey and I stopped on the water's edge and spun around to confront the oncoming dead. She was the first to put down one of the advancing zombies, the blast from the business end of the shotgun destroying the creature. Its head crumpled and disappeared, as well as the flesh covering its chest and upper arms. She slid two more shells into her shotgun, and that's where I came in. I moved forward, holding my machete like a warrior of old would hold their sword. I swung it when another zombie came within reach. I didn't even take note of the devastation I had caused as I pulled my machete back again. What was the point of remembering it when it was all so similar? The steady stream of undead heading towards us would be the same, whether it was my flesh or theirs.

I risked a look over my shoulder, past Tracey and towards the boat which stood still in the water. What was taking Gary so long?

****

Gary

Gary had always been a good swimmer. His mother made sure of that. She had constantly reminded him that her father had drowned in the family pond. She had later admitted that it was nothing to do with his lack of ability to swim, but he had passed out drunk. Regardless, the fear of God was put into Gary whenever he was near water, but Mama wasn't having any child of hers scared of water, so he had swimming lessons every day for fifteen years. Overreaction? She considered it proactive. Even into adulthood, Gary made sure he went swimming once a week. Old habits were hard to break.

Taking all that into consideration, Gary still found it difficult to swim out to the abandoned boat. The water would wash over him and push him back and under. He felt the growing frustration of not getting anywhere. The tide was just too strong. Every foot he gained, he lost half of that and sometimes more. He felt he was fighting a losing battle. Gary wasn't one for giving up, but he was cold, wet, and growing more tired. His arms burned and eyes stung. He was beginning to think they would have to find another way. They could retreat back to the boathouse and try again. Or they could –

Boom!

What in God's name was that? Gary felt the hair on his neck stand. He looked over his shoulder mid-breaststroke and saw his beautiful wife reloading the shotgun.

He had three immediate thoughts. The first was that he needed to swim faster for Tracey's sake. The second was that he should not have let Sam convince them to leave the safety of their home. The third? A completely irrational and insignificant realisation that an implement of death could make such a simple noise. The jet of cold and salty water that went up his nose and down his throat brought him back into the moment. His focus was the boat!

****

Sam

I saw Gary in the water, making his way to the boat. He looked as though he was fighting a losing battle. Who could fight the ocean and win?

Despite the impossibility of the situation, I could see Gary making progress. He was winning inch by inch, and his resolve never seemed to waver. Before long, I watched Gary grip the edge of the boat and hoist himself up. It was only the pounding of feet and snarls of the hungry closing in on me that tore my eyes away from the miracle that was Gary. I rolled my shoulders, ready for the next onslaught of the undead.

"Ready?" I said to Tracey, looking over my shoulder. She

nodded, clutching the shotgun. No, not *the* shotgun, *her* shotgun. She didn't hold it like it was a safety blanket anymore. She held it like a confident warrior. There was something in her eyes that hadn't been there before. A hardness. A hardness that would help her survive in a broken world. And in that moment, I saw the beauty in her that Gary saw. She was strong and confident. Standing on that waterfront, I knew I didn't want anyone else by my side. Not Gary. Not my mother. Not Alice. Not even Bear Grylls, the master of survival. Tracey was my backup, and I was happy.

I swung my machete at the first of the next wave of undead.

CHAPTER 26

Gary

Once Gary had pulled himself up onto the deck, the first thing he did was look back to the waterfront to see how his Tracey was faring. She was doing fine. Amazing in fact. Sam was doing a fantastic job of protecting her. Gary could see that he was out in front, stopping any zombies from getting to her. Deep in the blood and gore. But as much as Sam was keeping her safe, Gary had an odd feeling. He couldn't explain it, but something was gnawing away at him. There was something off about Sam. Not necessarily bad, but definitely not right.

When Gary had finally pulled his gaze away from his wife, he looked around the boat. He knew the model well. Had seen a fair few docked up around the boathouse. There was an enclosed cabin up five or six steps. A darkened window looked outward. The deckhouse. That's where he needed to go. And he almost went straight there, until he noticed the blood droplets leading to the lower cabin.

Gary hesitated for a moment, knowing the darkness that awaited him should he open the door. But he knew that he needed to go there. He had to make the boat safe for Tracey. He looked around the deck for some kind of weapon. Found nothing of use. He considered waiting for Sam to get on board.

At least then he would have backup. But if there were any zombies in there, they could get loose in the meantime. He sighed, then approached the door and placed his hand on the doorknob. He slowly twisted the knob, then suddenly let go. There was something … his survival instinct? Something was telling him not to walk in. He placed his ear to the door and tapped with his knuckles. Almost immediately there was the sound of thrashing and snarling, clinking of metal on metal.

Gary waited for the zombie to slam into the door. It didn't come, yet the thrashing continued. Was … was it stuck? Trapped? He wanted to wait longer, but the occasional boom of shotgun blasts reminded him that he had limited time. He gingerly twisted the doorknob and let the door swing inward. Although Gary was confident that the monster within was confined, he wasn't willing to bet his life on it.

The gloomy light of the outside world filled the darkness of the cabin. Gary could see that it was the dining room, with a door at the back leading to another room – the bedroom. There were strewn over chairs and shattered ornaments. Bloodied carpets and broken everything. But the décor's condition wasn't the main concern. What was the main concern was the zombie in the room. The literal zombie in the room.

The man had clearly bled out after killing himself. Deep slash marks on his wrists, a fisherman's knife by his side, and a dried pool of blood spread around him. The former man had removed his shirt. He had, what looked like, bite marks on his upper arms and torso. A chain looped over his shoulders and around his neck, with padlocks holding the loop in place. He had looped the other end around a table, the base of which had been bolted to the ground. Something to keep it in place if the waters were rough.

The entire scene had clearly been premeditated. The chains, the slashed wrists, even bringing the boat to a stop. Had the man killed himself because he'd been bitten? Did Sam's previous assumption about bites carry some truth? Or had this man thought the same? Regardless, the man had taken his own life. Gary said a short prayer for him. No one should suffer that fate.

The zombie continued to pull at its chains as if they weren't even there. It continued to gnash its teeth and snarl. The presence of Gary encouraging the creature's excitement.

Boom!

Gary had to act fast. Time was running out.

It didn't take long to find the keys to the padlocks. They were on the floor, by the door. The poor man had probably thrown them out of arm's length after he locked himself down. Gary still didn't have it in him to put one of the creatures down in cold blood. It wasn't an immediate threat to him, but he needed to dispose of it. He had a plan, even if he didn't like it.

Gary approached the zombie slowly, waiting for it to extend its chain to see how far it could reach. He also held a long pole in one hand, which he had found on the deck, and in the other was a small ornament. It had a hollow in it, the same way a vase did, and fit perfectly over the end of the pole, which Gary proceeded to do.

"Open wide," he whispered to the snarling zombie while pushing the object into the zombie's mouth. It clamped down, expecting to taste flesh, but found the tasteless and inedible ornament instead. It didn't matter to the zombie, though. It just tugged it free from the pole. With the ornament wedged in its mouth, it wasn't able to bite anything else.

Gary knew he should kill the zombie, but he just couldn't separate the person from the monster they'd become. He sighed as he walked forward, keeping the zombie at a distance by pushing the pole into its chest. Gary grabbed the keys and unlocked the padlock. The zombie, now free to roam, charged forward with its arms extended. Although Gary still had the pole pushed against its chest, the zombie pushed forward with all the force it could manage. The pole, sturdy and metal, sunk into the rotten flesh of the zombie's chest. It kept going until it hit bone.

Gary knew it was dead, but he couldn't comprehend how anything moving wasn't aware of the damage that was happening to it. But he also couldn't afford to linger, so he led the zombie out, using the pole to keep it at a distance. Each step shook bits of congealed gore off the zombie, hitting the deck and making a soft *splat.*

Once he had directed the zombie to the edge of the boat, Gary made one final move. He twisted the zombie sideways, the pole tearing a large gash into its chest cavity as it tumbled into the water. He collapsed to his knees, heaving until vomit hit the deck and joined the gore. He stood, knowing his momentary respite was just that, and wiped his mouth. All he needed to do was check the back bedroom and pull up the anchor. Then it was time to get to work.

****

Sam

"He's taking his time!" I panted, felling another zombie. I was covered in blackened blood and parts of decaying organs. There were bone fragments and flesh on the floor, trailed by corpses with pieces cleaved out of them. Have you ever seen decaying brain matter spilling onto the floor? The smell of decay never gets easier.

With each swing, I grew more tired. My shoulders ached from it. Arms felt like they'd been attached to weights. Every contact between blade and flesh and bone made me lose a little bit more of my will to survive. My skeletal frame felt as though I was being shaken to pieces. Movies made ripping the undead to pieces seem so easy, but it was incredibly tiring.

There was a blast from the shotgun as Tracey obliterated a zombie that had gotten too close for comfort. The shower of bone fragments was all I needed to know that I'd been saved.

"Cheers," I wiped my face with the back of my hand. It didn't help to remove the sweat and gore and probably made the matter worse.

"I hope he's okay," Tracey said, using her moment of respite to show concern for her husband. Almost in reply came the rumble of a boat engine starting up.

CHAPTER 27

It was such a beautiful sight, seeing that boat sail closer and closer. This was our salvation, and Gary was our very own Charon. He would guide us, the damned, to the other side … I really needed to stop with the mythological comparisons. At what point would it be too much of a stretch of the imagination to make them work?

I jammed the machete blade into yet another zombie, up through its chin and into its brain. Slain in one hit. I looked up and saw another couple of zombies run into view. We hadn't needed to fire a shot in a while, so what was drawing them in? It wasn't like they had echolocation. Or did they? It was hard to think with the roar of the boat engine thumping away behind me. Then it dawned on me. The boat engine! Damn. That was the noise drawing them in.

"You're drawing them here!" I shouted once the revelation hit me. "Turn off the engine. Let the momentum carry you."

Gary couldn't hear me. He could see me waving frantically, but couldn't understand my intent. He just continued onwards to save us but, unknowingly, probably dooming us instead. I turned to Tracey, ready to tell her to fight. I didn't need to, though. She already knew what needed to be done.

The next group of zombies got to us before Gary did. But we weren't going to be stopped that easily. Our bodies may've screamed with exhaustion, but that was better than death. Tracey brought down two zombies, with two succinct blasts, whilst I killed a third.

"Oh, come on," I growled as more zombies came into view. We couldn't kill any more undead without attracting more attention. On top of that, the boat would draw more. They would just keep coming. On the other hand, if we didn't kill any of the undead then we would to die then and there.

"What can we do?" Tracey shouted, panic swelling as the number of undead around us increased.

"Let's go!" I screamed as I grabbed a bag and tossed it over the huge gap between land and boat.

Like something out of a bank heist movie, the bag landed successfully on the boat. Tracey threw another, and I tossed the last one. I turned around to take down another zombie that had closed in.

"Come on!" Tracey screamed as she dived across the distance between land and boat.

"Here goes," I huffed quietly to myself as I also threw myself towards the boat.

The difference between Tracey and I is that she landed gracefully. My overall size on an injured leg prevented me from getting a proper liftoff, and I collided with the edge of the boat. My lower half was dunked in the icy water, and my top half held on for my life. I dropped the machete onto the boat's deck and pulled myself entirely on board.

I could hear the impact on water as the undead ran into the ocean to try and get at us. I didn't care, though. Gary was already pulling away from land and we were safe. I was cold and wet and had almost been killed, but I was safe. I laughed, and laughed, and laughed. I carried on laughing until tears streamed down my face, and before long, I was crying.

"Is everything okay?" Gary climbed down to see what the commotion was.

"I have no idea," I said between sobs. "I honestly thought that was it for us."

But I wasn't crying for the almost-loss of my own life. I cried because I would've died without ever seeing Alice again.

"Well … we made it," Tracey said uncertainly, shocked by my sudden outburst of emotion. I dug out Thundy and showed it to Gary and Tracey properly for the first time.

"I need to get this to my Alice, you see. She'll be scared without it," I explained, as if that would answer everything. They both looked at me worriedly before turning to each other and hugging.

"I was worried," Gary kissed his wife.

"Me, too," she returned the kiss. I looked away from the public display of affection and noticed the gore-slicked deck. There also appeared to be vomit, which one of our bags had landed in. I looked at Gary and noticed that he was a shade paler than when he left to get the boat. He didn't bring up the mess on the floor, nor did he even acknowledge it existed. Whatever had happened, I guessed Gary had defended the boat from the previous occupants and didn't want to talk about it. There might still be hope for Gary yet. He was certainly turning over a new leaf if the evidence aboard the boat was anything to go by. I was proud of him.

After Tracey and Gary had finished their affectionate greeting, and all the adrenaline had left my body, I pushed myself to my feet. It was time to explore my new mode of transport. It wasn't big at all, and three of us on it meant there was very little room. We would all be living very closely over the next … however long we were together.

Gary attended to the sailing of the boat, and Tracey was moving the bags into the cabin. I thought it would be best if I helped, so I picked up two holdalls and carried them through. The scene inside backed up some of my speculation about what had happened aboard when Gary arrived. The blood. The destruction. The chains? I would have to ask Gary about that. It was the only thing that didn't add up.

I followed Tracey into the backroom, which was a pristine bedroom. Untouched by the carnage that lay in the other room. There were photos and other personal knickknacks, which Tracey quickly took to packing away in a drawer. I dumped the bags on the bed and went back for the last one. On my second pass through the living room, I took to observing every little detail about it. After all, it would be my bedroom over the following days. I certainly wasn't getting the double bed to myself, so the bloody sofa it was. I would have to scrape and scrub most of it off before I slept on it of course. Wasn't great, but it would do.

After moving the bags and helping the others set up our belongings for the journey ahead, I started preparing my own bed. My main concern was, of course, the blood. No amount of scrubbing would get the blood out of the material and carpet. I had to try solving this by thinking outside the box, and what cleaning couldn't fix, had to go.

While tidying the mess away in that room, I found a small and deadly blade – fisherman's knife. After I cleaned it off, I used it to cut through the carpet and remove it in bloodstained sections. Most of it had sunk through, onto the surface below, but that just wiped away. I tossed the carpet and other bloody bits and pieces into the water. No one was around to complain about my ocean pollution. I used an untainted sofa cushion and a spare bedsheet as my bedding. I had already slept in worse. The sofa would be just fine. I kept the knife, using duct tape to create a makeshift sheath for it, and put it in one of my many boiler suit pockets. Finally, the finishing touch. I unwrapped Thundy and placed it on the table, facing my sofa.

"We're on our way," I said gently with a smile, stroking Thundy's soft face. "It won't be long now."

****

Tracey

Tracey never liked being on the water. The vastness of the ocean terrified her, yet she felt safer with Gary there. He had sailed for years and never had an issue. Her focus was to get the boat ready for them to live in for the following days. Or however long they were there. They had spent so long focussing on getting to the boat that they hadn't thought any further than that. They had relied so much on Sam that they'd essentially put their future in his hands. Whispers of doubt traced her mind as she heard him in the next room, talking to the bear he carried. Then again, Gary was there, too. Everything would be okay. It would have to be.

****

Gary

After setting the boat on a steady course, and ensuring

they were far enough out to avoid any hazards, such as rocks, Gary took to searching the cabin he was in. He found lots of things which were of no use, such as old parts that had been replaced over the years. It wasn't the cabin of an organised man. But when searching a drawer full of letters, maps, and other personal mementoes, Gary found something that would make their life much easier.

****

Sam

"You'll never guess what I found," Gary said, surprising me as he walked into the room. He had dragged me from my deep thoughts about the path ahead.

"What is it?" I stroked Thundy.

"This!" Gary held up a small black device. Tracey came to investigate the conversation.

"What is it?" I said again, reiterating my interest.

"A marine GPS. Basically a satnav for boats. We can find out where we're going and have a course made for us, too. Mixed with other things I found, we can find our way to a dock, or somewhere else to refuel," Gary beamed. I didn't entirely understand the importance, but Gary was pleased, so it had to be good.

"Nice find, man," I smiled. "We can decide what we need to do from here, then!"

"Tomorrow," Gary nodded. "I need to make sure everything is calibrated before anything else."

He turned and left.

Tracey stood there, staring at my hand.

"What's up?" I asked, uncomfortably.

"Your fingers … I think they're broken," Tracey said. I

looked down at the hand I was instinctively keeping closer to my body. Two fingers were twisted at an angle, and they were an angry purple.

"Oh, yeah, I forgot about that. It happened when we were waiting for Gary," I said dumbly. I touched them with my other hand and winced at the pain. How had my body kept that at bay all that time?

"Let me fix that for you," Tracey said before leaving to get some medical supplies to set the bones.

"Great," I sighed, ready for the upcoming pain.

CHAPTER 28

Looking back on my life, I can only remember one other time I went on a boat. No, make that two times. Although, they were both ferries and not the sort of boat I had escaped on. Neither time would be considered a success. The first of which was abroad, on a ferry trip around the island of Crete. The second was on a ferry to Germany for a school trip.

Nothing of interest happened on the first trip. I'm sure it was an amazing trip, but I was too young to appreciate the sightseeing tour. As a result, I spent most of my time in the playroom. Basically an unsupervised nursery for kids too young to be on the tour. But I was also probably too old for that playroom. Seconds passed to minutes, passed to hours. I was bored, so I devised a little game. I set up a fort made of toys and cushions on either side of the room, then proceeded to unleash all-out warfare on both forts, destroying them as best as I could by throwing various things at them.

Unfortunately, the forts weren't the only thing destroyed. What I didn't realise was that every time something hit the ceiling in my attack, it shook loose a tile. I threw one final thing, grazing the ceiling as it soared. Suddenly, the ceiling collapsed! Tile after tile fell in a cascade. *Thunk! Thunk! Thunk!* It sounded like a huge deck of cards hitting the floor. I ran from the falling ceiling like a hero in an adventure film of old escaping an advancing boulder. I stood in the doorway, panting and looking back at the destruction. I had singlehandedly destroyed a room on a ferry. I left after removing any evidence that I was there. When I later saw streams of staff heading towards that area, I made sure I was nowhere to be found.

The second occasion wasn't fantastic either, but it was also the time I discovered I was immune to seasickness on rough seas. A trait not all my friends possessed. It was a school trip, not that I remembered where we were going. The ferry's journey was, for lack of a better term, mental. The ship was going up and down, left and right. On several occasions, I felt like I was launched into the air. It wasn't a safe journey. The souvenir shop had to close due to items being thrown from the shelves. The restaurant had to close for similar reasons. The only thing that stayed opened was the arcade since every machine had been bolted down. I and the majority of my friends, the ones who could actually stand the bucking of the ship, were in the arcade playing away. While so absorbed in a game, we barely noticed we were almost falling over. About an hour into our arcade session, we heard a voice behind us.

"Guys, I don't feel too good," one friend said.

He had previously stayed in the lounge room due to not being able to handle the motion of the ocean. He must've gotten bored and found his way to us, because he stumbled through the door, doubled over, clutching his stomach. He opened his mouth to speak again, and that's when the most fantastical arc of vomit I had ever seen erupted from his mouth. Well, second most fantastical, but that's a story for another day. I swear he could've done two forward flips had he been capable before even touching everything he'd uneaten.

Not only did he have distance, but the volume. Had he bowed to the porcelain throne instead, I'm sure he would've filled it up and then some. Horrific … and amazing.

We all stared at him in disbelief, our silence broken when the owner spoke.

"Get out, you filthy pig!" he screamed, shooing my friend away. He then turned and looked at us with the rage of a man who knew he was going to be wrist-deep in vomit. He snarled, "Are you with him?!"

My friends and I all looked at each other before I answered for the group. "No. No, we're not."

With that, our friend left and we returned to playing our games.

CHAPTER 29

Although life on a boat wasn't bad, it wasn't something I wanted to do again sooner than I had to. What was truly difficult was having broken fingers. Every time I forgot, I was quickly reminded by the blinding pain.

We were on the boat for three days, not including our first day of getting on and setting sail or our final day of leaving the boat and being forced to land.

During our first day at sea, Gary taught me valuable skills which would help me survive the apocalypse. How to set up a fishing rod, how to fish, and general maintenance skills. Unfortunately, we didn't catch a thing. As far as I knew, his fishing skills were all a bluff to show off. The way Tracey rolled her eyes at his fishing was enough to make me think that was the case, but he definitely acted like he knew what he was doing.

Images floated across my mind of society reverting back to the hunter-gatherer way of life. Maybe kids would cast their line off of London Bridge and into the Thames when life returned to those waters. We would all become soldiers to survive and farmers to live. Maybe not soon, but eventually.

Tracey also felt she had skills to pass on, and I was her

student. She taught me to, as she called it, cook properly, and it really was properly. I never knew you could turn one meal into something so different depending on the spices used. Her cooking was amazing. Tracey was a superwoman, having a full-time career and she was also a fantastic cook. Gary was a lucky man.

It was nice having the escapism of cooking – proper kitchen cooking – even if the kitchen we were using was just a poor imitation of one. I doubted I would ever need those skills if the world carried on the way it was going. The only skills I would need was how to eat pork and beans out of a can around a campfire without wanting to blow my brains out.

Gary, not to be outdone by Tracey, decided to show me the basics of boating. Useful, although I don't understand the need for so many nautical terms. Maybe one day I would travel to a new land by boat. Just me and Alice on a lonely island where we could finally be away from all the death. Idyllic? Yes. Impractical? Incredibly. There was no way we could sustain ourselves on an island forever. Who knows, maybe we could simply wait for the undead to finally pass before returning to society, or die on the island, waiting. So many wonderful options for my future.

Night came and we planned our journey onward. We knew fuel was limited, and the small amount we had wouldn't last long. We weren't sure how far what we had would get us, and we didn't want to run out before it was too late to do anything about it. So we needed to go to the nearest dock, which we were sure would have fuel. A dock somewhere north. We found one on the navigation system that was a couple of days sailing depending on the weather. After that, who knew. We would just keep heading north I supposed, looking for signs of Alice and her family.

The second day gave me the direction I was looking for. Like everything in the apocalypse, it came in the way of a radio broadcast. What made it stand out was that it wasn't a repeated and automated broadcast, but an actual person talking. I didn't catch the whole broadcast, but what I heard of it said:

… Forthside Barracks and Redford Barracks. I repeat, Forthside Barracks and Redford Barracks is the destination for all existing military. They are both taking in civilians and military personnel. That means head to Scotland. If you spot our convoy, do not approach us directly or we will open fire. You must group together at various locations so that we can approach you. I repeat. Do not approach us directly. Remember to tune in every day at twelve hundred hours, and twenty-four hundred hours for confirmation of a checkpoint …

And that's when he would list the next lot of locations to wait for the convoy. We weren't near any of the checkpoints, but we could get to one eventually. I assumed there would be new checkpoints the further along the convoy made it. That's where Alice would be heading, if she wasn't part of the convoy already. I would meet her on the convoy or at their final destination.

What remained of the military had their act together, and they knew what they were doing. They may not operate under the British Army moniker, but they were still an organised group. The first bit of hope and the chance of meeting Alice again had become a reality. I smiled. When I told Tracey and Gary the news, they smiled too. We had a destination, and we had a path to follow. We were no longer lost. We not only had a destination, but a purpose as well. It was exhilarating.

"You hear that?!" I asked Thundy, picking him up and hugging him. "You're going home!"

Thundy just stared at me, glassy-eyed, but I swore he smiled.

****

Tracey and Gary

"Now that's love," Tracey beamed, putting her arm around Gary.

"What? With the bear?" Gary joked. Tracey dug him in the side with her elbow, and they both laughed. "He is so full of life when it comes to Alice."

"She'll save him from the dark places he goes," Tracey watched Sam's smile grow bigger and bigger the more he talked to the silly bear.

"I love you, Tracey," Gary kissed his wife passionately. She didn't need to say anything to express her love for her husband, she just kissed him back and pulled him close. If Sam wasn't there, Tracey would've taken Gary to the bedroom. Unfortunately, they would have to wait until they were on land again to show how much they loved each other. They smiled at the other, lost in the haze of the same love they'd had for each other since the day they met. Gary thought about how Tracey got more and more beautiful with each year, and how their love never dimmed, not even once.

If Alice is even half of what Tracey is, Sam's a lucky man, Gary thought with a smile. He made his way to the cabin so that he could make a few adjustments to keep them on track.

****

Sam

On the third day, fuel was running a lot lower than expected. The water and winds had been rougher than we'd planned for, and our stop for fuel was coming up fast. We worried if we would even make it at all. So Gary decided that we should start heading more towards the coast, in case we needed to make a split-second decision to return to land. The boat engine drew undead towards the waterfront, and they wandered straight into the water in an attempt to get at us. Like the stereotypical idea of lemmings following each other off a cliff, to their death – not true, I might add.

We agreed that when we reached our final destination, we would wait further out and have to swim in. We couldn't risk the engine drawing undead attention which would make it difficult to get on land.

There was a lot of waiting around, and everyone was anxious. We all agreed to go to land on the off-chance we found more stuff or extra fuel to carry back. Plus, we didn't want to risk getting separated. It wasn't the best plan, and we had debated it to the point that Gary stormed out of the room. The debate being, Tracey should stay behind on the boat to keep an eye on everything, while Gary and I went to land. Tracey's response was that Gary should stay behind since he knows how to use the boat. The counter to this being that Gary and I could carry the most, so we were the most valuable on land. Tracey was happy to go to land. Gary didn't want her to. I suggested we all go. We couldn't bring the boat in anyway, and there's safety in numbers. Finally, we agreed that getting more fuel earlier meant fewer land visits later. It was the lesser of two evils. I didn't like either option, but I felt we'd picked the safest option. Anchoring the boat would keep it in place for our return. We all wanted an early night and an early rise, but I doubted any of us would be able to sleep if Gary and Tracey felt the same pit of nerves that I did.

"Gather 'round boys!" Tracey dished out our meal. A mixture of tinned vegetables and corned beef. I hated corned beef. I couldn't complain, though. Cooked food was cooked food. She placed the food in front of me, but I knew better than to just dig in. We had to say grace first. We linked hands and closed our eyes.

"God," Gary began, "for what we are about to receive, may the Lord make us truly thankful."

I loosened my grip, but Gary held on. That was unusual. I opened my eyes to look around.

"I would also like to thank you for bringing Sam into our lives. Without him, we would be lost," Gary said. Tracey smiled.

They both said, "Amen."

"We mean it, you know," Tracey looked at me. "We would never have gotten this far without you."

"Thanks," I said. I hated being the centre of attention. "You guys saved me, too. With my leg and your food."

We all shared a laugh and ate. We were safe. We were content. The only worry was the following day. I miss days like that.

When we turned in for the night, we were merry and didn't even need any alcohol to reach that level of happiness. I laid down on the sofa, Thundy looking intensely at me.

"I haven't forgot about her," I muttered to him, turning away from his judgmental stare. Then I closed my eyes and instantly fell into another dreamless sleep.

Broadcast Three: Shaun, Frank, and Barbara 2

Barbara: It's one in the afternoon! Time to check in! How's everyone doing?

Shaun: Still living but wish I wasn't. Finished the last of my Oreos earlier. Pretty damn depressed about it.

Barbara: Well, that sucks. I wouldn't know your suffering, of course, because I swiped a whole crate from a supermarket.

Shaun: Why rub it in? That's like rubbing salt in my wound.

Barbara: I'm trying to prove a point. You're gonna have to leave eventually. You'll run out of food and fresh water soon, or the power will go.

Shaun: I'll cross that bridge when the time comes.

Barbara: We'll see. Where's Frank? Did his raid go okay?

Shaun: Not sure. Haven't heard anything either.

Frank: Well, well, well. Speak of the devil and he shall appear.

Barbara: Making me worry, Frank. Not cool!

Frank: I had to deal with some unwelcome guests. Could say they were drop-dead gorgeous.

Shaun: Not funny. What happened?

Frank: Not sure why, but the dead have started gathering outside my apartment block. Always one or two to begin with, but by the morning there's always about twenty or so. Like they're drawn here.

Barbara: Maybe you should start using your vibrator on a quieter setting. I'm sure your massive flappy lady parts could do with a break. Maybe man-up and you won't need it anymore.

A bark of laughter from Shaun and Frank.

Frank: Why are we friends with her again? She's disgusting.

Shaun: I'm only friends with her so that when you die and are out of my way, me and her can repopulate the Earth. I'll name the firstborn after you, Frank, don't worry.

Frank: And if it's a girl?

Barbara: Same name. Perfectly acceptable if we're naming her after you.

Frank: If I'm the only thing stopping you from finally getting laid, I'm willing to take one for the team and kill myself. I'll go head first out my window – for you, Shaun.

More laughter from all three of them before Barbara interrupted with a serious tone.

Barbara: Guy's, I'm leaving.

Shaun: Your house?

Barbara: No … the country.

Shaun: What?

Frank: Is this another joke?

Barbara: No, guys. I heard it's safe in America. A guy has a boat, and he's taking a few people with him.

Frank: You do realise how suspicious that sounds, right? Besides, who told you it's safe?

Shaun: Yeah, was it the same guy as the aliens?

Barbara: Don't say it so mockingly. I'm certain I saw one as well. Anyway, it was the boat guy who told me America was safe. I know how dangerous and stupid it sounds, but why would he risk a voyage to America if he didn't believe it himself?

Frank: In what way is it safe?

Barbara: He told me there was a man fighting a war against the dead. I have to believe something more is out there.

Shaun: Barb … please don't go.

Barbara: I don't want to go, but the reason I'm telling you two this is because I want you both to come with me. It could be an adventure.

Frank: I'm so sorry, but I can't go, Barbara. I need to wait here in case my kids find their way home. That's what I have to believe is out there.

Barbara: Shaun?

Shaun: I'm sorry, Barb, but I'm safe here. I don't want to leave.

Barbara: Fine, just remember, you'll have to leave eventually. This isn't going to just blow over. There isn't a cure. There's nothing but death. I love you both. You're like the only family I have left.

Frank: I care for you too, Barbara. Be careful out there.

Shaun: Yeah, be careful. I love you so much … like family.

Barbara: Thanks, guys. If either of you changes your mind, the boat leaves in a couple days. It's at the docks near me. I won't say over the broadcast because others could be listening. You both know where I mean, right?

Shaun: I do.

Frank: Sure.

Barbara: Well, I gotta go. I need to pack. Good luck out there, guys.

CHAPTER 30

Awake. Awake at first light.

"Ugh," I groaned as I rolled myself out of bed. What was the time? I looked around groggily, seeking the small clock on the wall. 4:53 a.m.?! I'd forgotten that anything before 7:00 a.m. even existed.

I stood up, joints popping. It felt amazing. Without the civilised world to direct my life, I woke up when nature dictated. I splashed water on my face to take the grogginess away. Normally I couldn't start my day without a shower, but there was no point that morning. I would do that when we returned from land after my double dip in the sea. I hated salty water.

I grabbed a bowl of some leftovers, and while walking out onto the deck, eating the cold mess, I noticed three things. Land was close. Cold temperature. The engine wasn't running. Had we arrived?

I sucked in a breath. The air was crisp and had a wintery feel to it. Getting into the water would be like a punch to my nervous system.

"Goddammit," I muttered.

"Language, Sam," someone laughed. I spun around and looked up, seeing Gary leaving the wheelhouse.

"Didn't see you there," I laughed, not sure who else it could've been. I gestured to the ocean. "Great day for a swim isn't it."

"Perfect if you have ice in your veins," Gary agreed with the same disgust I felt. "Been up long?"

"Not really," I shrugged. "You?"

"About an hour," Gary descended the ladder. "Had to prep the boat for our arrival."

He gestured towards the nearby land.

"That's it then, is it?" I asked, unimpressed. It wasn't what I was expecting. A few odd buildings. A few other boats on land, and cars dotted about. It was like a more lived-in version of the boatyard we'd come from. That also meant there could be undead anywhere.

"Yup," Gary nodded. "The fuel should be in one of those buildings. It would've been sold to boaters and whatnot. They'll have fuel canisters, like a jerry can, in there, too. We can fill those and get them back to the boat.

"And if there isn't?" I asked, the cold air bringing out my natural pessimism.

"We can syphon it out of the other boats. Don't worry, Sam, it'll be fine," Gary smiled and patted my shoulder. "Guess I better wake Tracey. Get ready for our little swim."

"Great," I sighed as Gary went inside, staring angrily at the ocean as though it had personally offended me and my bloodline.

I finished my food and returned to my temporary room. My own preparation consisted of plastic wrapping my phone and Thundy, as well as pocketing Harrington's bullet. They were my only true belongings, so I certainly wasn't leaving them behind. I tucked them into my boiler suit pockets, where they were comfortably at home.

Gary returned, pointing the shotgun casually at me.

"Muzzle sweep!" I called, panicking and ducking. He realised his mistake and lifted it so that the killing end was pointing at the ceiling.

"Sorry about that," his eyes bulged. "Should I bring it with us?"

"Yeah, of course," I nodded. "I'm bringing the machete. We need to be able to protect ourselves on land."

"Uh, will it be okay going in the water? Like, rusting up and that," Gary asked, clearly unsure.

"It'll be fine in the water as long as we clean it later. It's mostly just a movie myth," I smiled. "It'll be okay."

"Okay, good," Gary said as he left.

We were all ready to begin our swim to shore. Gary had pushed the anchor overboard, and we stood at the edge of the boat. I tried to stretch my muscles in the way I'd seen James do. He would've laughed at my attempts, and that thought hurt. But I limbered up as best as I could because I knew my muscles would try to seize up the moment I entered the frigid water.

It was still early, and even though the sun was shining, it wouldn't do much to warm the water. The more my mind lingered on it, the less I wanted to do it. I continued to stare at the water, trying to see past the murky layer and into the depths.

"Worse you'll find in there is seaweed. Maybe a few fish," Gary patted my back.

"I hate seaweed," I sighed. Could this day get any worse?

"You ready?" Gary asked with reluctance.

"Better now than later," I shrugged and then jumped into the ocean. I made sure to slam my eyes and hold my nose. I didn't want salty water jetting into my orifices.

The water was horrific. I'm fairly certain my butthole slammed shut in shock. I had jumped in to avoid the horrible sensation of easing my way in, but it didn't make it any better. The water was so cold that it knocked the air out of me, like a giant hand tightening around my chest. My body burned, and the boiler suit weighed me down. It was so hard to focus on anything except the cold! My chest hurt. I needed to breathe! I kicked my feet and thrashed about, pushing to the surface. I gasped, filling my lungs with the air it so desperately needed.

"How is it?" Tracey called. I could barely open my mouth to answer. Tracey optimistically added, "You'll soon warm up!"

I didn't warm up and it didn't get any better. It was equally horrific the whole time I was in there. I stayed still, just bobbing in the water and gasping for air. My legs and arms were going numb.

"Let's hurry," I growled through gritted teeth, something primal taking over as the cold worked its way into my bones. Gary and Tracey jumped. I kicked my feet to keep myself afloat while they went through exactly what I had. *Good, at least they knew what it was like.*

Once we had all caught our breath and got over the initial chill, we began to move. The cold made it difficult to swim. Hell, it made everything difficult. We couldn't take big strokes. It was like the cold kept our arms close to our body to preserve heat. But that didn't matter as much as I would've expected. We were actually getting somewhere with our doggy paddle swim.

As if everything was finally aligning to aide us, the icy waves washing up around our faces were also moving us forward. I kept pushing myself more and more, getting further and further ahead. I wanted – no, needed to be out of the water. Gary seemed to be doing the same. Tracey, although making progress, lagged behind.

It was hard to think about the others in the crushingly cold water. My legs were so numb I almost didn't notice that the material of my boiler suit was catching on stuff below. The water must've been getting shallower. Maybe it was seaweed trying to ensnare me. I shivered, not because of the cold, but the thought of the slimy seaweed. This made me wheeze a laugh.

"What?" Gary grunted.

"Nothing. Seaweed," I laughed again. He smiled. He had caught up with me, and we were almost there.

Although the water was still deep, my clothes still kept catching. An odd tug here and there. Leg brushing up against the seaweed at another point. I just wanted out of the water. I wasn't far from the land. I'd be there soon.

"My leg is caught!" Tracey shouted.

"Kick it loose. Probably seaweed," Gary called back, teeth chattering. We continued on.

"It's getting tighter!" Tracey yelled. Cogs began turning in my brain. Random pieces of information coming together.

"Just really pull your leg!" Gary yelled back.

Seaweed. Fish. Worse to worry about.

"It's really soft!" Tracey called again, panic growing in her voice. She was reaching down to pull at it.

Seafront. Water's edge. Deep. What was my brain trying to tell me?

"You can do it, Trace," Gary laughed.

Noise. Into the water.

"I'm free!" Tracey began swimming again. Something didn't feel right. I paused, and that's when something tugged at my leg. Not my leg getting caught. It felt like an actual pull! I looked down again. Something was just on the edge of my mind. It was when the murkiness of the water cleared momentarily, that it became obvious what lurked in the depths below.

"Undead!" I screamed as much as my lungs could manage, and began thrashing my legs to propel and protect myself. What I saw below the surface was dozens upon dozens of bloated, rotting faces. The undead reached towards us, grabbing. I flailed about, every twinge I imagined to be the undead. I didn't stop to think about anything. Just kicked and pushed to get away.

I wasn't far from the waterfront. Gary wasn't far from me. The sheer panic made me uncoordinated. I was taking longer than I needed. I just wanted to keep moving. I refused to be pulled down by the zombies. I kept splashing and trying to move forward until I finally pulled myself up onto the waterfront. I laid there, huffing and coughing out all the water I had swallowed.

Gary had also pulled himself up and out of the water, panting. He dragged himself about ten feet away from the edge before speaking. He was having a lot harder time recovering than I was.

"Where's Tracey?" he choked out. I pushed myself up and looked out into the water, where I saw Tracey thrashing and shouting. Calling for help. It was impossible to hear with the blood pounding in my ears. Gary was still on all fours, sputtering. Unaware of what was happening. Tracey was stationary. She was panicking so much and spending so much time flailing that she wasn't able to move

"Over here!" I shouted in an attempt to re-orientate her. If I had stopped to think, I would've been aware of attracting any undead. It didn't help. She continued to go side to side and in circles. Gary had finally taken notice and was staring at her.

Then, in one of the most surreal moments I had ever seen, she stopped flailing. Stopped moving altogether and stared at us. Our eyes locked, and it was like time froze. Then reality came speeding back as Tracey was wrenched below the surface.

"Tracey!" Gary screamed. He pushed himself to his feet and bolted forward, about to jump in after her.

I had a split second to decide, and I chose action. I dived on him, half a step from the water's edge. He fell to the floor, with me on top of him. He tried to throw me off him and crawl into the water to get to his wife. But I held on.

"Tracey! Tracey!" he kept screaming.

"It's too late for her!" I shouted. I needed to calm him. I needed him alive. He kept fighting me. I kept repeating myself and held him in place.

"I can still get to her!" Gary wailed, slamming his elbow into my nose. I fell back, blood streaming down my face.

"You'll just get yourself killed!" I shouted and pulled him back by his foot. He clawed at the concrete. In that moment, I was stronger than he was. His nails ripped off and fingertips bled, but I carried on pulling. He carried on screaming for his wife.

When he was far enough from the water, I dropped my knee onto his back and held him down with all the force I could muster. He just kept calling Tracey's name and sobbing hysterically. Tears were forming in my eyes, too, but I wiped them away. Grief came later. Survival came first.

CHAPTER 31

I don't know how long I stood there holding Gary in place while he sobbed, but it felt like eternity. He went through phases of struggling to get to the water and just lying there. Eventually, he lost all fight and went limp. He didn't even sob anymore.

I eased off him, my knee ached and my head hurt. I just wanted to lie down. Gary didn't attempt to get up. He just laid there, catatonic. If it wasn't for the free flow of tears, I would've thought he was dead.

I stood there for a little bit longer, before I finally spoke to Gary.

I said, trying to sound as sympathetic as possible, "Gary … we need to get going. I know how much you're hurting, but–"

"No, you don't," Gary snapped. He turned to glare at me, with red-rimmed eyes. "You don't know at all!"

He pushed himself up and walked towards me. His height now looked terrifying as he loomed over me, and I began backing up.

"We can deal with this later, but right now we need to go," I said quietly, suddenly aware of how quiet the rest of the world around us was.

"No, we can deal with it right now," Gary shouted, and shoved me. He had the shotgun in one hand, held by the barrel. With the rising anger, he probably didn't even realise.

"Whoa, don't touch me!" I said, with clenched fists. Heat flushed my face and I gritted my teeth.

"You sit there acting like everything is fine and dandy, talking to that fucking bear!" he screamed. "You don't give a damn about anyone else, do you?"

He tried to shove me again, but I had stepped back further before he could make contact.

He continued on with his tirade. "I thought about it. I mean, I *really* thought about it a lot, and you know what? I'm certain I didn't unplug that freezer. I keep replaying it over and over in my head. It was you, wasn't it? You were the one who wanted us to leave sooner. I shoulda known something was up."

Gary was approaching me fast, anger replacing all the sadness inside him. And he had had a lot of sadness.

"Gary," I said, desperately trying to calm him, aware that he still had the shotgun in his hand. "Can we please get into one of those buildings and talk about it. We're exposed out here."

"Well, here we bloody are. We left when you wanted, and look where it got us. Tracey is dead. I'm stuck with a manipulative piece of crap. You're going to pay for this," he swung at me.

I wish I could say I was fast enough to dodge the punch or even deflect it, but it hit me square on the chin. The impact of my jaw slamming into my pressure points sent a shockwave to my legs, turning them to jelly and causing me to collapse like a ton of bricks.

"You're scum!" Gary screamed, with all the dignity of an

enraged beast. He threw down the shotgun and slammed his boot into my side.

Cracked ribs. He stomped on my already injured leg. *Tissue tear.*

I tried to push myself up to defend myself, but he was on top of me in a second. He pulled me up by my head and smashed it into the ground. My vision pin-holed. I felt nauseous. He didn't care. He showered blow after blow onto me. I felt skin break and could taste blood. I couldn't fight back. Could barely defend myself, but I knew I had to, so I pulled my arms over my head. It didn't stop him from punching me, but it did stop my brain from hitting the back of my skull with every blow.

Am I going to die here? Probably. I was going to be beaten to death by the very man who had saved me. He was stronger than me, bigger than me. He had the advantage. No amount of planning and careful thinking would get me out of this.

I'm going to die. Why fight it anymore? This is what I deserve. I decided it was time to give up. I began to relax and accept my fate, when the punches suddenly stopped.

I was terrified to look past my arms in case it was a trick, but the weight on me had gone slack as well. Strange. I risked a look through my arms – my eyes had already started swelling – and saw that he was just swaying, eyes rolled into the back of his head.

"Gary?" I said through split lips. Had he broken? Had he finally snapped? Blood started leaking down the top of his head.

"Hit it again!" an unknown voice demanded. I noticed shadows looming behind Gary. Then there was a fleshy thud, and Gary's body fell sideways.

Standing over me were three men. The sun was behind them, so I couldn't make out their features.

"He's pretty messed up," one of the men said.

"Reckon he'll make it? We don't want him coming back as a meat-bag," another said. Then I heard the click of a gun.

"It's just a beating. It's only superficial," the third man said, overruling the others. They started discussing logistics and what to do with me. I didn't like that – I was right there. I eyed the shotgun, which wasn't far from where I laid.

"Don't even think about it," the apparent leader said, and scooped up the shotgun. I forced out a laugh. I was tiptoeing on the edge of mentally breaking down.

The leader leaned down close to my face and smiled. "You'll be just fine, won't you? Plenty of fight in you. Are you able to stand?"

"Yeah," I slurred through a swollen jaw.

"Good. Get up and we can get going," the leader held out his hand and pulled me up when I took it. He then turned to the others. "Call back the other guys and we can head back."

"What about the darky?" the first guy pointed to Gary's rapidly cooling body.

"Dump him in the water with the others. He'll be a meat-bag soon," the leader said.

"No!" I called as they began to lift his body. I wasn't letting the men who'd killed the man I'd once called a friend – even if he didn't see me that way in the end – dispose of him like he was nothing.

"We can't just leave him here," the leader said. "He'll be walking soon. We can't bury him – we don't know what it'll do to the soil. Besides, we don't have time."

He stopped walking and turned to me. At least he was listening.

"He was my friend. I should be the one who does it," I mumbled and began walking towards the men carrying Gary.

"It sure didn't look like you two were friends," the first guy said, but he was silenced by the leader.

The men dropped Gary's body to the floor and left him to me. I attempted to lift him, but the weight was too much. After a couple seconds, the leader approached, took Gary's legs and helped me to carry him, without saying a word. We placed him on the water's edge, and the leader stood back. I would bury him in the water where Tracey had died. Seemed fitting. At least they would be together again.

"If anyone deserves to go to heaven, it's you two," I wept. "I hope you find each other there."

I rolled him into the water, only walking away after he had sunk low enough that I couldn't see him anymore.

"That was nice, kid," the leader pulled me away from the water. He smiled awkwardly. "When we get back to base, we'll fix you up and we can talk about it over a beer if you like."

"Why didn't you let us just dump the darky in the water if that was what you were going to do?" the second man replied exasperated.

"That's enough of that, Bill," the leader said. "We're going back."

I was taken to a couple of beat-up vehicles, one of which was a flatbed truck. Several men gathered at them and climbed in, including me and my escort. I didn't even care where we were going. Didn't care who I was with. They seemed friendly, but where was my brutal paranoia that accompanied me to every encounter? I didn't even question them. I just didn't care.

I was sad for Tracey and Gary's passing, and I was sad

knowing at least one of them had died hating me. And I wasn't angry at my current hosts for killing him. It didn't seem personal. Sure, Bill had probably taken some satisfaction in killing *the darky*, but at the end of the day, it was just business to them. They had saved someone from their attacker, and the politics of the situation wasn't their concern. At least they'd allowed me to give him a semi-decent burial.

I didn't pay any attention to where we were going. What was the point? I didn't even seem like a concern to the men. They weren't even bothered by the new face. They didn't seem concerned with guarding me. Friendly men leading me to safety without question. I had been through that before. Almost like we had come full circle and I was back with James.

"We're almost there," the leader said over the engines' roar.

"At least you didn't whisper," I muttered, absentmindedly.

"What was that?" the leader looked at me. It was the first time I'd a chance to look at him properly, although my rapidly swelling eyes were attempting to prevent that. My face hurt so goddamn much. I squinted to take a clear look at him. He was a rough-looking man, like he had seen his fair share of fights and hardship. His weathered appearance looked pre-undead. Time to Sherlock of the situation. Greying hair, weathered appearance, and calloused hands. I guessed manual worker of some kind.

"Well ..." the leader prompted after I didn't answer.

"Nothing," I said. "Just thinking aloud."

"You got your secrets, I understand that. But when we get where we're going, we need to have a serious talk. I need to know who I'm letting into my little kingdom," he said. *Little kingdom? God or messiah complex? Great.* The leader laughed. "Don't look so intense. It's a joke amongst the guys. If you stay long enough, you'll understand it."

"I don't think you've told me your name," I said. "It would be nice to put a name to a face."

"Everyone around here calls me Boss. You can do the same if you like," he shrugged. "You?"

"Sam," I replied. It was amazing how times had changed. Pre-undead, I wouldn't have ever told people I didn't know my name due to fear of what they could do with that information. Whenever charities knocked on my door, I always gave the name Charles Diamondback. It sounded incredibly fake, but that was the point. Post-undead, I didn't mind telling potential scumbags my name. They couldn't do anything with that information anymore.

"Nice to meet you, Sam," Boss shook my hand, with a tight grip. "Well, welcome to my home."

I turned and looked over the driver's cabin. We were approaching a wall of shipping containers.

"This is it?" I asked, a bit thrown off by what I was seeing. There was a wall of different coloured shipping containers with men standing on top.

"Home sweet home," Boss said to me, then shouted, "Open up guys!"

I watched two parts of a container appear to separate, only to realise it was actually two container doors closing. The container doors had been left open, and they were the doors for the wall of containers. Impressive! Talk about using the environment to your advantage.

We passed through the gates and into a makeshift carpark, with more containers forming a secondary wall.

"How far do these containers go round?" I climbed out

of the flatbed and looked around.

"All the way," Boss said, walking next to me. "We're enclosed on all sides. There's another set of doors on the opposite side. I feel a lot safer having two ways out."

Men closed – or opened, depending on how you looked at it – the doors behind us.

"Or another way in," I muttered.

"You're a pessimistic sod, aren't you," he laughed. "I just didn't want the possibility of us being trapped with the dead outside. There are vehicles on that side, too. Ain't nothing half-assed around here."

We walked through the second doorway, and what I saw was amazing.

Broadcast Four: Tony with the Truth

Tony: So … zombies, eh. They're among us, and the Government still won't admit things have gone tits up. Well, I'm telling you to lock your windows and doors, ladies and gentlemen. This isn't some sort of infection that can be contained. The Government has lost control. We aren't trying to exterminate the undead anymore – they are exterminating us. This is Tony coming at you with the truth.

A distant gunshot in the background.

Tony: I keep hearing warfare out there. Not just undead on living, but man fighting man. I know, I know. We need to survive, and our own comes first, right? Wroooooong! We need to help each other. I ain't no hippy, but we can't be killing each other like this. At least take out the zombies first before getting back to killing each other.

The streets ain't safe. Even now, I'm locked away with enough food and water to live a long while, but this ain't me being selfish. Oh, no. I need to bring you the news about what's happening out there 'cause the Government certainly ain't doing that.

So here's a list of things that've happened out there. Well, there still ain't any news out of Bristol – the broadcasts have stopped, and the military abandoned their posts. Guess the rumours were true, so if any of you fine folk were hoping for some West Country cider, better cancel your plans.

A loud slurp of a drink as well as a louder gunshot.

Tony: Folks are awfully fighty out there today. Anyway, next on the list. Ooh, a little birdy has told me that the Government has gone to Scotland with the last of the military. Good to know that the rich and powerful are staying that way. Obviously, this is just speculation, but it does tie in with the rumours of large military movement up north from a week ago, as well as some very peculiar broadcasts. If you have to move out there, Scotland sounds like the safest place right now. If they don't shoot you on sight first.

Tony laughed. Then there was a gunshot much louder than the previous two.

Tony: Finally, this is a personal request from a lovely listener. The message reads, "Danny, we have tried to head to the coast. Love from Ruth." Well, Danny, if you're still out there, please let Ruth know you're okay. You shouldn't keep a lovely lady waiting. Please be safe out there, you guys, and … what the hell?

A loud banging in the background, possibly knocking on a barricaded door, followed by the shuffling of Tony's footsteps to investigate.

Tony: You can't just break your way in here! This is my property. I have a duty to the listeners.

The sound of a new voice.

Intruder: Well, you weren't lying about all your supplies. You really could live in here for years.

Sound of a gun cocking. Tony's tone went from brave to a whimper.

Tony: Please don't hurt me. Just take what you want, but don't hurt me.

A loud crash of something being pushed over.

Intruder: Trust me, I'll be taking everything. But I'm not just here for your goods. For the last two weeks, all I've had to listen to is your bullshit. Firing shot after shot, listening to your station to see how close I was getting. I am so sick of your nonsense. I'm sick of you! I'm sure other listeners are, too.

Sounds of a scuffle, and then a noise of something heavy hitting the ground. The footsteps got louder as the person walked closer to the microphone. A sigh before the speaker, imitating the news reader's low and throaty tone, spoke into the microphone.

Intruder: Now ladies and gentleman, time for a real show. Let me put a question out to the listeners. How many broken bones before he passes out?

The following twenty-five minutes was filled with crunches, laughter, screams, and crying as the intruder fulfilled his promise of a real show.

Intruder: The answer is seven. Seven bones before he passed out.

Chuckling.

Intruder: That's all folks.

A gunshot followed by a burst of static before the station died.

CHAPTER 32

The area I had walked into looked fantastic. It was essentially a small community. The area, which was protected by the container walls, encompassed a vast section of land. It was difficult to tell how big it truly was because of the maze of containers. But this didn't seem to trouble Boss, who navigated it with the ease that comes with familiarity. There were men entering different containers or carrying boxes between them, with clear intent.

"The containers come in pretty useful," Boss pointed to men going into one. "The ones over there, for example, were filled with food when we opened it. We took inventory and keep one guy on it at all times."

I gave him a strange look. Why would he need someone on guard?

He saw me looking at him and laughed, "It's not that I don't trust the men here, but … do you know much about psychology?"

"A little," I smiled. It would be interesting to see what kind of psychology he would try to fob off to me. I was so used to people having poor conceptions of what psychology was.

"Without rules, people … go off the deep end. Without something to occupy them, well, you can imagine," he began. I nodded. So far, so good. "So, in my infinite wisdom, I created certain roles and restrictions. This keeps the men in check and keeps them occupied."

"So why tell me all this?" I asked. Why would he possibly tell a newcomer about the ins and outs of his setup?

"I see a lot of me in you. I feel like I can trust you," he replied simply. He didn't even know me! He added, "Don't get me wrong, you could be absolutely nuts, and I'll still determine if you can stay."

"Fair enough," I nodded.

The place was amazing. All the men were busy like Boss had said. I noticed that they consistently walked the wall, watching for the undead. Or the living. Beyond the containers for storage, we reached an area with a lot of porta-cabins. I mean, a lot. More than I had ever seen before. They were all the same snap-together grey plastic material used on building sites.

"We got everything you could possibly need here," Boss said, clearly pleased. "Water – bottled and fresh. We have working electricity thanks to some portable generators we found. Electricity means music, television, and video games, which we have plenty of. The men won't get bored. Food, water, and entertainment. What more could they need?"

"What about women?" I suggested, finding a hole in his paradise. He laughed and slapped me on the back. We passed a container with a red circle with an 'X' through it.

"Don't go in those or near them," he pointed to the marked container.

"Any reason?" I asked when I realised I wasn't getting an explanation.

"Short version, they're full of meat bags," he said as if that was the most normal thing in the world.

"And the long version?" I asked with annoyance. What

was it about the post-apocalypse that meant people had to be vague?

"We put bodies in the containers, out the way. Haven't had time to move them. The dead are now undead and trapped in there. It sucks, but that's how it is currently," Boss shrugged. I would certainly be keeping away from any container marked as such. How did all the people sleep at night knowing the undead were so close? Then again, it was the same material that made up their walls. Suppose it was safe when you looked at it like that. We arrived at a porta-cabin, no different from the rest, and entered.

The room was set up like a doctor's office, although slightly less organised. Boxes, with various medical labels, were stacked along one side of the wall. A man sat at a makeshift desk, reading a medical textbook.

"This is our doctor-to-be, Dr. Mark," Boss said introducing us. He looked about twelve years old. "Everyone calls him Doc."

"I dropped out of my Ph.D.," Doc said, sheepishly. "Got drunk too much and realised medicine wasn't for me. Now here I am, doing it."

"I need you to fix up my friend here," Boss said to him. I, on the other hand, didn't want a medical school dropout to touch me.

"Sure thing," Doc closed the textbook, then looked me over, examining my face. "Should be easy enough. I need to reduce the swelling and throw in a few stitches, and we're good to go."

"You sure you're qualified for this?" I stared uneasily at him.

"God, no," he laughed, causing me to wince at the idea. He then added, more seriously, "But I am the best you got for miles … probably. Now sit down and let me get to work."

As nervous as I was – and so was he – he did a fantastic job. The swelling was already going down, and blood wasn't oozing out of my wounds once he was done. He gave me some painkillers and sent me on my way.

"He's a good kid," Boss said as we were walking away. "We found him wandering around, bloody and scared. We brought him in, and turns out he's helped tenfold of what we did for him. Now Sam, what can you bring to us?"

"Bugger all," I shrugged. "I was a graduate in a skill that's not relevant anymore."

"Well, you've survived this long. How?" he asked, probing to find out more about me.

"I fought my way here. Living and dead alike," It was true, and that was all he needed to know.

"Why did you end up here?" he asked. We seemed to just be walking without any real direction.

"I'm looking for … someone. It led me this way," I shrugged. Now I was being the elusive one. He didn't need to know all about me just yet.

"Fair enough. Do you have a problem killing?" he questioned bluntly.

"The living, yes. Undead. Yes, but I know I have to do it to survive," I answered, choosing my words carefully.

"You'll fit right in here, Sam," Boss smiled. "How long will you be staying?"

"I don't know. Forty-eight hours at the most," I shrugged again. "I really need to find her."

"That's fair enough, Sam. If you stay a little longer, we can set you up for your journey ahead," Boss offered.

"That's real nice, thanks. But I wouldn't want to impose," I wasn't about to owe anyone anything.

"Seriously, it's okay. We can get you a car, food, water, and a firearm," he insisted. "There's more than enough if you help out in the time you're here. You could consider it payment if you like."

"Thanks, Boss," I smiled. He seemed alright. "What would helping out consist of?"

"Well, emptying local buildings for supplies is our general way of doing things. You could be on guard detail," Boss explained. It was then I noticed we passed the doctor's porta-cabin again.

"You're clever," I said, with a sly smile.

"Why's that?" he grinned.

"We've passed that porta-cabin a couple of times already. We've literally been walking in circles while you pumped me for information," I was still smiling. It was so simple but such an effective way to get information.

"Psychology," he said, with a sly wink, then added with a laugh, "But are you up for guard detail?"

"I can do that. That's a fair trade," I nodded. "Two questions. Where can I stay? When can I help?"

"There are a few spare porta-cabins for newcomers to stay in. We can get some flat-pack furniture set up for you in a few minutes," he answered. He turned to a passerby and spoke to them. They nodded and left. "As for when, we're making a trip to some local houses in a bit if you like?"

"I'm up for that," I smiled. We carried on walking for a little longer.

"That's great, but you need some time to yourself. You'll need time to acclimatise to the events of your day so far," he put his hand on my shoulder. I almost asked why, before I remembered the events of the morning. Damn. I had forgotten about that. *Was I really that cold?*

"Thanks, Boss," I said, with a sad smile.

"And here we are," Boss said as we stopped at a porta-cabin. "There's a mattress, some water, and a chair in there. There will be more stuff later. I just need you to stay in there for now. I got some stuff to sort out. Someone will knock for you when it's time to leave."

"Cheers," I walked into the porta-cabin. As he walked away, I called, "In a bit."

He put his hand up without turning back to me.

I entered and looked at my temporary home. It was as bare as he had described. Barely anything in there. Even the mattress was so thin it looked like it was a waste of time. I crashed down onto it. No tears came that time. I was sad, heartbroken in fact, but no tears. I'd had enough heartbreak and just couldn't find the appropriate response anymore.

I laid there, muscles heavy, will worn, and body broken. I don't know what hurt more, their death or that Gary had died hating me. It kept playing through my mind. I would never be able to tell him what I thought. That chance was gone. Goddamn. Gary was gone. Tracey was gone.

Damn. Damn! DAMN!

CHAPTER 33

Catatonia. *Noun.* A syndrome characterised by muscular rigidity and mental stupor, sometimes alternating with great excitement and confusion. I was almost there – catatonic that is. I laid on the bed, unmoving and unthinking. Just feeling … and hurting. I could feel myself sinking lower and lower, with no net to save me. That was until a voice wrenched me from a downward spiral.

"New guy, Boss told me to come and get you. We're leaving in ten, so stop jerking it and get out here!" a gruff sounding man called while banging on the door like he was trying to tear it down.

"Okay, okay," I shouted in response, my earlier mental trauma almost forgotten.

I left the room and met with the older man outside. He had a cigarette hanging out the side of his mouth – he looked as though he had smoked from the day he left his mother's womb – and stained yellow fingertips.

"We need you to suit up before we leave," he looked me up and down in my still-wet boiler suit. It was beginning to get crusty from the salty water.

"We can swap out that for something dry," he suggested.

"I'd rather not," I pushed by him, all too aware of my belongings hidden within the pockets.

"Okay," he said, clearly taken aback by my refusal. "Well, you need to weapon-up before we go, anyway. Any preferences?"

It was then that I remembered the weapons I had arrived with. Once again, I had lost control of my position. I turned on the man who had come to get me.

"The stuff I came here with!" I snarled, barring my teeth like an animal.

"Whoa, man," he backed up. "I've only been told to get you. When did you get here? Today?"

"Yeah. Why?" I said, calming slightly.

"Then Boss probably still has it. We can see him before we leave if you like," he explained.

"Yeah. Sure," I said through gritted teeth. We began walking in what appeared to me as a random direction. I really had to learn my way around the place.

The walk was in silence. I tried to apologise to the man, but he wasn't interested. He just nodded and kept walking. We eventually came across Boss in a porta-cabin. He was marking areas on maps.

"Everything okay?" he said, looking at me.

"He wants the crap he came here him," the older man said.

"Weapon shed," Boss responded, returning to marking the map. "Ask Angel. He should still be there."

We left again and began our journey to Angel, who was stood outside a container.

"Weapons," the man escorting me said to Angel. "We want the stuff put in there today."

"Shotgun and machete?" the man smiled, opening the container doors.

"Yeah," I said. He handed me both without question. I managed a quick glance inside the container. It was a very mixed collection. A few military grade guns, some odd hunting rifles, plenty of ammunition cases, and a lot of heavy and blunt objects which could be used as weapons. *Nice.*

"Nice to meet you new guy, names Stephen. Everyone calls me Angel, as in Guardian, because I look after the weapons," Stephen said, introducing himself. There would be no way I was calling him Angel.

"Sam," I nodded, shaking his hand, before leaving.

We were off again. My escort speedwalked ahead of me, not allowing me to keep up.

"What's your problem?" I attempted to catch up with him. I knew I had offended him with my outburst, but surely not to this degree. I didn't get an answer so I pushed, "Well?"

"We're rapidly losing daylight," he turned to me, scowling. "Because of your crap, we're behind schedule. Less daylight means we're at a disadvantage with the dead. We'll probably even need flashlights now. So hurry the hell up."

"Okay," I shrugged with annoyance, shocked at his outburst. He was right, but if he knew what I'd been through, then he would know I had the right to be paranoid.

We exited through the other gateway from which I arrived. Outside, there was a truck and a large transit van. Standing around them were seven people, including us. They were all armed.

"Took your time, Luke," one of them laughed. "You up for this, newbie?"

"Nothing I haven't done before," I shrugged. "Where we going?"

"Housing estate about a thirty-minute drive away," said

the one who'd mocked Luke. "We saw it on a previous run and thought it'll probably have decent stuff for our taking. If the prior residents are dead."

"And if they're not?" I climbed into the back of the transit van. It was only me and him. An imposing man, tall and muscular. He looked like an action hero – square jaw, bulging arms, handsome. Someone dropped two duffle bags into the back of the van – the weapons.

"We tell them of our place of safety, and if they want to join, they're welcome to. If they don't, then we let them know they have some neighbours down the road should they need any help," he closed the door behind him.

"Ran into many people on your runs?" I asked. Something seemed odd about their altruism. Almost too good to be true.

"Not really. Once since I joined. I was picked up on one of their runs, ya know. They saved me. From what I heard, you were the same," he smiled. As the engine started up and we began moving, I thought about how fast news travelled.

"That's good," I breathed a sigh of relief. "So what sort of stuff are we looking for?"

"Medicine and medical equipment take top priority. We have so much of everything else that the rest can wait. For now anyway," he explained. "Obviously, if something sticks out, flag it to the others and we can either decide there and then or let Boss know for later."

"Why do you call him Boss?" I asked, redirecting the conversation.

"Because everyone else does," he shrugged.

"Any idea why *they* call him Boss?" I pushed.

"I think it's because he's their literal boss. From what I gather, most of the guys were workers at the container site.

After things hit the fan, the ones who didn't have family stayed here and made it their home. They were quite lucky with how things went for them. I'm Keith, by the way," Keith held out his hand.

"Sam, as I'm sure you know," I smiled, shaking his hand. He had a strong grip, with very calloused hands. I gestured to the world beyond the van. "So what did you do before all this?"

"Just things," he smiled and winked. "I'd have to kill you if I told you."

"Very funny," I laughed. The cliché was surprisingly funny when heard in a real conversation. "I was a student. Planned to become a head doctor eventually."

"There's good money in that," he nodded.

"Was. Not doing me much good now, is it," I shrugged. "Shoulda done something more useful. Power of retrospect, I guess."

The van slowed, and the rumble stopped. We were there.

CHAPTER 34

We climbed out of the van, taking the duffle bags with us. Everyone sorted through the bags until they found the guns they had chosen to bring with them. There were many standard issued guns from the British army. SA80 assault rifles and Browning Hi-Power handguns. Even a single Benelli M4 shotgun! Where the hell did they get all that? I seemed to be the only one who'd brought something that didn't fire bullets. I picked up my machete and my double-barrel shotgun. Next to the Benelli, my shotgun felt impotent.

"The plan is the same as normal. We take two houses at a time. Two go into each, clearing upstairs and down. Remember, watch your lines of sight. We don't want any accidents like before," the man said, looking at one of the men, and there were a few smiles. "I want everyone else to secure the surrounding area. Regroup out front once the inside is clear. Then we can clear it of any supplies. Don't be afraid to shout out should anyone need help. Everyone got it?"

There was a chorus of, "Yes."

"Right, I want Sam and Luke up in the first house, and Keith and I will take the house next to it," he continued. "Let's do this."

We broke and strode to the houses. Typical that I was stuck with the only one who didn't like me. Oh well. It had to be done.

The housing estate was similar to the one I grew up in. There was a row of houses either side of the road, with grassy patches outside of both. There were only about eight houses, four on each side. Detached housing, fancy looking. Now that I think about it, not much like my own at all. What a stupid mistake to make. I paused mid-stride to realign what my memory of home looked like. I hadn't even been gone all that long, but so much had happened. Maybe it was normal for memories to become skewed.

I carried on towards the house with Luke, who was wordless the entire time. We approached the door, either side of it, like we were a SWAT team. Luke pounded on the door. There was no answer or sound of stirring within.

"Anyone in there?" Luke shouted. Still no answer. I let Luke lead the way since he was experienced with the supply run. He tried the handle, and the door opened and swung inward. The stench of death was in the air. Whether it was from the undead or just dead was yet to be determined.

"I'll take upstairs," Luke whispered, then took the stairs two at a time, the Benelli clutched in his hands.

"Guess I have downstairs," I muttered, holding my shotgun by its barrel and twirling my machete.

There were only three rooms downstairs. Two had the door closed. I tapped on one door, waiting for a response. Nothing. I opened the door slowly. The room was devoid of life … or unlife. It was a dining room, and it was in disarray. Not like a struggle had occurred, but like it had been abandoned in the middle of being used. There were dinner plates still on a small table. Photos on the mantle place, of a mother with two daughters. All brunettes, petite pixie faces, and brown eyes. No sign of a male in their life. Good on them.

The next room, the kitchen, was in a similar situation. There was cookware everywhere. Pots and pans littered the side. A sign on the wall which read, *Families That Eat Together, Stay Together.* There were photos everywhere in there, too, albeit less serious and more fun. They all had face paint in one and were making silly faces in another. They were all so … human looking. It was the most emotion I'd felt in a while. The ice that had been freezing my heart for such a long time, melted ever so slightly. My mind kept flashing to my own family. I needed to know if they were okay. But it would have to wait.

The third and final room was a spare room with odd boxes and whatnot. No living or dead threats. I was about to leave, when I heard a thump upstairs. I didn't think anything of it until another few minutes passed without any sign of Luke.

"I know I shouldn't …" I said absentmindedly while staring at the stairs. I knew I should've gone outside and called for help, but curiosity was getting the best of me. Following Luke's footsteps, I took the stairs two at a time. At the top was an empty bathroom. Next room was a child's bedroom. Still nothing. One more room. It had to be the mother's room. From the angle I was walking, I couldn't see within, but I could smell the overpowering stench of death.

"Luke?" I called in a hushed voice. No answer. I called again, "Luke?"

I peeked around the doorframe and saw something terrible.

I … it was … Luke laid on the floor, motionless. Face up, limbs twitching as the three zombies tore into him. They pulled pieces of … Luke from deep within Luke, each ramming strips of flesh into their mouths. That wasn't the worst part. I had seen so much of that by that point. The worst part was the zombies.

There was the mother, with sullen and grey skin. Little tears on her neck and bare breasts – something that only little mouths could do. The other two zombies, they were children. Not even children, toddlers. Tiny girls. Both dressed as a princess from one of latest Disney films. Joining their mother in a feast, like a good family. Like a happy family. *Families that eat together* … I reached down slowly and picked up the Benelli, which had been cast to one side … *stay together.*

As I backed away, unnoticed, I pulled the door closed behind me. I didn't need to see that. No one needed to see that. I stumbled down the stairs. My head hurt. I practically fell through the front door. Others stopped to look at me.

"Are you okay?" Keith asked as I fell to my knees, with vomit rising in my throat.

"Luke … don't go …" I choked out. Two of the men rushed into the house and upstairs. I heard four gunshots. Mother, both daughters, and Luke. I just sat on the cool grass, heaving.

Keith rubbed my back. "It's okay, man. It can get hard even for the toughest of us. Wanna take guard duty? Someone else can clear the next house."

"No, no," I took deep breaths. "I got this."

I pushed up to my feet, using both shotguns as support. I looked down at the double barrel and dropped it. I took a deep breath. The Benelli was much more efficient and held less painful memories. Even though I felt green and like a horror film dropout, I pushed onward. I went into the next house, clearing each room and ignoring the signs of humanity in each. This made things so much easier.

The second house didn't have any undead, but the third more than made up for it. Four undead in the first room. The humans had clearly killed themselves together, with their wrists slashed open and dried blood everywhere. This family had taken the easy way out. They died together. They came back together. I didn't even pause before I fired the first blast from the shotgun. It was a panicked gutshot which tore the male zombie in half. Rotten innards spilt to the floor with a wet and heavy thud. They weren't the healthy pink and red hue you would expect, but a decomposed black and grey. And as always, the smell. Horrific. But in a weird way, I enjoyed it. It helped me focus. It was familiar. It kept me in the moment.

Severing the zombie in half didn't stop his upper half from coming for me. I slammed my machete into its skull, stopping it where it lay. Two more blasts from my shotgun. The first disintegrated another head and left a bloody smudge on the zombies behind it. The second removed the left half of another zombie from the rest of it, the force of the blast throwing her to the ground. I raced forward, arcing my blade into the final zombie, and ending the attack with my blade in the collapsed one.

My wrath ended them so swiftly that none of the zombies made it out of the room. I was covered in rotten gore.

"I live for this!" I panted, exhilaration and adrenaline making me feel alive. Was this the feeling that people call bloodlust?

I heard snarling behind me and then turned to see a zombie race in from the hallway. I smiled while slamming the machete into its head. I hit it so hard I crushed the skull, swiped right through the bone, and into the wooden doorframe. I wrenched it free and stepped over the dead zombie.

Kitchen? Empty. Downstairs bathroom? Zombie chained to the toilet.

"Is this being a bad sport?" I asked the trapped zombie as I slammed the butt of my shotgun into its skull. The first hit, I heard a loud crack of bone collapsing. The zombie didn't die, but there was a huge dent in its forehead. The second hit, the skull collapsed inward, and the zombie went limp. Surprisingly effective.

"Downstairs clear!" I shouted to Keith upstairs.

"Took your time," he said from the front door, waiting outside.

"Har-har. Any trouble?" I made my way to him.

"Not at all. You look like you had some, though," he nodded to my blood-spattered boiler suit.

"Yeah, just a bit," I shrugged. "What now?"

"We clear the house of stuff. Head back. It's getting darker, and we really shouldn't be out at night," he stared at the approaching dark skies.

"Is there, uh, any rules on what we can personally keep?" I asked, with a sheepish grin.

"Well, you can't take weapons back. No guns or blades within the walls. Unless you're going out on a run, of course," he rubbed his face. "Obviously, the stuff we're out here for goes to the site. Any extras you can carry, you can keep. Why? You got something in mind?"

"Wait here," I re-entered the second house. *Where the hell is it?*

While looking for the object of desire, I saw myself in the mirror. More gore than man. Only a stray patch of skin and clothing were untainted. I was like a crimson blood god of war. I held back a sob as my thoughts returned to the two girls and their mother.

I returned to the other guys, with a crate of beers I'd seen.

"Should we give Luke a send-off?" I held the crate up. The guys smiled and each took one. I didn't like Luke, not in the slightest, but they did. It would be a good way to win people over. My beer would be for Tracey and Gary.

The others drank, talking about Luke and what he had been like. I drank and stared at the double barrel shotgun I no longer wanted.

"Guess this truly is goodbye," I sighed. I had to move on. Was I doing it too quickly? Probably. Was it a necessity? I thought it was.

I was back in the moment, no longer thinking about the past or future. I looked at the setting sun, the world in an orange hue. It was warm, and I was out drinking beer with a group of lads. *I could get used to this existence.*

"Right, guys, it's time to get a move on," one of the men said once he'd finished his beer. "Darkness is approaching and we need to get back before we attract more meat-bags."

Everyone else downed theirs, and I placed my half-finished one next to the discarded shotgun. It would rust there, and I was happy with that.

"Problem with that shotgun?" Keith nodded to it.

"Yeah, doesn't work," I said.

"Well, maybe someone can repair it," he headed over to pick it up. I grabbed his arm, and he turned to me.

"Can we just leave it? Please," I pleaded. He stared at me and then nodded.

"Sure," my eyes must have radiated hurt, he didn't even question me.

Together, we entered the houses we had cleared and collected any medical supplies we could find. Half-finished medicine, over-the-counter medication, prescription medication, latex gloves, even a few surgical masks. Perhaps someone thought the infection was airborne. Or they had an odd kink?

We managed to get a lot of goods. Even had room for the crates of beer we'd found. That would go over extremely well back at base. But we had to get back first to enjoy them. We began climbing back into the vehicles now packed with supplies.

"Watch where you sit and what you touch," one of them said to me, noticing how gory I was. None of the others looked anything like I did. I was certainly making an impression on my fine hosts.

CHAPTER 35

When I emerged from the back of the van, I felt like a victorious centurion as all the eyes turned to watch me. The blood had congealed and stained me red. The looks of shock and horror turned to smiles and laughter as I lugged the crates of beer out of the van. The medicine, although appreciated, was far overshadowed by my find.

"Welcome back," Boss said with a huge grin, which grew even bigger when he saw what I was carrying. "You shouldn't have."

"Very funny," I smiled and handed him a crate of the alcohol. "It's for everyone."

"I'll spread it about tonight," he walked alongside me.

"Tonight?" I asked. What was happening tonight? Dancing around the fire and sacrificing goats, nude whilst …

"Once every few days, we have a gathering so that everyone can bond. I know we all live with each other, but we still need some communal time to keep up to date" Boss explained. "Our normal plan is gathering everyone. We talk about any news or changes, like deaths. It's surprising how much people miss even when we live together. We also discuss what our goal is for the next couple days. We want to work towards building something sustainable for our future, so it's a great way to keep everyone on task. Finally, we have a celebration to keep us all grounded and the morale up."

"Sounds like it could be fun," I smiled. I wasn't a fan of social gatherings and normally avoided them, but I didn't think I had a choice on that occasion.

"But first things first, Sam," Boss began, with an embarrassed smile. "You need to shower. You look disgusting, and you'll probably get shot – you look like a zombie."

"Cheers," I muttered. "Where can I wash?"

Boss again spoke to someone passing, and they nodded and stood patiently. I recognised him, but it took me a few moments to place his face. It was from earlier that day. It was Bill, the potential racist.

"Bill, will show you where to go," Boss smiled. "Normally we would wash offsite in one the buildings nearby. But I don't think anyone should be out at night. We have some portable shower-bag things. They're not great, but they do the job."

So Bill led me off, in all his racist glory. I couldn't help but glare at the back of his head. But I felt like a rat in a maze and needed his help getting around. I hadn't even been there twenty-four hours, so being lost was expected. Time flies when you're having fun.

The "shower-bag things" were basically camping showers. It was a twenty-litre bag on a hook that you would fill with water, hang from a tree, and turn the nozzle. The water would trickle out. The bags were black to absorb the sun's heat. Taking an emergency shower at night was going to be a cold and extremely unpleasant experience, but it had to be done. I hung the camping shower from the overhang of the roof of my little room. I stripped down and began washing. I was beyond caring about who was looking. Apparently, others didn't care about my nudity either. People milled by, oblivious to my nakedness, heading towards the big night in. I could smell smoke in the air. No one seemed bothered or panicked by that either. A bonfire, perhaps? Although a little apprehensive, I was excited to see what they had set up.

I washed the gore off as quickly as I could, even though the camp shower didn't make that easy. Patches of my skin were still red, but the various visceral chunks had been washed away. I blew my nose as hard as I could. There was some sort of blockage. I sucked in more air through my mouth before giving it one sharp and quick blow. No mucus or snot came out. What did come out was a fragment of something that shouldn't have been there.

"Gross," I said, mortified. I sent a jet of water up my nose, but it didn't make my insides feel clean.

When I was finished, I dumped my boiler suit in the corner of my room. It needed to be washed, but that could wait. I was happy to see that I had been left with a t-shirt and jeans. Both were too big for me, but it was better than nudity. Time to get the party started.

I followed the steady stream of people heading towards the social gathering. We arrived at a central area where the containers had created a large clearing. There was a roaring fire, and many men were laughing and smiling. No women or children, though.

There were a lot more people there than I had anticipated. Thirty or forty. A lot of people for a confined space, but they all seemed happy. Some were drinking, others were carrying boxes or other objects. I saw my crates of beer, as well as many others, being stacked nearby. The one stacking them was deliberate in ensuring they weren't too close to the fire. Good. We couldn't drink warm beer. We were in for an awesome night!

"Grab those, will you," said a man fiddling with a laptop and pointing to some large speakers. I shrugged and carried them over. Looking at the size of them, they were like something out of a nightclub. I placed both where he had pointed, and he proceeded to hook them up to the laptop. He tapped a few buttons on the laptop, and the static from the speakers came to life. He pressed a few more buttons, and the speaker next to me erupted with a *Bwaam!*

"Holy crap!" the tech-man wrenched the cable free of the laptop, then smiled sheepishly at me. "Need to balance the sounds a little or something."

"Please do," I winced as my ears rang.

I felt out of place, so I decided to take a step back and watch it all come together. I found a dark corner where I could sit down and chill out while I observed the scene build. The flames climbed higher. The speaker system got better. People got drunker, and the evening had yet to officially begin.

It was dark when the grand night was considered started. Everyone had gravitated to the clearing. All except the few who remained vigilant on the walls. They were our watchful protectors. The overall tone of mirth silenced when Boss climbed onto a container to rise above everyone.

"Gentlemen, and gentlemen!" he announced, with a huge smile. "The last few days have been quite eventful, have they not?"

There was a chorus of murmurs and laughs.

"Here's the news," Boss pulled out a scrap of paper, read it, and then continued. "Of course, we've had a new addition to our group. The survivor Sam, who you can thank for some of the excessive amount of alcohol!"

There were a few cheers, and someone even slapped my back as thanks.

"But," Boss interjected, silencing the jovial cheering, "we also lost one of our own. Luke died while bringing back medicine. It's sad, I know, but we have to move on to keep our group strong. So we'll drink to those who died, and keep moving forward."

Boss held up a bottle of alcohol in a toast, and so did everyone else. I did the same. Thirty seconds of silence passed with the glasses raised before everyone downed their drink in one.

"And now," Boss wiped the drink from his lips, "let's get this party started."

He climbed down from the container and walked towards me. The music began to build. Club music.

"How was that?" Boss asked me, with a huge grin.

"Very well put," I grinned back. He began guiding me more towards the central mass of people.

"Well, let's get dancing," then he walked off and disappeared into the crowd. People stood around, talking awkwardly, and all I could think was that there needed to be some women.

I never liked nightclubs. They were the worst way I could think of to spend an evening. So boring and primal. People would peacock to try and impress a mate by drawing attention to themselves through the mating ritual of dancing and dressing like an asshole. The perceived alpha males would try to assert their dominance through displays of aggression and stupid shows of bravado. The women would, unfortunately, fall for it and be wooed. God, nightclubs sucked. I wouldn't miss them post-apocalypse at all.

But the container party wasn't anything like that. Sure, it was a cockfest, but the competitive nature of nightclubs wasn't there. Probably because there weren't any women around for everyone to impress. It actually made the evening all right.

The guys stood around, chatting and laughing, telling stories from their past. Some did show off a little, but not in a way that was detrimental to others. I stood back, drinking and watching. I preferred it like that. I didn't want any attention on me. That didn't stop Boss from finding me amongst everyone and wanting to talk.

"So what do you think of our little shindig?" he asked, with a drunken smile.

"Pretty great," I said. "You're keeping the community together so well."

"It isn't hard when everyone gets along and there's plenty of resources. We'll see how well we all stay together when competition begins to set in," he replied, a little darkly.

"I'm sure you'll do it well," I said, trying to instil confidence, even though I could imagine any place going a little Lord of the Flies not before long.

I didn't think humans were great as it was – expert opinion from a human. It didn't matter, though. I wouldn't be around long enough to see it fall apart. I would be with Alice soon.

"If I had you by my side, we could pull it off," Boss looked at me and smiled. "I know, I know. You won't be here for long."

"Sorry about that, man," I laughed. At least he remembered and wouldn't forcibly keep me there like Harrington.

"Not a problem," he slapped my back, then began

walking off. "Remind me to start putting together a travel pack for you."

"Will do," I said quietly. Things were going to be okay.

We partied long into the night. Drank and ate until the sun started to rise. It felt fantastic. I felt buzzed, and not just from the alcohol. I actually felt normal. Like an actual human for once, instead of feeling like I was masquerading as one.

I returned to my room, the air tainted by the iron of blood. The blood on my boiler suit.

"Damn," I muttered, stumbling over to it, and then emptied the pockets of my three possessions. The thought of the boating excursion with Gary and Tracey came to mind. It was then I remembered something. I still had the fisherman's knife. I had originally kept it as a form of self-defence amongst the living. It almost seemed a little silly having it in the container community, but having a trump card never hurt.

I stashed the four items together. They would never leave my side again. My phone. Thundy. Harrington's bullet. The knife.

"So Thundy," I began, "Looks like we're getting somewhere. We can actually do this. We can make it to Alice."

Thundy stared back at me. He didn't speak, but I knew he was happy to be going home … home to Alice. I smiled and looked around, realising something was off. It took longer to hit me than it should have, but the room had been furnished. I had a bed frame for the mattress, which had been on the floor. I crawled into bed, head spinning from my alcohol intake.

"Whoops," I laughed, holding my head. My tolerance for alcohol clearly had lessened. It was good to be at peace and feel safe. I closed my eyes and drifted into slumber.

Broadcast Five: Aidez-moi – Help Me

Eric: *Bonjour, mon nom est Eric. Je suis coincé à sur mon campus universitaire. Les gens de l'extérieur ... ils essaient de manger l'autre. Je suis pris au piège. Se il vous plaît. Je suis terrifié. Ma famille me manque. Je souhaite que je restais à la maison. Pourquoi ai- je étudie dans ce pays de merde!*

Baiser cette. Je suis à court de nourriture. L'eau ne fonctionne plus. Tout ce que je ai, ce est de soude. Je pense qu'il ya quelqu'un à la porte. Mes colocataires sont partis il ya une couple d'heures. Je ne pense pas qu'ils ont fait. Tout ce que je ai entendu était cris . Se il vous plaît . Se il vous plaît envoyer de l'aide.

(Hello, my name is Eric. I am stuck at my university campus. People from outside ... they try to eat each other. I am trapped. Please. I'm terrified. I miss my family. I wish I stayed at home. Why did I study in this shitty country!

Fuck this. I am running out of food. The water doesn't work anymore. All I have is soda. I think there is someone at the door. My roommates left a couple of hours ago. I do not think they made it. All I heard was screaming. Please. Please send help.)

CHAPTER 36

For the first time in my life, I woke up with a hangover. I hated it, yet I felt alive again. I climbed out of bed, feeling like my head was a lead weight. I needed water, so I dragged myself to one of the bottles nearby and inhaled the hydration. Then I opened another and drank that. My head spun, and I felt nauseous.

I looked at the boiler suit and decided that I didn't need it anymore. The clothes I had been donated fit as well as I needed, and the boiler suit was disgusting. I did want another at some point. It had done me well.

When I felt capable of walking, I left my little home and decided to go exploring. I seemed to be up before anyone else, except for the few wandering the walls. My body ached from the night of heavy drinking, and I knew I needed it out of my system. Breathing and urination would get some out of me, but sweat is what I needed.

I started with a gentle jog – no effort to my amazingly sculpted body. I pushed up the speed a notch. That was easy, too. The question was whether I had the stamina to sustain the speed. I had done so much fighting and running over short distances that I didn't know if my muscles were trained to keep it up.

I began to lag, slowing bit by bit. I reduced to a jog again. I would take being able to keep moving longer, over a short time but faster, any day. I mentally mapped the place as I ran around it. I would take twisting and turning paths, sometimes doubling back on myself so that I would know every way around. Focussing on something else enabled me to just keep going.

I jogged about half an hour, only stopping when I nearly ran face first into the doctor.

"Sorry about that, Doc," I replied breathlessly, stopping to catch my breath.

"Not a problem, Sam," he smiled. "I see the leg is feeling better?"

"Completely better," I nodded, smiling. Although that wasn't true, I had barely thought about it, nor the circumstance of why I was alive to begin with. Thoughts of Gary and Tracey sent stabbing pain into my stomach.

"Your face?" Doc questioned. I noticed he had a slightly dishevelled look about him, like he had been up all night.

"Fine, too," I said, with a less enthusiastic smile this time – it was incredibly tender. "Been up long?"

"Early hours," he nodded and began yawning. "A couple of guys were convinced they were dying. Too much alcohol."

"Babies," I muttered. "What you doing now, Doc?"

"Not much," he shrugged. "A couple of us are going to get showers in one of the local houses while it's still quiet. Wanna come?"

"Definitely," I nodded enthusiastically. I could feel the crustiness on the surface of my skin from the previous days. I still had gore ingrained in my skin which needed to be erased.

"Okay, I'm just grabbing some towels," Doc rubbed his hair, which had just started to develop a greasy sheen. "Need anything?"

"Clippers and a razor," I said without hesitation. My hair was only a couple of inches, and stubble was beginning to grow, but it was far too long for my liking.

"Cool," Doc nodded.

"Do we need guns?" I felt naked without something to defend myself. It was easy to accept safety without a second's thought, and the idea of going out again was terrifying.

"Nah, we'll have an armed escort," Doc replied. "We're technically not supposed to be going out without Boss's say so, so we need to keep things to a minimum."

"Uh, fair enough," I shrugged. I felt like I was betraying Boss by doing things without his permission, but a shower sounded fantastic.

I met Doc and a couple of others at what everyone referred to as the North Gate. The same gate we left through for the housing estate.

"So where are we actually going?" I asked. There were me and five others all jammed into a family carrier. Doc was almost on my lap.

"Old folks home," Doc said. "We found it quite early on. All the residents were already gone. It's a gated place with electricity and water. It's all good."

"Why not live there, then?" I questioned.

"Way too small to live there fulltime. Could probably get fifteen people in there at most," Doc replied. "Boss considered making an outpost there at one point but decided we would all be better in one place. Which I agree with. Being social is a huge part of us staying alive."

I had to agree with him. I wasn't a social person, but humans were social creatures and having contact was essential.

"Anything worth taking there?" I asked absentmindedly.

"Already been pilfered. Wasn't really much worth having, anyway," Doc replied. Then added with sorrow in his voice, "It all looked so sad."

We sat in silence, waiting to arrive at the old people's home.

"Blossom Grove, where ageing means dignity," I said, reading the sign to the gated mini-community. What cheesy nonsense.

"The inside looks as boring as the sign suggests," one of the others snorted. We all climbed out and went through the padlocked gate. One of the men had the keys, so they were probably the ones who locked it to begin with. There was a quaint garden in the front – very small, but with lots of flowers. Overgrown.

Everyone strode confidently up to the front doors and walked in. The huge black fence around the building ensured that it hadn't been compromised. One of them clicked a light switch on without even looking, clearly a well-practised action. The lights revealed that the whole building looked like a grandparent's front room – cosy and inviting with the décor of many decades ago.

"Everyone gets a room to themselves," Doc said, as people began to separate and go their own way. "Here are the things you wanted."

He passed me the requested items and left for his room. I carried on until I found an unoccupied one. A cramped and ugly room filled with hundreds of pieces of someone's life. Photos. Ribbons. Birthday cards. Christmas Cards. *We love you, Nana!* Homemade gifts. Finger paintings. Letters. Medals. Photos of a man in uniform.

I picked up one of the photos. It appeared to be one of the more recent ones. The woman in it looked so old. She was wrinkled and gaunt. Looked ill except for the smile on her face which illuminated her eyes, even through the photograph. She had two young children either side of her, smiling toothless smiles. Grandkids? Great grandkids? It could be either. She was nowhere now. Hadn't taken anything with her. There wasn't any sign of a struggle. No blood, either. I hoped she had survived somehow.

My thoughts turned inwards. Would I ever be a parent? A grandparent? Probably not. Not just because of not having any children, but because I doubted that I would make it to middle-aged. Would I even want to bring kids into the world? It wouldn't be fair on them, and I doubted I could do it. I hadn't ever thought about having kids, but now that the world had taken that option from me, I wanted children so bad. Life wasn't fair. Why? Why did it have to happen?

"Dammit," I sighed, sitting on the edge of the bed. I would never experience life. I had been so excited to lose the responsibilities that the civilised world forced. I would never have to work or pay taxes, but I would never have a family or know true safety. The end of the world truly meant the end of all things. Not just the bad, but the good too.

After moping around in my self-pity for a while, I decided it was time to start getting ready. First things first was my hair. I ran the electric clippers over my head without even finding a mirror. I wasn't bothered about it looking good, but was more worried about efficiency.

I watched the sink fill with my blond hair, only for it to disappear down the drain when I turned on the tap. I ran my hand over my freshly shaved head, feeling for spots I'd missed. Next was a quick shave with a manual razor to remove the stubble on the top of my head as well my developing beard. Then I needed to shower. I pulled all the safety equipment from the bath-shower combo – all the supports and handles was clearly for the previous residence. I didn't need them and neither did anyone else anymore. I turned the shower on, extra hot, and enjoyed the cleansing heat that washed over me. I scrubbed away at my flesh until I felt truly clean.

Looking at the water that drained away, it shocked me at how filthy of a shade of brown it was. The filth must have been ingrained into my skin. Naturally, I peed in the shower, and no one has the right to act disgusted by that fact. There are two types of people in this world – those who pee in the shower, and goddamn liars.

I dried, dressed, and returned to the others, who were already done.

"Nice hair, killer," one of the guys laughed.

"What's that?" I smiled awkwardly.

"Your hair, makes you look like a psychopath," he reiterated. I didn't comment on his neck and knuckle tattoos. We all shared a laugh at my expense and then sat around waiting. One guy brought out some beer he had hidden previously and began drinking. I almost challenged him on drinking so early, only to realise I didn't have a clue what time it was. The only clock I could see, required winding, and that had stopped long before. It was none of my business, anyway.

Once everyone was ready, we headed back. We returned uninterrupted and had one of the guards let us back in. He knew the deal and often partook in the morning visits. We went our own separate ways, except in higher spirits than when we'd left. I found my way to the centre, where the social gathering took place. There wasn't any evidence of our previous night except for the ash from the fire. I hung around, just admiring the day and being at peace in the world.

Eventually, Boss found his way to me.

"You look chirpy today," he smiled at me, and then added, "And a little crazy. Haircut?"

"Just a bit," I smiled and rubbed my head. I wondered how many times I would hear a reference to how my hair made me look.

"Had anything to eat yet?" he asked. I shook my head. "I'm cooking up some bacon. Had to freeze the stuff to make it last. Gonna miss it when it's gone. You in?"

"Sure. If that's not a problem," I grinned. Bacon – the true way to my heart.

"Not a problem at all. Besides, I wanna see if you're up for a few things today," he replied and began walking off. I wanted to show my newfound knowledge of the place, so I took the lead. Surprisingly, I got there without an issue and smiled to myself. I finally kind of knew where I was going.

CHAPTER 37

"Good?" Boss asked. I had scoffed the bacon down in seconds. It was glorious, and I so badly wanted more. I nodded, with a huge smile.

Boss also grinned. "Excellent. So how'd you feel about helping out today? It's quite a big task and important for my future plans for the group."

"Uh, sure," I said, a surprising change in tone. I began to realise that the bacon may've been more of a bribe than a friendly offer of delicious meats.

"Great!" he cleared the table and proceeded to pull out a map from a filing cabinet.

The room was infinitely better furnished than mine. He had so much unnecessary stuff in there, exactly the sort of stuff that made a house a home, I suppose. He laid the map out, using salt shakers to hold the corners down. Several areas were highlighted, with circles drawn around the highlighted areas, including the container site.

"So what am I looking at?" I asked after a minute of silence.

"This is the area we're currently in," he pointed to an X. "The circle around it represents the houses we've cleared and taken supplies from."

"Mm-hm," I nodded. I could clearly see that.

"Over here," he moved his fingers to a red circle, "is a mall. I've had a couple of guys watching it for a while. Before you got here, anyway. Apparently, it's filled with meat-bags. It was open when the dead got in there, so now they're still in there. I want that mall. It's full of food, equipment, and there's a hardware superstore not far from it. If we took it over, we would be completely protected. We'd get the shutters down and use stuff from the hardware store where we needed. If it was designed to keep the living out, it can keep the dead out, too."

"So what's stopping you?" I asked.

Having a mall seemed perfect, and incredibly cliché. They just needed a helicopter on the roof or some buses in the parking lot and they were good to go!

"We have the people, but we don't have the firepower to take it," he sighed, sitting back. "We've been waiting to see if the meat-bags let themselves out, but they seem quite content to be in there. So now we need to forcibly remove them. That is where the plan today comes in."

"Which is?" I asked, deeply frustrated that no one ever elaborated on anything without pausing.

"This," he pointed to another red circle on the map, "is a military outpost. We saw it the other day while driving back from clearing out some houses. It looked like a temporary setup, but there weren't any soldiers in there. I think they were overrun and killed or something."

I had finally clocked on to what he was saying and said as much, "You want the abandoned military equipment to help you retake the mall, right?"

"Exactly!" Boss beamed. "Now the question is, do you want to go along with the group today? I ask you since you seem to have the most experience fighting meat-bags."

"I can do that," I smiled, receiving a nice ego boost.

"It'll do us a huge favour," Boss continued, "and yourself, too. After all, you can take a share of it when you leave."

"That's awesome, thanks," I smiled. "I'll have to leave soon, you know."

"I know, I know," Boss nodded and laughed. "Feel free to leave after we've taken the mall."

"Sure, Boss. Cheers!" I said with a smile.

After a few moments of silence, my gaze fell to other areas marked on the map.

"What are those for?" I said, nodding at the map.

"Nothing important really," Boss shrugged. "Previous areas we've looted. Potential areas of interest should we need to leave here. Some we're using as storehouses in case we have to evacuate and need another supply of stuff."

"Ah, makes sense," I said, you didn't want all your eggs in one basket. "So when are we going to the base?"

"A couple hours. I want to chat with the entire group before we go," Boss explained. "I'll be going too, but I want everyone to understand what we're doing before we leave."

"So meet at the centre in a couple hours?" I asked. Boss nodded. I didn't know what to do with that time. It was the first free time I'd have where I was safe. An idea hit me. "Are there any spare pens or paper lying around? I wanna make a shopping list."

Boss laughed. "Fine by me."

He got me what I asked for, and I returned to my porta-cabin.

I sat there, a little sunlight coming through the window, but most of the world was obscured by surrounding containers and other cabins. I wasn't in a prime location at all. Perhaps if I was living there, I could trade for a better cabin. It didn't matter, I was leaving soon and needed to make a list. It wasn't a shopping list as I'd told Boss, but more of a travel list. Stuff I wanted to leave with, whether thanks to Boss or from what I took from the mall. With a vehicle, I would have a lot more space to carry things as opposed to the backpack I previously had. The obvious things on the list were food and water, and a lot of it. Next was a gun and ammunition as well as sharp objects for when combat got up close and personal. Then there were other items which, although not necessary, would make my life easier – a flashlight, binoculars, a radio, and transmitter. Next were other items which, although not necessarily important to survival, would make life more comfortable – a raincoat, some thermal undergarments, two sets of clothes, a toothbrush and toothpaste, even some all-in-one body and hair wash. I would have to see what medicine I could scrounge as well. I was fully aware that luxury items would have to go amiss for the more essential stuff.

Goodbye delicious, guts-destroying fizzy drinks. Could I justify taking some whisky? It did have a dual purpose – delicious beverage and anaesthetic. But I was pushing it. I would have to go without. I could do with a satnav or a map, which would make travelling much easier. I preferred a satnav, but a map didn't need recharging or recalibrating. The map it was, but it meant I needed a compass also. The list of what-ifs would go on and on.

I eventually just put my list to one side for later and went to wait in the centre for Boss and his big talk. A few others were there too, also waiting around. We greeted each other and acknowledged that we were all going to the same thing. The only one I recognised out of the group was Keith. We stood side by side and caught up. It hadn't been long since we'd seen each other, but it felt like so much had happened since then.

Keith said he was asked to go because he knew a lot about guns. I told him I was asked because of my experience with the undead. He smiled. *That was odd.* Even Doc had some influence over what was to happen with the list of medical supplies he wanted.

Eventually, Boss turned up with the others. There was about fourteen of us altogether.

"So guys, today is quite a big day as we all know, hence you all being here," he announced. Boss definitely had a way of talking to people. He could've made shovelling dung fun. "We're going to take the military base not far from here. We need guns. We need equipment, and we need hardware. As a few of you know, we're going to use it to take a bigger prize."

"What is it?" one of the men called out.

"I'll get to that in a bit. Either way, we need the weapons," Boss replied. "So there are a few things we need to be careful of. As far as we can tell, there isn't anyone living on the base. We've checked on it every couple days and haven't seen anyone. That doesn't mean there aren't a few still left. If there is, we'll leave or ask them to join us. But it isn't worth the unnecessary deaths. If there isn't anyone alive, we still need to be careful – there will probably be meat-bags there. So we take it slow and steady. We'll have someone on guard at the gate, and always stay in groups. We can watch each other's backs. Finally, don't forget to announce yourself if you see any other group. We don't want any mishaps. We all clear?"

A combination of "aye" and "yeah" rang out.

"Let's get going, then!" Boss called. We all left for the North Gate, guns and weapons already prepped for our journey. We climbed in, spread out between three vehicles, and left.

CHAPTER 38

"See anything?" Boss asked me. I had ended up in his group, with Keith and a few others. I was looking through a set of binoculars at the apparently abandoned military base. We had parked out of sight and were watching from a distance. The other half of the group had approached from the rear and were doing similar.

"Nothing," I replied simply. "Undead and that's it."

The base consisted of three buildings and enclosed by a chain-link fence. I think it was probably an outpost or a supply depot, and never intended to be more. Even calling it a military base seemed a glorification. There wasn't even a gate, but an opening for vehicles to drive in with sandbags either side. I could see corpses, and not just the shambling kind. The military had definitely lost that one. Luckily for us, no one else had the foresight to pick it clean – if they had, then they'd also been killed by zombies. There were guns scattered here and there, and some still clung to the undead thanks to the strap. Boss stood up and began walking to the base, everyone else followed. The other group appeared and made their way to the entrance also. We already had our weapons drawn – me with my trusty machete and the Benelli shotgun I had claimed ownership of. I didn't feel I needed the shotgun as there were so many of us and so few of the undead, the machete would be the way forward.

"Remember lads, once we're sure the place is empty of anything other than us, we meet in the middle and leave our weapons. No accidents today," Boss reiterated. He was really against any accidental injuries occurring – I wonder how many times that had happened before. I didn't mind, I didn't want someone to accidentally discharge their weapon into me either.

"Can I put forward a suggestion?" I asked, an idea coming to me.

"Go ahead Sam," Boss nodded, giving me the floor.

"I think we should only use guns as a last resort," I began, gaining a few odd looks. "In my encounters with the undead, they're drawn by sound. Gunshots included. If we take them out silently, we will potentially save ourselves more hassle later."

A few people nodded approval and Boss said, "Sounds like a plan. Only use a firearm when you really have too."

We all moved out and entered the base slowly. A few of the undead noticed our arrival. I wasn't at the front of the group, so I got to see the visceral evisceration of the undead skulls being done by someone else for once. The first attack was two rapid strikes from a hammer. The first dented the zombie's forehead, the skin sunk slightly where the skull had fractured below the surface. The second strike sunk through the flesh and into the rotting brain beneath. The zombie dropped, pulling the hammer and the man still holding it tightly, to the floor. The hammer was stuck pretty damn good. All I could think about was how ill-prepared the man was for fighting the undead, and that you shouldn't use hammers! I snapped back from the momentary lapse in reality. A snarling zombie had dived on the person, pulling itself and the man towards each other, jaws snapping hungrily. I was reminded of piranhas. The man was doomed. That was it, he would be eaten. However, that wasn't the case. Another two of the men dived forward and pulled the zombie off of their fallen friend. He stood up and brushed himself off, smiling awkwardly. He was perfectly fine! The two guys held the thrashing zombie down while the man used the hammer to kill it once and for all. The face was left in a bloody mess and beyond recognition by the time he was done, but the zombie wasn't moving and no one had died. Huh … I guess being in a team could be necessary for survival. I always wanted to be alone, but a team of people you trusted could work! I mean, he only survived because there was someone to watch his back, and they trusted each other enough to do that. All I needed was a team I could fully trust.

The men moved further and further into the base, dealing with any undead they found. I was teamed up with Boss, and we encountered no trouble at all. All the undead had either been killed or were not there – the men may have been inexperienced but they were very efficient. The only place left to check was a large shed-like structure … the one with munitions printed in thick block letters above the door.

"The motherlode?" I said to Boss with a huge smile.

"Let's open it," Boss grinned excitedly. I nodded and gave the metallic door a few taps. Nothing stirred inside. We were set. Boss stood by the door, ready to swing at any attackers, and I gripped the handle. I signalled to him a countdown before pushing the door. It bulged inwards slightly at where I pushed the handle, but it didn't move. I tried again, pulling it – nothing.

"I think it's locked from the inside," I said with disappointment. Boss aimed his gun at the door. I shouted, voice high-pitched with panic, "No! If you hit anything inside, it's gonna be very bad for us."

"Ah," Boss concluded and lowered his gun. Smart people could do surprisingly dumb things. "I think there is a crowbar in one of the trucks."

Boss turned to leave and I followed.

CHAPTER 39

Do you ever get that feeling that you're being watched? Not just a paranoid feeling, but a genuine sense of unease. That is how I felt leaving the base to get the crowbar. Like I was being stalked. My initial thoughts turned to any returning soldiers, coming to claim what was theirs. No one announced themselves, nor shoot us had there been any hiding. The undead didn't exactly plan an attack either – they would have come straight for us.

"Something isn't right," I finally said to Boss, stopping in my tracks.

"Don't be silly," Boss laughed and carried on straight to the truck. I began looking around. If I was watching someone, where would I hide? The answer was obvious, I had already been watching the same base. I turned and stared directly at our former hiding spot. That is where I saw it. Hidden in the shrubbery, but not very well, were two faces. I couldn't make out any features other than fear when spotted. Their faces disappeared further into the greenery.

"Boss, there's someone over there," I called to him, and began jogging in their direction – my shotgun out and ready.

"Did they look threatening?" he asked, alarmed by the readiness of my gun.

"They hid when they saw us," I said, staring at the place they had been.

"Then put your gun away," he hissed at me. "You'll scare them."

I stopped, confused by his lack of fear.

"They could be–" I began, but was interrupted by Boss shouting to them.

"Hey, are you ok?" he called. No response. He tried again, "Look, we know you're there. There's no sense in hiding. There's way more of us."

"They're not gonna come out," I replied angrily. "We could be as much a threat to them, as they are to us."

"Hush," Boss whispered. This was the first time I had seen him genuinely annoyed – I could see the wheels rapidly turning behind his eyes. He then said aloud, "Look, we know that you think we could be a threat. We feel the same about you. I'm coming to you alone, I have water and no weapons. My people will attack if I'm not safely returned."

With that, Boss dropped his weapons and picked up a couple of bottles of water.

"Talk about being blunt," I said to him, shaking my head in disbelief. He was so ready to risk himself just to talk to someone!

He turned to me and said, "If I'm not back in five minutes, get the people out of here. I don't want any trouble for them. You understand?"

I nodded, and he put his hand on my shoulder and smiled. He began walking away. Some of the guys had taken notice and had started wandering over.

"Stay in there," I called to them. They carried on advancing.

"Listen to him!" Boss shouted to them when he realised they weren't going to listen to me. "While I'm gone, listen to Sam. He's in charge."

The men paused, they didn't return to what they were doing, but they stopped approaching. They looked at me questioningly. I looked at Boss with the same expression, I didn't want the responsibility of all those people!

"Goddamn," I huffed, leaning against the truck, waiting for Boss to return. I looked at the clock in the truck. He had exactly five minutes, and then I was going over there to see if he was ok, regardless of what Boss said.

CHAPTER 40

Four minutes and thirty-eight seconds passed. I was just getting ready to go after Boss, when he and two figures returned. I stood there, impatiently, with my hand clutching my shotgun. They got closer and closer. Boss had a smile on his face, and he was being trailed by two women – one in her twenties, the other in her thirties. Both were extremely dirty. Muddy, not bloody. The older one was average height and blonde. She carried a tyre iron and looked like she knew how to use it. Her face was hardened, eyes had the sharpness of a blade. The younger one was tall and brunette. She wore a rucksack and had a sad, distant look in her eyes. She looked soft, emotionally and physically. They had done well to get as far as they had. They both looked, not exactly at ease, but happy for that moment.

"All good?" I asked Boss.

"I think so," Boss looked between me and them. "I would like to introduce Kirsty and Stephanie."

Kirsty was the blonde one, and Stephanie the brunette.

"Nice to meet you both," I said, with a tight smile.

I knew it was really stupid, and maybe a biological flaw as a man, but I felt a lot safer knowing the people watching us were women. Sexist? Extremely. No idea where it came from, but I felt as though men would be a lot more murder-ey, and the two women in front of me looked trustworthy.

"You, too," Kirsty said, sternly. She didn't smile. Even had a look of anger in her eyes. Stephanie just nodded.

"You two related?" I asked, trying to break the ice. "Where are you going?"

"No," Kirsty replied with no further explanation. If I felt men were untrustworthy in the end times, I wondered how she felt.

"We're heading south," Stephanie said, quietly.

"I don't think there's anything down there," I said. The information that Bristol had been lost came back to me in a sudden flash.

"We're going to find something. North wasn't any good, so we have to try," Kirsty stared at me as if I had done terrible things to her bed and hadn't told her until it was too late.

"Fair enough," I said – at least I tried. "What now?"

"Well," Boss replied thoughtfully. "I'm going to escort them back to our base so they can shower and get a few supplies for their journey."

"Is that wise?" I bore holes into him with my eyes. Not only were they rude and still a potential threat to Boss, but I felt extremely possessive of our supplies. And by *our supplies* I meant the things I would need when I left. Besides, we didn't know if there were more people out there waiting for us.

"We have plenty to share, Sam," Boss said, with a huge smile. He might've been smiling, but there was forcefulness in his voice. He turned to the women. "Don't worry about him. He's been through a lot, and now he's a bit defensive."

"Stood right here, prick," I said, under my breath. Boss was grating on me big time. He was behaving irresponsibly and showing off. What was it with people and showing off in front of others? Did he think he was going to get laid?

"I'll meet you back at the base anyway," he locked eyes with me. "You're in charge, Sam. Above all, remember that the wellbeing and safety of my men is more important than anything else. I'll go to great lengths to keep them happy, okay?"

"Yeah, yeah," I waved him away. He and the women climbed into the truck and started it up.

"Before I go, take this," Boss reached onto the floor of the truck and passed me a crowbar. "Get that shed open."

I took the crowbar and began walking back to the military outpost. I gave a short wave over my shoulder as they pulled away. *If he dies, it's his fault.*

"Dumbass," I huffed.

I was questioned numerous times by the men in the outpost about what had just happened. I just kept telling them to ask Boss about it later and that everything was fine. People resumed the collection of what resources they could take, although a lot less enthusiastically than before. There were whispers and mutterings about what had happened, but I ignored them. As much as Boss liked me, I wasn't a leader to these men and they knew it. It didn't matter. I was going to get the munitions shed open.

"I'm coming in," I said to the shed, tapping the door with the crowbar for extra emphasis. Still no movement within. I wedged the crowbar into the line where the doors met, and pulled, prying the metal apart inch by inch. A foetid stink came through the hole I had created. My eyes watered and I quietly retched, but I pushed through it. I tore enough of the metal apart to see it had been chained from the inside, but there was no padlock. I unravelled the chain from the door handle and it fell to the floor. *Thunk.* The entire time, I was expecting teeth to sink into my flesh while my appendage hung in the darkness.

I finally pulled the door open, and a light came on with the detection of movement, lighting up the small shed. Boxes from floor to ceiling were everywhere. Various sizes and numerical denominations on the side. *Holy crap.* We had found enough ammunition for the next few years, depending on the level of combat. It truly was the motherlode. But there were no guns in there, and I was hoping the men had found them in one of the other structures.

I circled some of the stacks, eyes still streaming from the smell, and eventually found the source. Leaning against one of the stacks was a soldier. A *very* dead one. His uniform was soaked in his blood, but had long since dried. In one hand was a pistol, the other held a photo of a small child. The wall behind him was sprayed with an upward jet of brain and blood and skull. The gaping hole in the back of his head suggested he had taken the lesser-of-two-evils route out of the world.

"Poor bugger," I sighed, sympathetically. I stared silently for a few moments before moving on with my journey. I pried the pistol from his hand and pocketed it. *Finders keepers.* I stepped outside and saw some of the men carrying boxes of what appeared to be guns according to the outer-writing. *Good.*

"Ammunition?" Keith asked as I exited. I nodded. "A lot?"

"Mh-hm," I nodded again. "We better start packing things up and head back."

"We're not gonna get all this back in one trip," Keith said. "There might be some vehicles nearby if we send a group out to look."

"Boss said not to risk anyone unnecessarily and to get

back safely," I explained, "I think we should just head back."

"He won't know," Keith grinned. "Come on. I'll go to look for it myself."

"Fine, go for it," I shrugged. I wasn't in the mood to play leader in the most normal of circumstances, let alone the apocalypse. So having that thrust on me unexpectedly just made me resentful.

"Okay, I'll be back before you even realise I was gone," Keith took his gun and hammer before jogging off.

I waited until he was far enough away before calling, "Right, everyone start packing up and filling the vehicles. We need to get back sooner rather than later."

The packing began.

An hour later, and after a lot of convincing, the rest of the men returned to the base. I had opted to stay behind at the outpost. They hadn't got anywhere near enough into the vans because of the number of men and because Boss had left with the third vehicle. More importantly, Keith still hadn't returned. I had given him the go-ahead to leave, albeit begrudgingly, so it was my responsibility to see if he returned. It looked to be about mid-afternoon, judging by the position of the sun, and I just sat there and waited. I was debating on how long was an acceptable amount of time to assume someone was dead and leave, when I heard a vehicle approaching. A large white transit van pulled up, driven by Keith.

"Miss me?" he smiled.

"Had some trouble?" I questioned, looking at the bloody smears and handprints down the side of the van.

"I've been in worse," he laughed. Then alarm crossed his face. "Where's everyone else?"

"I sent them back. Wasn't expecting you to be alive," I said bluntly and with a shrug. He just stared at me.

"So why'd you wait?" he squinted at me.

"Letting you go was my decision," I said through gritted teeth. "I'm not going to let others die due to my bad choices, but I'm not going to abandon someone either. Let's pack up the rest of the crap and leave."

I carried ammunition crates to the van, surprised at how heavy something so small could be. One by one, I dropped the metal boxes into the back of the van, the metal clanging. Keith did the same. We were an efficient team. Although he did warn me about dropping them so hard because of the chance it could set the contents off. I pretended to ignore him, but when he wasn't looking, I sure as hell made sure I put them down gently.

We both carried some of the larger weapon crates, far too heavy for just one of us. I was happy to keep carrying boxes, unsure of their contents, when Keith stopped me on one.

"That's tear gas," Keith stated.

"And?" I questioned, still carrying it.

"We don't need it," Keith stated simply again.

"Why not?" I stopped in my tracks to look at him, but I couldn't stay like that for long. The box was heavy!

"They'll be useless," Keith explained. "Against human combatants? Brilliant. The dead? Won't do a thing, I'm betting. We'd be better off using the space for ammo instead."

He had a fair point, so I dropped the box where I stood. I know it was silly, and out of spite. But I did take a few out of the box for personal use when Keith wasn't looking. He may not be planning on fighting humans any time soon, but I had a long road ahead of me and I would need them.

Eventually, we set off back to base, the van filled with

extra weapons and ammunition. There was a grinding noise because the van was far beyond the recommended safety weight. I couldn't help but think that the van would break down at any moment, and if it didn't, then the damage from the weight would certainly be permanent.

We headed back for our grand return. Boss didn't even notice our absence. He was still doing his thing. Nothing more was spoken of it, and I stashed the tear gas and handgun in my cabin. I crashed in bed for a few hours, while others brought the cargo in. They couldn't expect me to do everything. Besides, I needed to sleep.

"Tomorrow is the most important day for our little community!" Boss said to everyone. I mean, literally, everyone – we had all gathered in the centre, even the guards were down from the walls to listen in. Boss had returned a couple of hours into my nap, a satisfied look on his face. Probably had a threesome or something along those lines. He had woke me up to tell me to gather and for me to tell anyone I saw to do the same.

"As some of you know, there's a large mall not far from here. No one living inside, but certainly filled with undead. This will be our new home. Our scouts have confirmed that we can get in there easily enough. All we have to do is clear out anything walking that shouldn't be. Once the shutters are down, we'll have our own personal fortress."

There was an eruption of cheers. Even I did a fist pump or two. *When in Rome …*

"Because it's such a big target, we'll need almost everyone there," he looked at each person in the crowd. "We'll leave one or two people here on the walls to keep the place looking occupied, but the rest of us will be doing an assault on the mall. We will clear it. We will take it. But we won't be able to move in straight away. We'll need to move everything bit by bit. We'll be vulnerable in this time since our forces will be split between two areas, so it's imperative that both groups stay in contact in case the other needs them. We'll be defending two bases for the time being. This won't be easy. Any objections?"

Not a single person spoke.

Boss shouted, "Now get some rest. We have an early start tomorrow."

People cheered with Boss, laughed, and celebrated.

Good. I wanted a word with Boss about the actual plan, as well as give a few ideas of my own. I fought through the dispersing crowd to reach for him.

"Hey, Sam, sorry about running out on you earlier. I planned to return but ended up helping take the ladies a little further than expected," Boss apologised. He looked sheepish. "I'm sure you understand."

"Completely," I lied but carried on past it. "I got a few suggestions on how to make our assault easier tomorrow."

"Excellent. Come with me, and we can discuss it in depth," Boss led me away from the crowd.

Broadcast Six: Shaun, Frank, and Barbara 3

Shaun: Hey, Frank, you still out there, man?

Frank: Yeah, still here. Sorry about leaving abruptly yesterday. Had a couple of zeds outside. Had to deal with them.

Shaun: Did it go okay?

Frank: Yeah, fine. Almost got bit. Again.

Shaun: Oh, yeah, about that. If anyone out there is listening in, a bite doesn't infect. My buddy has been bit twice –

Frank: Three times.

Shaun: Three times! Clean the wound, and if you do it properly, you'll be fine. It's nothing like the movies.

Frank: Who are you talking to? The other people on the radio? They're not listening. They're too busy hearing their own voices. We might be the only people left.

Shaun: No, man. I heard America has survivors.

Frank: Yeah, you heard that from Barb, same as me. You shouldn't believe everything she said. She was also sure that aliens were roaming around out there and that the undead weren't the real threat. Besides, it's too late. The boat left days ago.

Shaun: I have to believe there are other survivors out there, and not just in America. Remember the guy leading the war? What if she was right? Why would that guy just make that up? What if he is out there, winning this war? What if there's a chance to live happily ever after, and it's in America? We need to find a boat or something, and then we can be safe.

Frank: Yeah, just don't go chasing after a girl you never met, okay. I don't want to get my hopes up because … what the frick?

Shaun: What is it, man? Everything okay?

Frank: Yeah, just zeds outside again. They must've followed the noise from when I dealt with the last lot.

Shaun: You need to be more careful. That's three days running now. You're going to get overrun.

Frank: I'll be fine. I'll just go out and draw them away.

CHAPTER 41

We were in the car park, waiting at the far back and watching the entrance through binoculars. We had our rifles trained on the entrance – the ones we had pilfered from the military outpost. Proper military hardware.

Once again, I was reunited with an SA80. It was almost exactly the same as the one I had before, except this one had a scope. It felt comfortable in my hands and familiar – an old, death-dealing friend. Would it be weird to describe a gun as sexy? Because that was exactly how I described it in front of some of the men, only to be met with strange looks. Regardless, the SA80 was becoming my favourite weapon!

I had wanted to be the one to set up the trap since it was my idea, but Boss wanted me back with most of the others. His logic being that I was the better shot, after he had strategically extracted my previous gun experience from me.

The morning had consisted of trying to see which of the men were good shots and who needed training. I realised barely any of them were a decent shot. It was all well and good giving off the impression of strength by having armed guards on the walls, but it would become apparent that they were more of a visual deterrent than a real defence force.

So an evaluation session was done. Each man was given twenty rounds and one rifle for training purposes. Most were awful, except for Keith, one or two others, and myself. I suggested we delay taking the mall until the men were more prepared and familiar with the guns, but Boss wouldn't have that. He was sure someone else would take it if they didn't act first. I knew it would be a disaster.

When it came to the assault on the mall, we were asked to stand back, with our sights trained on the entrance. The worst shots were up front, setting up the same speaker system previously used during the party night. They were armed with shotguns and anything effective from close range. They felt they were heroes being at the front and risking themselves, but they didn't realise it was because that was all they seemed capable of.

After some tinkering with the electronics, they waved to us, climbed into their truck, and began to drive towards us. Over the rumble of the engine, I could hear a steady tune building. Violins to begin with, slowly building with accompanying pieces of the orchestra and rising to an operatic high. *Ride of the Valkyries*. So goddamn appropriate. Zombies started running toward the truck, drawn out by the music. The slower ones fell to the floor as their faster brethren collided with them. We fired.

See, that was the plan. We already knew sound attracted the undead, and the building was filled with them, so we had to find a way to draw them out. It was like poison from a wound. As the song climbed higher and higher, more and more undead came out of the mall. I was resting my gun on the bonnet of the car to steady my aim, staring through the scope. I had become adept at scoring headshots. One would step out, I would let off a pop, and a split second later, zombies would fall to the ground, with an arching spray of gore as the bullet tore through it.

Shooting and killing zombies to the *Ride of the Valkyries* was one of the most epic feelings I'd ever experienced. The hair on my arms stood on end! I felt so heroic with the crescendo that I didn't even feel a little bit bad for killing the undead. I could see why it was used in classic war films.

The full glass front of the mall was being coated in decaying gore with each shot. Any zombies I didn't take down on the first shot were dispatched by Keith. He was a hell of a shot. I didn't think he missed one. He was even better than me, and that was saying something. I had learned through survival. He had learned through training.

Eventually, the tide of zombies slowed and eventually stopped. We waited as long as reasonably possible before we decided to approach the mall. Someone disconnected the music, and the silence that followed was eerie, like all sound had been removed from the world. I even pressed my finger into my ear to create some noise. I felt deaf. Vulnerable, like I was on show and being observed. Maybe I was.

We split into three teams of varying sizes. My team was the largest and would go through the mall and secure it from any lingering undead. Another team, led by Keith, would stay out front and ensure no more zombies entered. And the final team would circle the area for similar reasons.

Once my team was inside, we were to ensure that all doors to each store were locked, and the ones that weren't, we were to make sure the store was clear of any undead. We would then clear the locked stores systematically. Our ultimate goal was to get to whatever security room there was, turn the lights on, and survey the security cameras for anything of interest. Then the shutters would go down. We would be working in near darkness until then, so it was vital we got it done sooner rather than later.

The recon team had told us where they predicted the security room would be. This assumption was based on the staff entrance behind the mall, which we didn't want to force open because it would compromise overall building safety.

"Right, lads," Boss called. "We all know the plan – get in there, play it safe, and don't shoot each other. We have some flashlights for a few of the guns, but not many. So stick with someone who has one. We don't want anyone being mistaken for a meat-bag."

I was one of the lucky few handed a flashlight. Awesome.

We all began to creep into the mall through the bloody entrance, the piles of undead corpses making it difficult. *Sign of times.*

"Once more into the breach," I muttered softly to myself, flicking the flashlight on and entering.

Entering the mall felt like I was stepping into an indie horror game. For those of you not in the know, there was an odd period for gaming when there was an explosion of independent game companies making horror games where you didn't fight. You simply ran and hid. It created an atmosphere of tension and fear. You would be equipped with a flashlight, or smartphone, or video camera with some form of night vision – something to allow you to be able to see in the dark and create a sense of urgency when the battery level got low.

So when I stepped through the door and into total darkness, with only the flashlight illuminating small sections at a time – which cast long and grotesque shadows – I was scared. Not video game emulated fear, but genuine primal fear.

I was twisting my entire body as I walked, cutting huge swathes of the mall to be lit up as I moved. Everything looked like a humanoid figure in the dark. I took deep breaths to calm down, but the darkness was getting to me. Or more accurately, what could be hiding in the dark. *Breathe, Sam.*

The men started checking shop doors, skipping the shuttered ones and those that didn't open. Every now and again, I would see someone disappear into a shop. Even less often, I would hear a roar and a gunshot. Whoever had gone in would then leave the store and give a thumbs-up. The door would then shut behind that person.

We carried on like a poorly trained SWAT team. Room by room, we cleared. For once, I didn't come across a single zombie in the stores I'd entered. But as I moved on, I built a mental map of all the shops I needed to visit. Even some I just wanted to visit. *Ahem,* video game store, *ahem.*

A smaller team worked their way towards the security room, slaying any undead on the way. They pushed through like an arrow. We cleared the area they'd left behind them so nothing could sneak up on them. I came across a zombie thrashing about in a water fountain. Where had I seen this before? I put it down, its bloody sludge discolouring the water. By flashlight, everything looked so surreal. The longer I stood and stared at the zombie in the water, with the occasional shot ringing out in the background, the more ill I felt. Not sick or queasy, just … abnormal. My vision swam, and I felt like I'd been hit by a wave of vertigo.

"The frick?" I muttered, squeezing my eyes shut. *What was that?* I moved on, hoping that distancing myself from the bloody fountain would help. It didn't.

I followed the team, pushing forward as they slowly reached the end of the mall, running out stores to check. Eventually they took a turn, which I almost didn't see. It was like a small access corridor. They reached the end of a corridor and disappeared into the doorway at the end. I stood around, waiting, marvelling at why zombie apocalypses always led to a mall. Sure, they were full of useful goods, and humans seemed to gravitate towards them, but being somewhere that was dark and quiet when it should've been filled with light and noise was so eerie.

There was a shout, some gunfire, and then silence. I considered going in after them, charging in like a damn hero, but I really didn't want to fall into the same trap that they may have. Besides, just looking down the long corridor into the extended darkness made me feel sick and unsteady on my feet. Was I coming down with something? Had it been something I ate? I didn't know, but every gunshot felt so loud. So I waited, and waited, and waited. Others were still wandering around and double checking. I didn't want any part of that. I slouched onto one of the many benches and sat there. The work carried on around me, ignorant of my existence.

After what felt like an age, the lights came on. I heard the static hum of speakers turning on, and splashing as the water fountain came to life.

"Welcome to the mall, your new home of luxury and survival," Boss said over the intercom system. "Gentlemen, there is life in this place yet."

Some of the men clapped and whooped, and I smiled with relief, the sickness temporarily gone but not forgotten.

Boss came out to greet us with a huge smile. It was possibly his greatest achievement, and he definitely knew it.

"Congrats," I said to him and smiled, shaking his hand.

"Couldn't have done all this without you," Boss replied, using the royal 'you', if that is even a thing.

"So what's the next part of the plan?" I switched the flashlight off and slung the SA80 over my shoulder.

"One more sweep in the light to make sure the building is clear, and then we'll look into securing the place," he rubbed his chin and looked around. "We need to check the locked and shuttered stores as well."

"Sounds like a plan," I nodded. "How we planning on getting into the locked ones?"

"Few of the dead guys look like security or staff. We can check them for keys," he pointed to one of the dead zombies. It wore a security jacket, and there was an identification card in a florescent wallet on his sleeve.

Boss walked off to talk to the other men. I bent down and checked the zombie to see what he had on him. A walkie-talkie, a personal phone, a wallet, and … some goddamn keys.

"Well, what do you know?" I smiled. Life had its ups and downs, but things were finally getting on track. I walked away before my discovery was noticed by the group, and started on my shopping trip, ignoring most of the shops I passed. I was sure someone else would find a set of keys. At that moment, I wanted to get on with what I needed. First stop was a sports store.

CHAPTER 42

I rolled up the shutters, the clatter echoing around the mostly empty mall, and crept in. The lights were on, and there weren't any zombies inside. Well, not immediately, but I was certain they would've been drawn by the shutter noise if there were any.

It was one of those crappy little sports stores that always seemed to have a closing down sale sign in the window. Didn't mean the stock cost any less than another. Hell, I was getting it for free.

I browsed through the shelves for a bag, like a holdall, just something to carry anything I wanted. I found what I was looking for and put a pack of thermal boxers, socks, and t-shirts in there. I would need those for the colder days to come. The cold could be deadly if I wasn't careful.

They had plenty of raincoats, gloves, and hats, but I knew the hiking shop would have much better quality. The same also went for a backpack. The ones in the sports shop were mostly for fashion as opposed to functionality.

I admired all the different trainers and other footwear they had on show. I was never one for having the most expensive pair of trainers. I considered it a waste of money.

However, having them ready for the taking made them a lot more desirable. I smiled and moved on, looking for anything else useful in the store. I saw a tennis racket and tennis balls. Not exactly useful to me, but I took them anyway. For … reasons.

I stepped out of the store, dropped the holdall and started bouncing the tennis ball the way you would often see tennis players do before serving. Then I threw it up and hit it as hard as I could with the racket. It soared high and flew far. Kept going until it bounced off a wall and disappeared out of sight. I grinned. Now *that* was fun.

I meandered towards the hiking store and started bouncing another ball. I swung. This one curved and bounced off a shop window, making a *plunk* noise, but didn't break anything. I sent the last ball back the way I came, and I swore I heard a shout of annoyance in the distance. I dropped the racket, picked up my bag, and carried on. I should've gotten a bicycle or something.

The hiking store didn't have shutters and wasn't locked, so I opened the door and wandered in, a putrid smell in the air. It was one of the rooms that had been cleared. I was still wary, though. I hadn't cleared the place myself, and I found it hard to rely on someone else's handiwork.

I surveyed the area and found one corpse twisted up on a small camping display, with its head and a large portion of its body missing. Definitely dead. I walked around the rest of the store, gun primed and ready to fire. Didn't find anything. Even checked the changing rooms just to be certain. I lowered my gun, feeling safe again.

I needed to speed things up if I wanted to get everywhere without my absence being noticed. I snatched up a raincoat and put it on to make sure it fit. It was thermal and waterproof, with a hood as well. Perfect. I also found a hat and gloves, thin but the label assured me they were thermal. I flicked the safety on the gun and tried on one glove. My finger fit into the trigger guard, albeit snugly. I could work it out somehow. Also put waterproof trousers and a waterproofing wax into the bag. Hiking boots on top of that – I would need to wear them in if I didn't want to make every step painful. These were all just-in-cases for the future.

The days were cold, but they would begin to warm up. I needed a few summer clothes too, but they were out of season and would be harder to find. New stock hadn't been delivered in ages, so the store was stuck in time. A few extra t-shirts and maybe a pair of shorts would be perfect, but I would have to find them later. I grabbed a large hiking backpack also. It felt comfortable on me, and I could fit a lot in there. I knew I would be in a vehicle from that point onward, but there was always a *just in case*. Life was full of those now.

I threw in a British Map Guide to Hiking and a compass as well. On the way out, I saw a small basket by the door, filled with little balls of netting. Mosquito nets. I picked one up and dropped it into my bag. *Eh, why not?*

I came across a small pharmacy-like shop also, which kind of looked like a homoeopathy store. Lots of herbs and other nonsense. What could I say? I was a psychologist. The placebo effect could only fix so much, and it was no cure for cancer. But I knew they would have other things of use. I began filling my bag with bottles of multivitamins. I knew I would still be able to eat, but odds were I wouldn't get every bit of nutrition my body needed. So those would help for a while. They didn't have anything else medicinal, such as paracetamol, but they had a root which claimed it would help – I wasn't taking that. Would rather suffer from the headache. There was also a protein section full of different powders and shakes. I took a few of the bars.

Ironically, next door to the homoeopathy shop was an actual chemist. So I took different medicines and other hygiene items from there, including a toothbrush, a large tube of toothpaste, and some all-in-one body and hair wash. I couldn't deal with a different scrub for everything – body wash, exfoliating gel, shampoo, conditioner, toothpaste, shaving foam, moisturiser, and maybe even a hand lotion. I would prefer an eight-in-one wash. I wouldn't mind using the same stuff on my teeth as my backside. Life would be so much simpler. If they could somehow add a car polish into it, they'd be onto a winner. But I would be burdened with the multi-product buy until that day, which would probably never come with the dead walking. So into the bag went a razor and many different heads for it, shaving foam also, as well as the makings of a first aid kit. My bag was getting pretty heavy.

I almost ignored the store when I went by it, but there was a shop that sold nothing but fine spirits. Imported stuff. Local stuff. Vodka, brandy, liqueurs, and whisky. Goddamn! I dropped my bag and went into the store. The draw of the whisky overpowered the putrid smell of the dead-dead corpse by the door. I admired all the golden bottles. They all looked so damn beautiful. I couldn't even decide what to take. In the end, I took the most expensive one I could find – a litre bottle of some whisky I had never heard of for the low-low price of seven-hundred and fifty pounds. It was the only one of its kind in the store and was even behind glass, on its own pedestal. I opened the small glass door and took it. Held it lovingly and stared at it with a huge smile. I reached behind the counter and put it into a small wooden box filled with paper shredding, and sealed it. Normally it would be for gift wrapping, but I needed to protect it. Into my bag it went.

I rushed to the next store, and the one I'd anticipated most – the video game store. That was just for me, not my survival. I wanted to retain some part of who I once was, and video games made up a lot of that. Being in an unattended video game store was my equivalent of being a kid in a candy store. I just couldn't wait!

On the way, I noticed a motorsports store. In the window were leather-clad mannequins. I had a sudden flash of brilliance and decided I needed to go in. It was an in-and-out job because I just needed a couple of things in there. Boss would come and find me when he needed me but, for those moments, I was my own person.

I left my bag outside, jogged in with weapon drawn. It had been one of the locked stores, but I was prepared for any threat. I was disappointed by the lack of undead in the shops. How dare it all be safe? I laughed. No zombies, no need for my gun. I let it fall on its strap, and it clung to me. I started looking through everything until I found exactly what I needed – a heavy duty leather motorcycle jacket and gloves. The jacket hugged me like a leathery embrace, albeit a lot less kinky sounding. I took two – one my size, and the other it didn't matter. Also took a repair kit for jackets. Next, I grabbed a pair of heavy duty motorbike jeans. I had brilliant plans for it. I would even say revolutionise the war on the undead. I grinned and continued onwards. Video game store next.

CHAPTER 43

The store was unlocked. There were no zombies present. The bright clinical light illuminated the shelves of games. I think my heaven would be like that. I walked around and grinned. It was just so quiet. So peaceful. A reasonably sized store. After all, the games industry was a huge business. The walls were lined with various games. Mostly preowned games, some chart releases, with a few different setups for demo games. There were different sections for each console, too.

I always found it strange trying to explain the idea of different consoles and their various games. Could never think of another type of media with the same type of system. I always tried to use DVD's as an example, telling people to imagine that there are three types out there called BVD, CVD and DVD. They're all of equal quality and equal value, except certain films would only appear on one of these types. Some films would come out on a DVD, whereas others would only be on a CVD. Some films would come out on all three. However, you would need a player for each format. That's how the different consoles worked. You normally found fans of only one system. I was always a fan of the Xbox. Great system, great games, and most of my friends had one. Sad to think that there wouldn't be any new games being developed and released.

I looked at the posters of launch dates and games I would probably never get the chance to play. I saw one on the shelf, a first-person shooter. I was so excited when it was announced. It was the newest sequel in a series I loved. I smiled at the case and opened it. Empty. *Damn.* Only a display case. They weren't going to keep games in reach of someone to take. I turned around to look behind the counter. There was a door, probably leading to the staffroom or where the discs were kept. I grinned. Looked like today was my lucky day.

I hopped over the counter and tried the door. Locked. Not by a key, but a security code, which meant my bunch of keys were no good here. I didn't have the code, and the employees apparently didn't use code 1-2-3-4 either. With five different numbers and two letters, and assuming it was a four-digit code, like the one in the supermarket I used to work at, that was a hell of a lot of combinations and permutations. I didn't want to shoot the lock – the beautiful games within could be damaged. I braced myself against the counter and kicked the door three times in rapid succession. On the third strike, the door flung inward and a zombie came out.

I tumbled backwards over the counter and hit the floor, my gun digging into my back.

"Crap!" I gasped, the air knocked out of me. I tried to take huge rasping breaths to fill my lungs. The zombie carried on towards me, snapping its jaws like a demonic beast. It had the game shops uniform on and a badge. *My name is Chris :).* I tried to twist the gun out from under me, but it was trapped by my body. I rolled over. The zombie fell over the counter, making a wet thud as it hit the ground.

I could feel the sickness I felt earlier creeping in, but

adrenaline pushed it aside. The zombie climbed to its feet. It was still coming after me. I managed to raise my gun. Didn't have time to aim for its head, so I fired a burst shot. All three bullets ripped through its knee. Anything below that point was severed and fell away.

The zombie, still moving forward, fell to the ground. It couldn't support itself anymore, but it kept coming. I fired another burst shot into its head. It stopped moving. I panted. That was close. So easy to get caught off-guard. I didn't stop there, though. I grabbed it by its remaining ankle and dragged it out of the store, a long and bloody trail behind it. I left it outside and returned. I finally managed to catch my breath. The store still smelled bad, but with the body out, it was bearable.

I looked down at my bloody hands and clothes. Dammit. I used my sleeve to wipe away any gore on my face. Believe me, I knew it was there. I could feel it coating me. I pushed myself back over the counter, determination now filling me. Turning on the internal light of the room, I looked in the cupboard. There were even more games in there. I let loose a smug smile and reached for the one I wanted. From the extra weight, I knew that the game and manual were in there. I took it, pulled it open and disposed of the cellophane. Walked up to the demo-stand and pried open the plastic case. The Xbox was already powered on and running the demo video. I pushed the disc into the slot, and held the controller as the music started up.

I was there, in the moment. Time disappeared as I was pulled into the immersive qualities of the game. Everything from the music, to the sounds, to the visuals. Everything looked so fake. That was just what I needed. A fake world I could disappear into, just to forget reality for a few moments, like I had done in school when bullied, and when I was upset and there were problems at home. Now, in the middle of the apocalypse where the dead were walking and I needed to carry a gun to survive, I could get lost in this sci-fi world. I was the hero. I would save the world. I couldn't die. I would survive.

Then before I knew it, it was over. I had finished the game. *How long have I been here?* I rubbed my eyes. They burned since I'd had them open for so long. Surely I hadn't been there that long? Games had been getting shorter and shorter. Was that the case? It didn't matter, I had enjoyed it. I was beaming.

It was lush just to be immersed in that world one more time. Sure, it had ended on a cliffhanger, ready for the sequel that would never come, but in a way, it had concluded a lot of the open storylines. The developer had given the series a great send-off, even if they didn't realise that was the send-off into the apocalypse. I removed the disc, returned it to the case, and put it on the counter. On a scrap of paper, I wrote *Highly recommend! From Sam the zombie slayer.* I smiled as I stuck it to the case and left. I picked up all my belongings and ambled back to the security room.

There were people everywhere upon my return. They were writing stuff down and pointing to areas. I went unnoticed amongst the crowd. I made it back to the security room and entered. Boss was sat at a desk, flicking through the security cameras. It showed most places – entrances to the shops, outside, and other areas. The only place it didn't show was inside the stores.

"Done a bit of shopping I see," Boss said without turning

around. I almost asked him how he knew, but realised he was staring at security footage.

"Just a bit," I smiled. "Few things to make my journey ahead easier."

"Fair enough," he turned to look at me and gestured to a chair.

"So what's the news on this place?" I took a seat.

"I think we've gotten really lucky by getting this now," he yawned. I caught sight of the clock. I had been gone for close to five hours. Classic sign of a great gaming session.

"What about defending it?" I looked at the notes on the page in front of him. He had drawn a pencil doodle of the mall, with X's here and there.

"Should be fine," he nodded. "Biggest problem is the all-glass front. Pretty sure it's double or triple glazed, so no meat-bags coming through there. The door is the weakest point, but it has shutters. I still would rather something to cover it. There's also an issue with the loading bay. The shutters are really weak. The dead might not be able to get in, but the living … it's definitely a weak spot. Luckily, the bay is easily defendable, with only one way in. We'd have to use that as our main entrance. As for the security door, we can weld that shut good and proper. Get some guys on the roof for watch. I think we can hold this place for a long, long time. Anything extra we need, we can make when we claim a hardware store."

"That's great, Boss," I smiled. I was ecstatic for them. They had a home and the skills to keep it. If things went bad with Alice, then I would come back to Boss. I felt a little at home with these people.

As if reading my mind, he said, "You know you're welcome to stay here or return here, right?"

"Thanks for the offer, man. I hope to see you again when

I do come back this way," I gave him a playful punch.

"Great! We need to head back soon. We can sort out your ride for the journey," he grinned. "We can leave a small force here, and the rest of us return home. It'll keep this place safe."

Over the intercom, Boss called for everyone and we all rounded up. From the volunteers, he chose who would remain. People were happy to stay. I suppose they were experiencing real safety for the first time. It was a hard thing to give up. Or they wanted to claim a few things for themselves while we were absent.

About half of the group stayed when the rest of us headed back. We still had hours of daylight left, but Boss had a lot to plan for. In addition to that, he wanted a big celebration that night. He said we actually had cause for celebration, so it would be a real party rather than just passing the time. I did wonder if those staying behind would feel left out. That was before I saw several of them heading into the spirits store on our way out. They would be just fine.

I dumped my holdall into the back of the truck and received questioning glances. Then we headed back to the base, leaving their future home behind for the time being.

CHAPTER 44

When we got back, I immediately went to my room. Dropped the holdall onto my bed and dragged out both leather jackets, the jeans, the gloves, and the repair kit. I laid them out on the floor side by side and stared at them, smiling. Then I put on the leather jacket and gloves. Surprisingly comfortable. Sure, they restricted my movement a little, and the feel of leather was just weird, but it wasn't all that bad.

I flexed and moved parts of my upper body. The shoulder sections were sturdy, and I could easily rotate my shoulders, which was great since I would need maximum mobility to survive. The only issue was fully extending my arms up. My hands were well-protected also, and the knuckles were reinforced. I kept clenching and unclenching my hand to stretch the leather out. I was concerned that pulling a trigger was going to be difficult. The jeans were extremely comfortable, albeit thick. They would be unbearable to wear in the summer. But I could bend my knees fine. I supposed that it all worked together to keep you in one piece should you come off your motorcycle.

I picked up the pen I had previously used to write my shopping list and started to write down the areas that hindered my movements. Then I took the jacket, jeans, and gloves, and laid them back on the floor. Took out the fisherman's knife and began to make small incisions in the leather. Under the arms was the main place. I cut all the way through until there was an opening I could see through. I put the jacket back on and flexed again. Mobility had mostly returned. The only problem was that I had sacrificed protection for movement. But I had planned for that.

I removed the jacket again, then began slicing patches from the spare motorcycle jacket. Next, I used the repair kit to affix the patches of leather to where I had created the slices. It looked ugly and broken, like a poorly made patchwork quilt. I waited until I had fixed all the holes before trying it on. Still comfortable. Still mobile. Still protected.

I smiled, "There's my super suit."

I then used the excess leather from the leftover jacket to create protective portions on the jeans – patches on the knees, up the front of the shins and thighs. It looked extremely unappealing, but it worked. The logic behind having a leather jacket and patches on the jeans was due to its thickness. I didn't believe that a zombie could bite through the leather. After all, they only had human teeth and human strength. Sure they could bruise and break bones through the leather, but I doubt they could tear flesh. The only problem was that I had no way to test it safely. I attempted to bite the jacket, but stopped for fear of breaking my teeth – something the undead never had to worry about.

It didn't matter, though. I felt a lot safer about my journey ahead with an extra level of protection. Bites weren't infectious, not in terms of creating more zombies, but they were still deadly in terms of all the bacteria nested in the undead's mouths. I would be protected against that going forward. I felt happy with my *purchase*, but there was one more finishing touch I wanted to add. All I needed was some spray paint and cardboard.

Twenty minutes later, I returned with both. Cut out a pattern on the cardboard to create two stencils. The first, in large writing, said ZOMBIE SQUAD. I took the leathers outside and used the white spray paint to stencil the words onto the upper back of the protective gear. After a few minutes, it had air dried. I used the second stencil to spray the letters ZS onto the right front breast. Did it look silly? Probably. Did I think it looked cool? Of course. I felt like I had an official end-of-days uniform and that I was prepared for anything. Undead world, here I come!

My next job was getting my boiler suit cleaned. I didn't have long before I left, because I was hoping to leave in the next forty-eight hours. The earlier the better, and I had a lot to do. I bagged up the boiler suit and gave it to someone heading out on a scouting run. I asked him if he didn't mind putting it on a wash and drying it in one of the local houses. He didn't mind, although there was also a trade of beer in the way of payment. The next job was finding Boss.

I found him writing lists and directing guys in his porta-cabin. He was planning the great exodus to the mall and keeping in contact with the group there via walkie-talkies, military ones. When there was a lull in the conversation, I finally stepped in.

"Hey," I said quickly, taking the brief chance I had. "Do you mind if I start packing up one of the trucks? Ya know, ready for when I leave?"

"Mh-mm, go for it," Boss said, absentmindedly. He barely noticed my existence where he was so wrapped up in his plans. Looked like he had gained ten years in the previous few hours. The stress of responsibility. I did feel a fraction of guilt for going ahead and packing when he didn't seem to have a clue what I'd said, but he knew the deal, so he shouldn't mind.

I made my way to the North Gate to let them know I needed to leave. On the way, I got lost and came across Bill hanging around one of the shipping containers, with a gun. Something wasn't right. When I got closer, I realised the container had been marked as one containing the undead.

"Uh, everything okay, Bill?" I was eyeing his gun. He jumped.

"Yeah, everything is fine," he said, gruffly. He clearly was not comfortable with me being there, like I had caught him up to no good.

"No guns inside the walls, remember?" I said, trying to make a joke of it.

"Yeah, well, Boss said the meat-bags in this container had been acting up quite a lot lately, so he wants someone to keep an eye on it. Just in case they get out and we don't notice until it's too late," Bill explained rapidly. Then added, "He doesn't want anyone knowing in case people start freaking out."

"Makes sense," I nodded. That explained his nervous behaviour, I wouldn't want to be so close to the undead either. Turning away, I said, "Well, shout if they get loose. I got stuff to do."

"Yeah, I will," Bill continued to hang around the container, with his weapon drawn. I hadn't walked far before Bill spoke again, "Sam?"

"What is it, Bill?" I asked, looking back at him.

"I'm not a bad person," Bill said – I wasn't sure if it was a statement or a question. I would argue he was based on some of his life choices, but who was I to judge?

"I'm sure you're not," I said with a tight smile.

He looked at me, genuine pain in his eyes and asked me another question. "Do you think good people do bad things for good reasons?"

"I'm sure they do, but who gets to decide they're a good person?" I said with a shrug. I continued on my way, leaving Bill to ponder his philosophical dilemma.

I continued on, forgetting about Bill, and asked to go out the North Gate. I told them Boss was okay with it, and they didn't even question me. I wasn't sure which vehicle to take since each one had its merits and downfalls. It may seem odd, but I chose the transit van. It wasn't fast or durable, but it had one thing the others didn't – somewhere I could sleep safely. I could go in the back, close the doors, and feels safe knowing I was protected on all sides. With time, I could probably make it safer with modifications and extra plating or something. It also had a lot of storage room in the back, and it wasn't going to fall out like it could with a flatbed. I could carry food, fuel, water, even people. If I was going a long way, I needed to carry a lot, and Murder Van would probably even look good on the side. That probably sounded a little psychotic, but it would keep others away.

I loaded my bag into the back, which looked fairly lonely being the only item in there. I still needed everything else. All it took was a quick word with the guy watching over the vehicles, and he returned with three jerry cans of fuel, which were loaded into the back.

I returned to the base and visited Stephen. He handed me

a bag with the Benelli M4 shotgun, three SA80 assault rifles, as well as boxes of rounds and cartridges for each. He even gave me a small box containing attachments for the SA80's, a flashlight, a silencer, a scope, and a bayonet. I felt I should protest that I couldn't take it all from them, but who was I kidding? I wanted it, they had plenty of extra, and I had helped them get said extras. I deserved it all. I had someone help me carry them to the van and put them in the back, which also contained the teargas. I was probably going to be the deadliest guy roaming the world at the rate my arsenal was growing.

I had to think long and hard about how much food and water I needed. Areas definitely still had running water, but that didn't mean it would last for long. So I couldn't rely on finding water. I needed to take a lot with me. Humans need, on average, two litres of water a day. I could have less than that if I needed to. People have survived on a cap of water for a few days when they have really needed to. Not that I wanted it to come to that. So say I had a month of travelling ahead of me, should the journey go well, if I had one litre of water a day, that was thirty-one litres. Boss had containers full of the five-litre water bottles. I would take seven of them; just to be on the safe side.

Next, was food. An average male needed twenty-five hundred calories a day. Monthly, that's … a lot. There was no more fresh food, so everything was tinned, canned, and salted. That was a lot to carry. Did I even have a can opener? I'd have to wing it. Water was easy. Food and nutrition were a lot harder. I would take as many MRE's, tins, and bars as I could. It wasn't that far into the end of the world – food would still be about. So a couple of pallets and crates would do it. I also stole a few dustsheets for covering myself should at night, for warmth and camouflage

I stood back, admiring my transit van of supplies. I couldn't believe it. Before long, I would be on my way. I just stood there and smiled. I really couldn't believe it. I would soon be travelling to see Alice again.

All I had left was my super suit, the bullet, Thundy, my phone, the knife, and my boiler suit when it returned to me. I would be leaving the following day. I wanted to stick around for the party and plan my journey, and then I was gone.

I was sad to be leaving the place Boss had made safe. It had done so much for me, and so had the people. Especially Boss. I was sad to leave him, but I would say my goodbyes. Besides, goodbye didn't mean forever. I could see them again. I couldn't stop smiling. Also couldn't stop yawning. Time for a few hours of shuteye before the party.

Broadcast Seven: Wartime Broadcasting Service

This is the Wartime Broadcasting Service. This country has been affected by an unknown pathogen. Communications have been severely disrupted, and the number of casualties and the extent of the damage are not yet known. We shall bring you further information as soon as possible. Meanwhile, stay tuned to this wavelength. Stay calm and stay in your own house.

Remember, there is nothing to be gained by trying to get away. By leaving your homes you could be exposing yourself to greater danger. Keep away from those who are believed to be infected. It does not matter if they are family or friends. They are a threat to yourself and others.

If you leave, you may find yourself without food, without water, without accommodation, and without protection. It is not believed that the pathogen is airborne, but it is not confirmed. Roofs and walls offer substantial protection from the infected. The safest place is indoors, preferably somewhere you know. Make sure gas and other fuel supplies are turned off and that all fires are extinguished. If mains water is available, this can be used for fire-fighting. You should also refill all your drinking water containers after the fires have been put out, because the mains water supply may not be available for very long.

Water must not be used for flushing lavatories. Until you are told that lavatories may be used again, other toilet arrangements must be made. Use your water only for essential drinking and cooking purposes. Water means life. Do not waste it.

Make your food stocks last. Ration your supply because it may have to last for fourteen days or more. If you have fresh food in the house, use this first to avoid wasting it. Food in tins will keep.

If you live in an area where there are confirmed sightings of the infected, ensure you remain unseen and silent. When the immediate danger has passed, the sirens will sound a steady note. The "All Clear" message will also be given on this wavelength. If you leave your home to go to the lavatory or to replenish food or water supplies, do not remain outside the room for a minute longer than is necessary. You will attract the attention of any infected the longer you are outside.

Do not, in any circumstances, interact with the infected. If you do interact with the infected, you will bring danger to your family and you may die. Stay in your house or shelter until you are told it is safe to come out or you hear the "All Clear" on the sirens. The military and government are doing their best to contain and quarantine the situation. Help is coming. Keep hope alive.

Here are the main points again. Stay in your own homes, and if you live in an area where the infected have been spotted, then a warning has been given stay in your house until you are told it is safe to come out. The message that the immediate danger has passed will be given by the sirens and repeated on this wavelength. Make sure that the gas and all fuel supplies are turned off and that all fires are extinguished. Water must be rationed and used only for essential drinking and cooking purposes. It must not be used for flushing lavatories. Ration your food supply – it may have to last for fourteen days or more.

We shall be on the air every hour, on the hour. Stay tuned to this wavelength, but switch your radios off now to save your batteries.

That is the end of this broadcast.

CHAPTER 45

I awoke to the sound of people passing my porta-cabin. I remembered Bill guarding the container of undead, and then I remembered the celebration. Once my adrenaline spike had disappeared, I realised I was actually excited to have another party. I needed time to chill out again. Time to say my goodbyes.

When I reached the central area, I wondered how I'd ever get used to the place? Not that I needed to since I was leaving. I noticed the layout was a little different than the previous party night. Hanging down one container was a huge white sheet, with the techie guy from before fiddling with a projector. Sweet! Looked like movie night. I preferred movies over music. As always, crates of beer were being stacked nearby. There were tons of chairs set about, like a makeshift open-air cinema. Once again, people were milling about. I truly felt like one of the guys the second time around and didn't mind helping out at all. I wanted to do my part.

"I'll get those," I said to the techie guy, pointing to some large speakers. He smiled and continued playing with his laptop and projector. I carried them over and put them where he had wanted them previously. He tapped a few buttons on a laptop, and images were projected onto the white cloth. The speaker started playing some music, indicating the start of the film, with no horrible feedback from the speakers that time. The techie smiled at his progress.

"Nice one," I smiled and patted his shoulder. He grinned at me.

I left to assist others. I helped carry boxes of food – tons of cinema style snacks without the outrageous prices. There were even people setting up coolers filled with alcoholic beverages as well as soft drinks. Everything was coming together perfectly.

Darkness began to fall, and movie night would soon begin. Once again, a few stood watch on the walls. Boss silenced everyone.

"Gentlemen, and gentlemen!" he announced, with a huge smile. "There's not much news to tell this week. As we all know, we have secured the mall, our soon to be new home."

"Hell yeah!" someone shouted.

"Quiet down there," Boss laughed, raising his hand. "Naturally, this is big news, and we need to discuss our plan of what's next. But not tonight. Tonight is for alcohol and movies."

Pentecostal cheers of the faithful.

"Let's do this! Keep moving forward!" Boss leapt down from the container. Music from the film sounded. Boss approached me.

"Pretty epic," I smiled. Boss began guiding me to the projector screen.

"Well, let's settle down and end this night with a movie," he pushed me down into a chair before disappearing. He had a habit of vanishing like that. I think he even enjoyed the celebrity status he felt he had. Someone pushed a beer into my hand, and the movie played on the big screen. I watched the footage and realised something – I knew the film. *28 Days Later.* I loved it. What an amazing apocalypse film!

The film opened up with the protagonist waking from a coma. He had awoken in the post-apocalypse world and didn't know what had happened. The streets of London were empty, which I couldn't help but reflect on how different it was from my own experience. He wandered aimlessly, grabbing unnecessary items such as money. He soon ended up in a church, looking down over tons of dead bodies. I felt uneasy watching the scene for some reason. Not because I knew what was coming, but for another reason. Something wasn't right. It was hard to explain, but the bodies just didn't look real. I know they weren't real. It was a film, but they lacked any realism. The film played out the same way it always had and always would. The reveal of the zombies, or the infected, depending on what stance you took on the whole undead–infected human debate. I always came down on the infected side for that film. Wounds other than headshots killed these movie monsters, so they weren't zombies.

The protagonist is in a church when he calls out, almost like a joke meant just for the audience, and that's when we first see the infected. They rise from the piles of bodies and begin chasing the protagonist.

I … something felt wrong about the film. It just didn't have the right feel. Sure, the film hadn't aged particularly well, but that was part of the charm. Proper British cinema. The blood and gore looked ridiculously fake. It … what was wrong with the film? I was … I watched the infected get chopped to pieces and gore fly. I began to feel uncomfortable, anxious even. I was sweaty. Such a sudden onset. Was I sick? I felt that way in the mall. The explosions and shouts, they were too loud. Too bright. *Damn.* Every gunshot, I jumped. I needed to get out of there. I'd had anxiety attacks before, but nothing like what I was experiencing then. Was it even an anxiety attack? There was an intense pounding in my head, and the film was making it worse. I felt nauseous.

I got up. World spinning. I tumbled. Dropped my beer. People sped by. A few turned to look. I needed to get away. I kept going. Stumbling and walking until I couldn't see the film. Until I couldn't hear it. I leaned against a container, panting. Sweat pouring off me. Trembling.

"Fuck!" I said through gritted teeth. The pounding in my head began to subside, and my breathing slowed. I breathed out slowly, "Fuuuck."

I just wanted to be alone and lie down. I stumbled back through the twisting and turning maze of containers, which seemed to go on forever, until I found my room. I opened the door and fell in. I crawled into my bed and made myself as small as possible. What was happening to me?

I don't know how long I laid there for, but I didn't sleep. The drained and terrified feeling remained. I felt so exhausted but couldn't drift off. *Bang! Bang! Bang!* Gunfire. I jolted up and scrambled for the knife, feeling around in the dark. Then realisation dawned. No, not gunfire. Someone knocking on the door.

"Who is it?" I asked, trying to hide a groan.

"Boss," he opened the door and stumbled in, a drunken swagger to his steps. He hadn't been drunk when I'd left. How long had I been gone? My mind kept flashing to the knife. I had to find it. I was hypersensitive. I couldn't think straight.

"Uh," I grunted in reply.

"You left in a hurry earlier," Boss slurred.

"Wasn't feeling too good," I said truthfully.

"Ah, you'll feel better after a sleep," he replied, waving away my issues. "You're leaving tomorrow, right?"

"That's the plan," I agreed.

"I really wish you'd stay, man," Boss said sadly – he clearly liked me, although I felt I'd given him no reason to. "I wish I could convince you. It's just tail you're chasing, right?"

There was no sense in trying to correct a drunk person, so I forced smile, "In a way."

"Ah, you can get that anywhere!" he laughed, waving his hands to the imaginary hordes of women around us.

"I know," I laughed, not at the validity of his statement, but at the way he acted.

"Hey," he said suddenly. "I got something to show ya. If you promise to keep it a secret."

"Uh, sure," I smiled. I was confused by the sudden shift in conversation and tone, but I always found alcohol made people inconsistent.

"No!" he stooped to my level and grabbed my shoulder. He stared into my eyes. "Say it like you mean it."

"I promise I won't tell anyone your secret," I rolled my eyes. I didn't like his touch. Still felt clammy and ill.

"*Our* secret," he stood up straight and held out his hand. After I took it, he pulled me to my feet. My head still spun.

"Let's go and see *our* secret," I said. I still felt awful, like I'd lost an emotional and mental fight, but I felt a little better with each passing minute. Boss draped his arm around me and began leading me in the direction of whatever he wanted to show me.

Everywhere was eerily quiet. Everyone had gone to bed except for the odd one or two people patrolling the walls. I only knew they were there by the clang of their footsteps on the metal containers. The term *dead of night* echoed through the passages of my mind. Ignorant to the creepiness that had set in, Boss strode along – a lot steadier than expected for a drunk man. He was guiding me with an excited purpose.

We passed the doctor's room, heading towards the remotest part of the base. The part which hadn't yet been designated for use, and the containers were disorganised. No one had any reason to be there. As far as I knew, neither did we.

"Here it is!" Boss stopped outside of a container. There wasn't anything special about it. Except it had a red mark on it to indicate there were zombies within. The mark looked a lot fresher and less weathered than any of the others. Had others died recently? Stranger, I couldn't shake the feeling I'd seen the container before.

"Where are we?" the hair on my neck was standing up. There wasn't a chill in the air, but something wasn't right.

"You'll see," he giggled, sounding manic. Then it hit me why the area seemed familiar. It was the container Bill had been guarding. Boss reached for the door pulley and began to open it. I reached for my knife, but it wasn't on me. I had to stop the drunken madman.

I moved to barrel him out of the way and then slam down into the door. I couldn't let him let the dead out. But it was too late. The door was open, and he had slipped in. I turned to run, but there were no screams, no wet chewing of flesh. Did the undead get him that fast? No, that wasn't right. They would've come out the moment we were illuminated by the moonlight.

"Boss?" I walked into the container. It was dark in there, and it smelled bad. Not undead bad. Definitely not the rot of flesh, but human waste bad. Piss and shit and sweat. I covered my nose.

Fear crept into my voice. "Boss?"

He turned on a light. A lantern or flashlight, or a goddamn candle for all I knew, because that wasn't what my eyes were on.

"Boss?" I asked again, voice getting higher. I refused to believe what I was seeing.

"Wonderful, isn't it?" Boss said, with a smug smile. *No! No, it isn't!*

"When did this happen? How long?" My mind raced with rage and disbelief.

"A couple days. Not all that long ago," he turned to me, a dreamy look in his eyes.

"Who … who else knows?" I had stopped the shaking in my voice, and I had control over my disgust now. But that didn't stop the tremble of a primordial rage from reaching my hands.

"Just you and me. A couple others. Bill knows, too," Boss took a swig of beer. "I'm gonna slowly tell others, but I don't want everyone knowing at once. What do you think?"

"Unexpected. Definitely a new development," I chose my words carefully, my hand balled into a fist and trembled. My knuckles were white.

"I'm showing you this so that you don't have to leave so soon," he wrapped his arm around me. He whispered into my ear, his hot breath sticking to me. "Do you think you'll stick around?"

I thought about his question for what felt like an age, but it was probably only a couple seconds. I stared at the two women, Kirsty and Stephanie. Their wrists bloody from fighting against their restraints. They were on their knees, sitting in their own waste and filth. Faces red and blotchy, partly from an assault and partly from crying. They were mostly naked. A large potato sack-like piece of material covered them, giving people easy access to their … their … I stared at the fear on their face and the hatred in their eyes before finally answering.

"Sure, I think I can stay a bit longer," I said with an iciness that only I was aware of.

"Brilliant!" Boss cheered, and drunkenly hugged me. A shiver spread over my body. "I knew we were the same. I knew you would want to stay. After all, you gave me the idea. Men need more than food, water, and shelter. They need women! This will be your legacy just as much as mine."

A pit crept into my gut. The shiver travelling up my spine met the chill in my neck. The coldness spread throughout me and down to my bones. I needed to do something.

We didn't talk much more that night. I headed back to my cabin, and Boss to his. I returned with a couple things I hadn't left with before – a bottle of vodka and a bestial, boiling black-tar pit of unstoppable rage.

I never took my eyes off the container as I retreated. I felt numb. Sickened to my core. What I saw in that container, that I had inadvertently given Boss the idea for … part of me died that day.

CHAPTER 46

I awoke, a blinding headache pulsing across my head. I pulled myself away from the mattress. The motion caused me to vomit, emptying my insides onto my outsides. I looked around the room and saw the destruction.

The night prior hadn't been a dream. I'd so desperately hoped that the last twenty-four hours had been a figment created by my twisted mind and empowered by alcohol to induce the hallucination. The chair had been smashed to pieces. Broken glass littered the floor. It really wasn't a dream. I wasn't going to wake up from the reality I existed in.

The super suit – no, the leather jacket no longer read ZOMBIE SQUAD, but had a white smear. I had emptied some of the vodka on it in a drunken rage and washed it away. The apocalypse wasn't child's play. Wasn't a game. Why did I ever think it was? There are monsters out there, and they aren't the undead. People are the monsters. People like Boss and Harrington. Evil people. They were doing much worse things than any mindless monster could. They were cold and calculating beasts, prowling the world under the guise of humans. I couldn't let them carry on. No way. I had to –

"Hey, dude," someone said as they stepped through my door. Boss. He was smiling. He seemed so … normal. I stared at him, trying to see through the friendly façade he projected. I expected it to shift, revealing some kind of creature beneath the skin. But there was no fault in it. He was human. He looked around the room and smiled. "Bit of a mess, ain't it? Too much to drink?"

"Something like that," I nodded stiffly. *I could kill him. My knife isn't far. I could plunge it into his –*

"The reason I stopped by is to drop off this," he threw me my boiler suit. It was clean and smelled amazing. I smiled. It disappeared when I thought of the conversation from the previous night. *Why did you have to do it?* How could he just stand there and talk as if his little reveal from the night before had never happened? Everything he had said. Everything he had been, it was lies. All of it. Where did the persona of Boss end and the real Boss begin? Maybe he didn't remember telling me about his sick secret.

"Thanks," I nodded, forcing a smile. *Seriously, I could kill him right in my cabin and no one would be any wiser.*

I couldn't do it, though. Not yet. I needed him to lead me to the girls again. A combination of exhaustion, darkness, and rage had blurred the memories from the night before.

"You better get tidying anyway," he looked around. "Since you're staying longer, my offer still stands."

A pit opened up in my stomach. He remembered! The sick, twisted twat remembered. Even sober, he … I needed to stop him.

"Yeah, I'm still staying," I said, a huge fake smile spreading across my face. I had to seem convincing at least. It was painful, though. I had to try and get more information and convince Boss of my loyalty in the process. Not that he didn't trust me. In his eyes, I was his best friend.

"So can I pay them a little visit this morning? I have some

stress to work off," I felt evil saying it. Disgusting. I felt no better than Boss was, but I had to say it.

"Eager, aren't you!" he laughed and patted me on the shoulder. I had won his trust. I only had to make that one statement to do it, and I felt so dirty doing so. I just wanted to end everything there and then.

"You could say," I also laughed, feigning embarrassment. *I'm going to stab him through the eye, and I'll enjoy it.*

"If we're quick, then yeah. I don't want to draw attention to it just yet," he checked his watch. "Get dressed, and we can get going."

Once Boss left, I pulled on the boiler suit and hid the knife in my boot. I would be ready. I met him outside, and he pulled me by my arm, to the container. I memorised the route and made sure it would be burned into my neural pathways forever. The very few people we saw didn't question us.

"Try to be gentle with them," he smiled as we approached the container. "They need to last us."

"I see what you mean," I said through gritted teeth. It took every ounce of willpower to stay my hand from his throat. I placed my hand on the container, ready to go in, but Boss stopped me.

"You'll need this," Boss passed me a foil packet. A condom. A goddamn condom. He laughed. "I don't want what you got, you dirty bastard."

"Ha-ha," I nodded. *Put the condom on the knife and stab him. How much would he be laughing then?*

"Let's do this," Boss said encouragingly. I didn't know what to say. Didn't know how to act.

I just said, "Give me some privacy, and I'll be back out."

"Try not to take too long. We have a long day ahead," he squeezed my shoulder as I slipped inside the container.

I had hoped it was a nightmare. Every second was a new horror etched into my brain.

"Please," Stephanie begged the moment she saw me. Tears streamed down her face. "Just let us go. We won't tell anyone."

Kirsty, on the other hand, just stared at me with pure hatred. She never blinked. Never moved. Just stared at me like a hawk watching her prey. It was unnerving, but she had every right to be like that. She could've burned the whole world to a cinder, and I'm sure whatever god existed would have forgiven her.

The smell was getting to me, but I couldn't leave until enough time had passed.

"It may not seem it, but I'm here to help you," I said quietly.

"Really?" Stephanie's eyes glimmered with a light of hope.

"Don't believe him," Kirsty said calmly, eyes never leaving me. "He's lying."

"I'm not," I swore, I needed them to trust me. "Believe me, I want to help."

"Of course you do," Kirsty said, still as calm.

"Are you gonna get us out of here?" Stephanie asked. "Just untie us, and we can go now."

"I can't just yet," my heart broke the moment I uttered the words. "I need more time to prepare before we leave. Later. I promise. I just need you to be ready for–"

"Is this how you get off?" Kirsty interrupted. "You act like our white knight, but you're no better. You're sicker than the others. Do what you're going to do, but don't lie to me."

I sighed and pulled out the condom. Stephanie's eyes widened. Kirsty's had a look of resignation.

"Told you," Kirsty said quietly.

"This isn't for you. It's for him," I whispered, and then spat. I gestured toward the door. I tore open the condom, the foil tearing louder than the pounding in my ears. Kirsty closed her eyes expectantly, and Stephanie began to cry again. I squeezed the packet tightly in my balled hand and held the slimy condom in my hand. I worked up some spit in my dry mouth and spat into the condom. It wouldn't pass under close inspection, but I doubt Boss would be inspecting my semen up close. I met both of their gazes. "Be ready. I promise."

I left them, my head low, and I felt dirty.

Boss was eagerly waiting outside, and he still smiled.

"How'd it go, minute man?" he laughed.

"Well needed," I sighed and held up the empty condom wrapper. I couldn't play the game for much longer. I was so tired. So fed up. So angry. It was eating away at my soul.

"Cheer up!" Boss hit me on the back. "You just got laid."

"Yeah," I laughed. It was forced. I sounded maniacal. Boss even gave me a sideways look.

"So what're you doing today?" he asked.

Preparing to kill you. I shrugged, "Probably unload the van. I don't really know."

"That's a good idea," he nodded. "I need to plan our move to the mall some more. I'm so happy you're staying man! It's amazing."

We went our separate ways. I continued on to the van and unloaded some things, but I doubted it was anything Boss expected. I loaded both SA80's and the handgun into my backpack. I didn't want to have to kill anyone. I wanted to get myself and both girls out of there. If that meant shooting someone, then I would shoot.

As I carried the guns back to the base and to my cabin, rage almost blinded me. Not just for what Boss had done with the girls, but for ruining everything. For dragging me into it. I just wanted to go. Wanted to see Alice. Didn't want to have to deal with the worst the world had to offer. But I had to. I couldn't leave them behind.

In a perfect world, I would give myself another two days to ready my escape. I would plan my route. Find the quickest and quietest way out of there. Wouldn't ever get caught. I didn't have time for that, though. The longer I waited, the more harm would come to those girls. The more they would suffer. The more they would get raped. I loaded every gun systematically. I would be prepared.

I sat on the edge of my bed and stared into nothingness. The void engulfed me. Everything looped around and around in my head. It was like a sick movie on repeat. I was waiting. They were suffering. I carried on waiting. They carried on suffering.

"I can't take it anymore," I said to Thundy. "The time is now. I'm going to save them."

I stripped down to underwear and a t-shirt. Pulled on my modified leather jacket and jeans. Flexed. Put my boiler suit on over my gear. I would draw less attention that way. The boiler suit looked unnaturally bulky, but I doubted anyone would question it. I scooped Thundy up and placed him in one of my pockets. Did the same for my phone and Harrington's bullet. I pulled the backpack on, which sagged with the weight of the guns, and strode out of the cabin, towards the girls.

I walked by everyone. Ignored every greeting and never adverted my steely gaze. I saw Keith. He took one look at me and just walked away. Maybe he sensed my fury? It didn't matter. He wasn't in my way, so I carried on. On to the hellhole I would free Kirsty and Stephanie from.

Broadcast Eight: Shaun, Frank, and Barbara 4

Frank: Shaun, are you there?

After a long silence, Shaun answered.

Shaun: It's three in the morning. Of course I'm here. You woke me. What's –

Frank: I'm so scared, man.

Shaun: Why?

Frank: There's more of them now. I heard noises, so I … Shaun, they're inside. Downstairs. I'm terrified. I'm hiding.

Shaun: Zombies? Damn, man. Take a deep breath and relax. They haven't found you yet. It means you still have time. Can you get out the window?

Frank: Yeah, I think so. It's a long way down. I'll break my legs.

Shaun: It's either chance it with the window, or stay and die for certain.

Frank: You're right. You've been a good friend.

Shaun: So have you. Just don't act like this is the end, dude. I've told you where I live. If you can make it, we can finally hang out in person. I've got a second controller for the Xbox, so I can stomp you when I see you.

Frank: Yeah, man, that sounds good. I look forward to kicking your pasty white ass when I get there.

Shaun: That would be awesome, but small problem, dude. I'm black.

Frank: Well, blow me sideways! I did not expect that. You sure? You don't sound black.

Shaun: That's strange, you don't normally sound like a racist.

Frank: I'll kick your ass no matter the colour when I get there. I gotta go, man. I can hear them coming up the stairs. Before I go, Shaun, one last thing.

Shaun: What?

Frank: They're not zombies, you uncultured swine.

Shaun: Whatever, dead man. Good luck.

Frank screamed as he fell from the window. The sounds of wood splintering as the undead tore through the final door to Frank's room. It didn't matter at that point, though. Frank was gone. The undead moved around the room before a burst of static sounded. The undead had knocked over whatever radio setup Frank had.

CHAPTER 47

Someone was leaving the girls container as I approached. It was Doc. He was doing up his belt. He had a smile on his face and a faraway look in his eyes.

"Oh, hey," he said, nervously, and looked around. "What are you doing here?"

"Don't worry," I forced a laugh. "Boss told me about things over here, and I wanted a little visit. Ya know?"

"Yeah, I do," he smiled, visually relaxing. "Have fun, man."

"I will," I nodded. He began to walk away. *What if he told Boss I was back over with the girls?* I had to act fast. I said quickly, "Hey, can you do me a favour?"

"Uh, sure," he replied uncertainly.

"I'm really claustrophobic, and I'm terrified the door is going to shut and I'll be trapped inside. Can you, ya know, wait until I finish and let me out should it happen? I'll knock on the door once I'm done," I lied.

"Yeah, that's fine," he smiled. "I can probably help you with that claustrophobia later."

"Cheers," I nodded and entered the container.

The moment I was inside, I shut the door behind me and flicked a flashlight on.

"Back already, you sicko?" Kirsty snarled.

"Are you here to help?" Stephanie asked, desperately and hopefully.

"Yes, yes I am," I dropped my bag and unzipped it, then withdrew all the guns. Fear flashed across their faces. I looked them both in the eyes. "You don't need to be scared."

I pulled the knife out and approached them.

"Don't you dare touch me with that," Kirsty growled.

I approached Kirsty slowly, and she struggled as I got closer. I ignored her reaction and swiftly cut her binds. She stumbled forward and glared at me. I cut Stephanie's restraints.

"Is this a trick?" Stephanie gasped, tears rolling down her face.

"No, it's not," I said, with a small smile. "Can you walk?"

"We'll have to," Kirsty nodded, then looked at the guns. "Anything for us?"

"Take your pick," I gestured to the guns. Kirsty took an SA80. Stephanie, the handgun. I asked her why. There was a bigger gun there, and she had ignored it.

"I was a junior shooting champion," she said. "I know this gun."

"Well, damn," I was taken aback, and I smiled. Both of them shared a tightlipped and exhausted smile.

"Before we get out of here," I said, "I want to keep the noise to a minimum. We don't want to draw attention to us. That way we can get out as quickly and quietly as possible. Doc is outside. I'll lock him in here. Okay?"

They nodded. I hated Doc for what he had done, but I didn't want to kill him. I tapped twice on the door. Doc opened it.

"You were quick," he laughed, but his face dropped when he saw the girls holding guns.

"Shut up," I snarled. I grabbed him by his throat and dragged him into the container, my fingertips digging into the flesh either side of his Adam's apple, nearly ripping it out. I shoved him into the corner that the girls had been bound. He began to weep. I started walking out, when I heard an ear-shattering blast behind me, my ears ringing with the reverberation. A gunshot.

I turned around, expecting to see Doc with a gun and one of the girls dead. What I saw was Doc lying down, brains sprayed up the wall and blood pumping out of him with each beat of his failing heart.

"I-I'm sorry," Stephanie gasped. "I saw him lying there, and I just got so angry. I felt so much hate, and I – I pulled the trigger. I didn't even think about it, but I did it."

"It's okay," Kirsty tried to soothe her.

"Damn. Damn. Damn," I said. That was loud. People would've heard it. They would be coming our way to investigate. I snapped into action. "Change of plan. We run. You two follow me."

I started to run.

"What are you doing?!" a voice from up high shouted. It was one of the guards who walked the walls. He was aiming his gun at us. He started to lift a walkie-talkie to his mouth, but Kirsty never gave him that chance. She opened fire with the SA80. The bullets cut a line through the air as they trailed to where she aimed. Three rounds hit the guard in the chest, and he fell back and disappeared.

We're in trouble. I began sprinting. *We need a distraction.*

I glanced over my shoulder to see the girls still following closely. As I rounded the corner, I caught a momentary flash of a red mark on one of the container doors. I slowed down.

"Zombies," I turned to the girls. "I want you to carry on running away from here. I won't be far behind. Try not to draw any attention to yourselves."

"We can handle them," Kirsty spat, venom lacing her words.

"There's about to be zombies in the mix," I said. "If we can have the men and the zombies spend their time fighting each other, then we can get out of here, unnoticed. They may even think the gunshots were in response to the zombies. Okay?"

Kirsty nodded.

I waited until they were out of sight and around one of the corner before I started kicking the container doors. I wanted the undead riled up and ready to attack. Once I heard enough of them slamming into the door, I gripped the handle and pulled, hiding behind it. Zombies sprinted out, into various directions. None of them saw me.

I waited until their putrid stink was diluted before sprinting to the girls. It was then that I realised there was one straggler zombie waiting by the container. It saw me before I saw it, and it lunged for me. I pulled my arm up to shield myself from the assault. The zombie sunk its teeth into my limb, and I shouted in anticipation of the pain, but I didn't feel it. It continued to gnaw through the boiler suit and was eventually chewing on the leather.

"Well, what do you know," I said, smiling. Turned out, the leather was decent enough protection from a bite.

It carried on, trying to chew through the leathers, but with no result. I pulled up the SA80 and blew its skull apart. It collapsed to the floor, dead. I stared at my arm. Barely a mark on the material. I nodded in satisfaction before running after the girls again.

I began to hear a lot of gunfire around the base. The zombies had made contact. I needed more help, so I opened up two more containers before finding the girls hiding behind one of them.

"What's wrong?" I questioned. I assumed they'd locked up with fear.

"We're held down," Kirsty said. "There's guys around the corner shooting zombies."

"How many?" I asked.

"Four or five," Stephanie said. "Kirsty already shot at them, so they know we're here."

"Goddamn," I huffed. I turned to Stephanie. "How good of a shot are you still?"

"I'm okay," she shrugged.

"She's amazing," Kirsty glared at Stephanie. "She hit every zombie in the head with one shot each."

"Good. She fast?" I questioned Kirsty – there wasn't time for Stephanie to be modest.

"Extremely," Kirsty nodded.

"Right, Steph," I looked at her. "I need you to hit all those guys in the head. First time, or I'll die."

"What do you mean?" she asked.

"I'm going to draw their attention. You shoot," I explained. I levelled my SA80 and bolted from our cover. I was aiming to get behind a container about twenty feet away.

I heard shots being fired in my direction. If I could hear the shots, at least I was alive. *It's the shot you don't hear that kills you.* I heard five handgun shots. Then there weren't any more shots being fired at me. Five bodies slumped to the floor, dead.

They wouldn't even be getting up as zombies.

"Nice shooting!" I heard Kirsty say.

"Keep moving," I demanded, and kept going. As I ran by the dead men, I could see pools of blood expanding around their corpses. That was something you never saw with the undead. The blood inside the undead had already begun to dry and rot.

I kept running. Shot several zombies who were getting to close to me. They dropped to the floor like dead weights. I kept running. I rounded a corner, and bullets peppered the container next to me.

"Stay where you are!" someone shouted. I didn't know if I recognised the voice. I couldn't think. Had word spread already about my betrayal?

"Uh, why?" I called out to the shooter.

"Goddamn," he hissed. "Is that you Sam?"

"Yeah, man!" I called back, feigning happiness at hearing the voice.

"Come out, dude. It's Stephen. I thought you were one of the attackers," he called back. I turned to look at the girls.

"What do I do?" I whispered to them.

"Just go out there," Kirsty said. "We can shoot him while he's distracted."

"Please don't hit me," I whispered. Kirsty nodded. I stepped out.

"What's happening, man?" I said to Stephen, recognising him the moment I saw his face.

He had veins bulging on his forehead. "I don't know. The zombies got out somehow. We're trying to contain–"

A bullet passed through his skull. I felt a pang of sadness when I saw his body hit the floor. Odds are he hadn't even done anything wrong. Probably didn't even know about the girls, but he would've stopped our escape. He had to be stopped.

"Sam," Kirsty said calmly. I turned and looked at her. "We need to get going. We can't just wait around, okay?"

I nodded.

We carried on moving. I felt lost and turned around. I needed to focus, so I breathed deeply and closed my eyes. I could hear gunfire, and I could smell the undead. I opened my eyes and smiled. I recognised where I was.

As we ran between the containers, I killed any undead I found, and we did our best to avoid the living. The girls had no issue shooting either of them. To them, it was necessary revenge. I, on the other hand, had yet to raise my gun to the living. I just couldn't. I didn't want to cross that bridge. Besides, the girls were quite content with doing that for me.

Plumes of smoke rose into the air. Where had it come from? The acrid smell of burning flesh. Undead were burning. Fire. That was the last thing we needed. We ran past my old cabin, and it was in flames. I didn't feel any loss for the place I'd slept. I had discarded all attachment to everything about the place.

More zombies. A few single shots from my SA80 put them down. The smell of burning smoke overpowered the stench of rotting flesh. Two men ran into view. Stopped and stared at me. I pulled up my gun and aimed at them, finger hovering over the trigger. I couldn't pull it, but they didn't have the same hesitation, and they opened fire. I dived out of the way. Kirsty fired and took them both out.

"Thanks," I said to her. She helped me up and nodded. *Keep moving.*

CHAPTER 48

I could see the North Gate. It had been left wide open. No guards, and no one to watch over it. Fire raging behind me. Gunshots and undead snarls echoed around. It all felt disorientating. None of it mattered, though. We were leaving.

Nothing was ever simple though. Bill crept out from behind a container to my right. He aimed his gun at me. I didn't have time to raise my gun in response. His finger waited near the trigger. His eyes grew wide as Kirsty and Stephanie rounded the corner into the same encounter. None of us moved. We didn't want to raise our guns in case Bill shot us in response. But he continued to aim at us. His eyes were wild and kept darting between the two women. I could see an internal battle raging within him. Suddenly, his questions on morality made sense. Then he lowered his gun.

"Go," he said simply. I walked past and nodded at him. He nodded in return, and then disappeared back into the base. I guess his conscience got the better of him.

I left through the gate and sprinted ahead, the girls shooting any undead nearby. I needed to start the van, so I rounded on the driver's side door. *Is it ajar?* I reached for the handle, and it sprung open. I didn't have time to react before it smashed straight into my face. I fell to the ground, bleeding and broken nose, bloody and split lips.

"Shit," I groaned. Boss climbed out of the driver's side, calmly and deliberately.

"Hello, Sam," he was acting calm, but I could see the bulging veins in his neck and the hate in his eyes. "You've really screwed us here."

"Go die in a ditch, you rapist," I snarled, the primal part of my brain bleeding into the logical part. My heart pounded and stomach knotted. Every indiscretion started coming back. The killing of Gary. Making a fool of me. Kidnapping the women. He would have to pay.

"I'm just doing what I need to do to keep my men alive and happy," he shouted before kicking me in the ribs. I couldn't catch my breath. He snarled, "I don't like what I have to do. I don't like these responsibilities. But I have to be the one who does it. It's not just about me anymore. I need to look after everyone!"

How could he not see that he was in the wrong here? His lack of responsibility fuelled my rage even further. My fists trembled wildly. He was a monster who couldn't see his transgressions. He was sick.

I tried to push myself to my knees, but Boss kicked me again.

"You're not going anywhere, you sick bastard," he growled. I saw his hands shook also. It was then I noticed the gun he held.

He's going to execute me! Where are the girls? I began cackling. He looked confused by my sudden onslaught of merriment.

"What's so funny?" he snapped.

"Me? Sick?" I said, still laughing. It ended in a spluttered cough.

"Yes, you," he snarled. "Look around you. You've

destroyed our home. *Your* home. We took you in, and look what you've done. How many did you kill? How many of your friends?"

"They aren't my friends!" I shouted. "You never were. If I knew what you were like at the beginning, I'd have killed you the moment I met you."

My words appeared to sting him. He took a step back and winced. I used that.

In one swift motion, I climbed to my feet and tackled Boss. He fell to the ground. I assaulted him. Punched him in the ribs, in the throat, in the head. All he could do was block my attack.

My gut felt as though it had a molten ball of hatred weighing me down and scorching my insides. I wasn't letting this evil scum go. *This is how Gary felt in his final moments.* I ignored the stray thought and continued. I pummelled him. Boss tried to raise his gun, but I slammed his hand down. He released the handgun. I grabbed it. Aimed it at his head.

"Just do it!" Boss dared me, with a small smile. I stared him in the eyes.

The hate ebbed away. I couldn't shoot him. He needed to die, but I couldn't do it. I relaxed, thinking over the moral dilemma. He took that as a sign of weakness and pushed the gun aside and grabbed me by my throat. Shoved me off him and onto my back. Stomped on my hand, pushed it into the ground, and twisted his foot back and forth. I could feel the skin on my hand tearing through the glove. I winced and gritted my teeth.

"I thought we were the same," Boss stared at me, with sadness in his eyes. "I thought we would run this place, side by side. You're nothing like me."

"Thank God for that," I laughed, manically. He kicked me in the ribs one more time, for good measure. It could only end one of two ways – Boss would kill me, or the girls would save me. I wasn't a killer.

I sighed. I didn't have any more fight in me. I was happy to just lie there and be done with it. Fighting was hard. Each hit I received felt like irreversible damage had been done. I could feel bones crack and skin bruise.

Boss straddled me and wrapped his hands around my throat. He didn't look angry or hateful at that point. He was just doing what he felt needed to be done. I just laid there and tried to accept it, but my survival instincts had different plans.

As my throat seized up and airways closed, my body instinctually began to struggle and try to fight him off. My hands clawed at his throat and face, but it was no help. He just tightened his grip and slammed my head into the ground. I saw stars, but that didn't stop me from trying to fight back. I started patting the area around me to try and find a weapon. A rock. A twig. Anything. I brought my knees up to try to push him off. No use. I felt something digging into my leg. Grabbed for it and tugged. The fisherman's knife. I brought it up. My vision was pin-holing. *Now or never.* I slammed the blade into his ribs. The knife ricocheted off them, but he screamed and relented slightly. I brought the knife back up, slick with his blood, and pushed it into his thigh. He screamed again, and blood began to pump out of him a lot faster. He was getting weaker, clutching at his leg. I shoved him off of me, then pushed the knife to his throat. I stared at him. He wasn't fighting me. He was smiling. I thought about it. I really did.

Slashing his sick throat, that is. But I didn't. I stood up and walked away. No point in killing him. He would die soon.

I turned around and saw the girls just standing there, staring at me.

"Didn't fancy helping?" I choked out.

"We were busy," Kirsty said. They were covered in blood and gore. None of it their own. She looked at Boss squirming on the floor. "Not going to finish him off?"

"No," I sighed. "He'll die soon. He needs to suffer."

"Just do it," Boss growled.

"Get in the van, you two," I said. They did so without question.

"You just gonna leave me to die?" Boss said. "Just kill me, or save me. You gotta do one."

"No, I really don't," I walked away, climbed into the van, and started it up.

I felt empty and weary. I retrieved Thundy from my pocket and put him on the dashboard. I looked at Boss in the wing mirror. Zombies were leaving the base and heading towards him. I started up the van and began to pull away. I could hear Boss shouting something. I sighed. Turned the van around until we were facing him.

"Are you–" Kirsty began, eyes wide, mouth agape.

"No. I'm not going to save him," I said, not allowing her to finish her question.

"Then why?" Kirsty asked.

"We need to watch this," I said solemnly.

The zombies continued to approach Boss, who was kicking at them and trying to crawl away, but he wasn't getting anywhere.

"I don't want too," Stephanie squirmed in her seat.

"You have to," I said. *I have to*. "The world is a bad place. We need to view the consequences of our actions. Otherwise, we'll act without morality. We can't act without remorse or guilt. We need to see what's out there. This is what's ahead of us."

No one said anything more.

We sat there and watched the zombies swarm over Boss. He was screaming as they ripped the flesh from him. We waited until they were done. Didn't take long. Then they began moving towards us. There was nothing left but bones and a bloody smear where Boss had once been. I reversed, turned onto the road, and drove away from the base.

CHAPTER 49

I continued driving. Didn't even think about where I was going. I just didn't want to be *there* anymore. I felt truly lost in the world. Had no real direction, and my actions of the previous twenty-four hours began to dawn on me. The cold distance that adrenaline provided me during those moments had worn off, and the seeds I'd sown had taken root.

I looked at Thundy, who was still on the dashboard. His black eyes held my reflection – something I didn't want to see. My hands were still sticky from the blood of the man whose death I had contributed to, and I hadn't given a thought to washing it off. I could feel a darkness growing inside me. A deep rot had set in. A rot which couldn't be cleaned, and the stench that followed would be as bad as that of the undead. I knew it would affect anyone I came near. But I had no choice. I had to save the women. It was the right thing to do. That wasn't the problem. The problem wasn't my actions or the life I had allowed to be taken. It was the enjoyment I gained from it. I would play and replay the slaughter in my head, much like a teenage boy would do of his first sexual encounter. It was a different kind of pleasure, though. A sick, twisted pleasure. One of power and vengeance.

Justice had been done, but it still scared me. The undead

were hard enough to kill. Killing a once-life tormented me emotionally for days when I'd first done it. Now, that was no longer a problem. I knew I technically didn't end his life, but I did put him in a situation to die. Stuck a blade in him. Most importantly, I didn't save him. I enjoyed his death.

I wasn't so naïve to think that I would survive without having to end a life. It was an inevitability of survival. I just hoped it wouldn't have happened so soon. I didn't want to kill another human, but I knew it would happen again. Just didn't know when. One thing was certain – it would be easier next time. It had to be.

I looked to my left and saw the two women clutching each other. They sat, huddled together on the passenger seat. Kirsty was stroking Stephanie's face, trying to calm her. She was clearly the stronger of the two. It was good they had each other, because I wasn't emotionally fit to provide them with any form of comfort. And with what they had been through, I doubted they would want another man to even go near them. After all, I probably seemed just as psychotic as the men they had escaped from. I had to be as brutal as I was to get us out of there. The same images of some ancient god of war from before came to mind. Was that how they saw me? I doubted it. A heartless and remorseless bastard was probably closer to the truth.

Wild and depressing thoughts were running rampant.

But you did save them, Thundy said to me. At first I thought it was mocking. Then I realised it was comforting me. That was true. I had saved them. I had dragged them out of a hell. Whether I was leading them into another had yet to be seen. I would just face that when it came. For now, I had saved them.

They were alive because of me.

"I will protect them," I said to Thundy. The women looked at me wearily, and I realised I had said it aloud. I said it again, to the women this time. "I swear I will protect you both. On my head be it."

They relaxed slightly. I'm sure they believed my intent, and I believed I meant it. We were all lost and alone in this world, but at least we had each other now. I had people to protect. It wasn't all about me anymore. I managed a smile. Tomorrow seemed more hopeful, and that was all we could ask for. Just one more day. We continued heading north, without a word. Driving into the sunset – a symbolic end to a terrible day.

****

"What the hell was that?" I jumped out of my attempt at sleep. There had been a metallic bang, as if something had struck the van, but there were no undead around.

"It came from the back," Kirsty whispered. She didn't appear to have even attempted sleep. I got out of the van.

We were all exhausted. We had driven far enough that the burning and the smoke of the container site was just a dot on the horizon, and then we drove further. I walked around the van once and saw nothing. Then I realised it had come from within the van. I crept silently to the back doors, where our supplies were. My vision had adjusted to the night, and the moon gave enough light to see by. The silence allowed me to hear the slightest of movement from inside the van.

Kirsty followed closely, clutching a wrench, ready to strike. She approached the doors. I pointed my handgun toward the door. I signalled for Kirsty to open the door on three.

One …

Two …

She snatched the door open, and I jammed the barrel of my gun into the van.

Inside laid a man, cold and shivering. His muscular, tattooed arms were wrapped around himself, partially covered by a dustsheet. He looked terrified, but his huge and menacing physique cancelled that out. I couldn't see who he was, so I grabbed what little hair he had and twisted his head to one side while jamming the barrel of my gun against the underside of his chin. I still couldn't tell who he was. Kirsty looked at me, unsure of what to do.

I pulled him out into the moonlight and grabbed him by the chin, twisting his face into the light. I realised that I knew him from the camp, and smirked. I pushed the gun even harder against the soft flesh of his throat, and snarled, "Now, what shall we do with you?"

ABOUT THE AUTHOR

I always enjoyed reading fictional worlds, but creating my own was always my passion. My Year 8 English teacher told me I should pursue writing after a short story I had written for a school project.

Things changed and life moved on, but even while I was graduating from my Bachelor's and Master's in Psychology, I still wrote stories and I still loved doing it. Writing is my passion, and everything else I do is a means for me to carry on with that passion.

I'm also prepared to move to a secure location at a zombie's notice …

If you've gotten this far, please leave me a review and message me. I love hearing what people think!

Website:

www.AmongTheDead.co.uk

Regular updates:

www.facebook.com/AmongTheDeadATD

www.twitter.com/AmongTheDeadATD.

Email me:

AmongTheDeadATD@hotmail.com

YOU

Printed in Great Britain
by Amazon

47901077R00169